THE CELTIC PHOENIX
A SHERLOCK HOLMES ADVENTURE

INTRODUCING TESSA WIGGINS:
THE IRREGULAR DETECTIVE

By

Kim Krisco

Paperback ISBN 978-1-78705-381-6
ePub ISBN 978-1-78705-382-3
PDF ISBN 978-1-78705-383-0

Published in the UK by MX Publishing
335 Princess Park Manor, Royal Drive,
London, N11 3GX
www.mxpublishing.co.uk

Cover design by Brian Belanger

NOTE FROM THE AUTHOR

Interest in all things Celtic has never been stronger. Some of our fascination derives from the fact that the ancient Celts remain a relative mystery. Our knowledge about this diverse group of tribes is incomplete. This is because the Celts were an ancient people, dating back to the 13th century BCE, and because they left few decipherable written records.

More than three thousand years ago, Celtic tribes spread across most of central and western Europe—far beyond Ireland, Scotland, Wales, Cornwall, Isle of Man and Brittany. The Celts were not a homogeneous race as we think of it today. There were distinct differences among the various tribes, but they shared a common cultural heritage and, in some cases, a common language.

The Celts were contemporaries of the Mediterranean cultures of the Greeks and Romans. Indeed, much of what we know of the Celts comes to us from Greek and Roman historians, geographers, and military leaders like Julius Caesar. These accounts are both helpful and problematic because the Romans saw the Gauls (their word for the Celts) as barbarians. The Romans wanted to justify their efforts to conquer and enslave them, so the Celts were often portrayed in false and/or disparaging terms. Nonetheless, we are fortunate to have the writings of such historians as Strabo, Diodorus Siculus, and Cassius Dio. As you will come to see, I draw word-for-word from portions of their accounts in this novel. This is in keeping with my commitment to write historically accurate stories—weaving actual historical people, places and events within my tales.

While the Romans judged the Celts to be less civilized overall, they respected them as warriors and philosophers. In particular, it was the Celts' spiritual beliefs that captured the imagination of the Romans. Celtic religious views and traditions hold that same allure for many people today. Additionally, there are other aspects of the

Celtic culture that speak directly to crucial issues with which our world is currently grappling.

The Celts ethos, as it relates to the earth and Nature, seems more relevant now than it may have been when the Celtics reigned. The priests of the Celts, the druids, embodied the belief that human beings must live in communion with the earth and everything that dwells on or within it. It should not be surprising to learn that their respect and reverence for Nature would shape how women, the bearers of life, were regarded in the Celtic culture. Unlike the patriarchal traditions that dominate the world today, Celtic women held equal status with men in many arenas. Here again, the three thousand year-old Celtic traditions echo today's fight for justice and equal rights for women around the world.

Finally, one caveat before you begin: Because this is a work of fiction, some parts of this story are pure fantasy. For example, while the Celtic calendar is real and still in use today, we know little about the cyclical rituals as they were actually practiced by the ancient Celts. I necessarily took poetic license when writing about such celebrations as *Samhain* and *Imbolc*. However, having conducted deep research before setting out to write this novel, I endeavored to have my depictions of these, and other Celtic practices, in keeping with my understanding and appreciation of who the Celts were as a people.

PROLOGUE

JULY 7, 1939

PEOPLE WHO NEVER KNEW HIM came to help with the boxing of his estate. *Voyeurs, all of them.* I nodded. They knew him only as an enigmatic man who solved mysteries. Their vulgar curiosity and insensible conversations drove me from the parlor.

I found myself motionless on the threshold of his office holding an empty crate already heavy with memories—a penny in my palm . . . his almost-smile . . . the way he could wither you with the words: "Oh really?" I smiled and stepped inside his office and quickly shut the door, falling back against it.

Chintz curtains fractured the light, stripping the room of color and rounding all the edges. The bitter tang of his shag tobacco still hung in the air. On either side of me, dusty bookshelves spanned floor to ceiling. I paced the perimeter of the room, running my finger across the leather spines: Pope, Poe, Shaw, Swinburne, Fabian Essays, and Dumas. They would miss his touch. On the far wall sat a tidy shelf of thick glass jars with human brains buoyed in an amber liquid—his infamous collection.

The floorboards creaked under my feet as I made my way to his writing desk. There, sitting in the corner, sat his never-ever-finished tome. The manuscript cover was embroidered with a border of twisting vines and tiny yellow flowers—cowslips. In the center was a shield with a bishop's mitre poised above it. And, the oddest thing—angel faces poking out from the four corners, as if the embroidery had peeled away to reveal their presence.

I opened it.

Theories of Crime it read in the center of the first page. I underlined his name with the tip of my finger: *Sherlock Holmes*.

I picked up the leatherback knife on the blotter. He used it to slit envelopes from which poured the hope-filled entreaties of princes and humble folk alike—the knife that helped to save his life.

I turned the pages, not reading, not even looking. Then . . . a torn piece of foolscap—ragged edges, paler than the other paper.

My poem. He kept it.

I cradled the piece of paper in the palm of my hand, turning it to catch the light so I might read the haunting lines:

> *Wet from the womb*
> *a baby knows*
> *the quintessence*
> *of the human animal.*
>
> *And it cries.*

The Tear—a message from the heart that cannot be expressed in language.

I recalled the very tear that prompted this poem. While I've shed an ocean of tears in my lifetime—this particular one, shed twenty years ago, still lingers on my cheek, as does the memory of the woman for whom it was shed.

PART ONE

OCTOBER 23, 1919

CHAPTER 1

THE CITIZENS OF LONDON were going about their business as if the ravages of the war were but a bad dream. Their necessary disregard was occasionally confronted when they walked past the burnt out shell of a building, but most went on with a buoyant resolve to reclaim their former lives. It was not so easy for Mr. Holmes. He was retired, or so he declared, when he left London for the Sussex seashore prior to the war. His contributions to the Great War were cloaked in secrecy, and he was content to let them remain so, as he again returned to his cottage on the Sussex Downs.

Retirement had little to do with his aging body. At sixty-five, Holmes possessed all his faculties. The pace of his daily labors may have slowed, but it was frenetic when compared to those half his age. We who know and love him doubted that Sherlock Holmes would find true peace among the quiet and gentle folk in the south. Dr. Watson himself openly expressed doubts about Holmes's choice—but, of course, that never deterred his emigration to countryside.

For a while, he cast aside our doubts that he would be able to wedge himself into the seamless landscape crowning the English Channel. Then, an extraordinary event occurred on a gloomy October morning that mirrored his mood. His melancholia was provoked when Dr. Watson telephoned to cancel his much-anticipated visit. Ever since the Doctor had diagnosed himself with arrhythmias of the heart, he became indisposed to move beyond the Borough of Richmond where his flat is situated. "He's a humbug," Holmes pronounced, as he replaced the handset on the oaken Erickson that had been banished to the back porch.

Returning to his morning cup, Sherlock Holmes tapped the collection of Shakespeare's plays he had recently retrieved from the library. Hamlet has been on his mind of late. Taking the book in hand, he returned it to the library mumbling: "that undiscovered country from whose bourn, no traveller returns." While there are many memorable speeches in the play, his choice was prompted by Watson's frequent reflection upon his impending death. Such contemplations annoyed Holmes who had always accepted the matter-of-factness of death. But, while he did not fear death, he was not immune to that which comes with the prospect of it. Regret had been surfacing of late as he strove to recall past cases and adventures for inclusion in his magnum opus on criminology.

Sherlock Holmes could rightfully take pride in the fact that his singular methods and practices had found their way into the wider arena of twentieth century crime detection. Thanks to him, a new breed was emerging in Scotland Yard. In particular, he held some hope for Inspector Joshua Walls who had successfully climbed the bureaucratic ladder to the top of number four Whitehall Place. However, Walls, like all those harnessed to a governmental wagon, wore blinkers that had him focused solely on the letter of the law. Holmes, who balked at any harness, always saw the *purpose* of the law as his aim. He once remarked: "It is in the intent of the law where justice resides."

A clattering of the latch on the front door interrupted his blue musings. Still huffing from her trek, Mrs. Thornton bustled into the parlor like a great Graylag goose flapping her charcoal tartan cape to shake off the mist. "The grower's year wanna end early this year, sir," his housekeeper remarked, as she made her way toward the kitchen. "I saw Wiley up the road. It appears he's headin' this way."

Most days the windswept road leading to Sherlock Holmes's cottage offered little promise of a diversion, so this was welcome news. Holmes reversed his trek to his office and went to the window to survey the Eastbourne to Brighton Road. His perusal validated Mrs. Thorton's prognostication. Wiley was pedaling his way toward the cottage.

Since the war, his retirement was marked by only one case. Not a case so much as an escapade. It ended in the death of Rory Wiggins, the former captain of his backstreet brigade. Rory's passing haunted him still.

As he turned from the window, he heard a clattering and humming in the kitchen that told him Mrs. Thornton was already at work preparing his afternoon meal. However, not wishing to appear too eager, he decided to let Wiley's rap bring his housekeeper to the door.

Hearing the messenger fighting his way through the bramble in the front yard, Holmes bustled back toward his office. He was behind his desk by the time the first knock came—followed by another—and finally, more emphatic rapping.

"Would you mind getting that, Mrs. Thorton?"

Holmes buried his face in his manuscript as his housekeeper's harrumph echoed from the kitchen. It took all of Mrs. Thorton's Christian resolve to keep from glaring at the *master of the manor* taking refuge behind his desk.

As she opened the door, sunlight cast a halo around the cheery face of a square-shouldered man with keen, expectant eyes. He held a package wrapped in brown paper and tied with twine.

"What have we now, Wiley?" Mrs. Thornton grunted.

"Good mornin', ma'am." The messenger swept his flap-cap from his head and proffered the package. "For Mr. Holmes."

"Of course it is. I suppose you expect—"

"There is a shilling on the tray for Wiley," Holmes interjected rising from his chair.

The burly woman snatched the package from Wiley's hand, lurching with surprise at the weight of it. She hefted it in her hand as she made her way to the sideboard. As she retrieved the coin, Holmes appeared and took it from her fingers.

Wiley accepted the coin from Mr. Holmes with the proper amount of gratitude. "Thank ya, sir, God bless ya," Wiley said, as a smoldering cutty bobbed in his teeth.

"I see the missus is visiting her mother again," Holmes noted.

The man's face screwed up into a knot. He straightened up, holding his arms out to better survey his attire. Wiley's hallmark grin reappeared. "Ah-h-h," the messenger exclaimed, pulling on a thread that had once fastened a coat button. He tapped his finger on the side of his nose, and gave a knowing wink. "Right ya are, sir—as always."

Holmes nodded goodbye to Wiley and turned from the door. He smiled as he noticed his housekeeper inquisitively poking the package on the sideboard. "Would you like me to open it, sir?"

"Please do." Holmes replied, closing the front door and returning to his desk.

Mrs. Thornton's curiosity bubbled up in utterances indicative of delight as the last of the twine and brown wrapping paper was peeled away. Her curiosity was rewarded. "My, my, my."

Holmes awaited a more definitive report.

"It seems to be a rather handsome metal jewelry casket. Brass, I believe. It is sealed with wax, sir."

"Well, open it."

"I will take it in the kitchen if you don't mind, sir."

Holmes set his pen down and watched the stout matron stride into the kitchen with true British proficiency.

Grunts, oohs, and ahs accompanied the scraping of an implement before a pop could be heard.

"My heavens!" she exclaimed. "Something's gone off, sir."

A rancid smell brought Holmes to attention: "Good god woman, what is it?"

Her final report took the form of a rare expletive: "Bloody hell!"

Waving her arms like a spastic preacher, the housekeeper shot off into the back porch as Holmes entered the kitchen. "You. You and your strange ways will be the death of me-e-e-e!"

"Finally, something interesting," Holmes said aloud, walking to the kitchen to reconnoiter.

Immediately he noticed the exquisite nature of the jewelry casket resting on the table. It appeared ancient, as it was adorned with archaic symbols. His further assessment was checked by the mounting odor of death and decay. "This is marvelous," he said, putting a handkerchief to his nose.

Lying inside the box was two fleshy objects the size of walnuts. He poked the objects with the tip of a kitchen knife.

Mrs. Thornton's blathering continued as she paced about pointlessly on the porch.

Holmes continued to prod and probe the objects with the blade. "I believe these are . . ."

"Please sir, I know what they are! Please sir, I beg you," the housekeeper said from her refuge on the porch. "Take them away. I'll not have them in my kitchen."

Holmes retrieved an empty canning jar from the pantry and poured the contents of the casket in. "It's all sorted, Mrs. Thornton. You may return to your kitchen."

Holmes twisted a cap onto the jar and held it up to the light as the housekeeper tentatively poked her head through the doorframe.

"No doubt about it. Testes . . . human, I believe."

CHAPTER 2

IT IS SAFE TO SAY that Sherlock Holmes was fully in the grip of euphoria as he gazed into the canning jar—a torrent of questions raced through his mind:

Why send these to me?

What is the message?

Why the archaic box?

Who is the former owner?

Then a ghastly possibility arose.

He brushed past Mrs. Thorton who remained dumbfounded at the rear entrance to the kitchen. He grabbed the barrel of the Erickson on the wall, put it to his ear, and leaned toward the mouthpiece.

"Number please," a nasal voice sounded in his ear.

"London, 5-1-8-5-3."

"London-5-1-8-5-3, the hello girl repeated.

As it rang, Holmes held his breath.

A click—then: "Hello. Watson here!"

Holmes's body unwound. "John, Sherlock here. You are well?"

Stunned momentarily by Holmes's rare familiarity, Dr. Watson replied: "Yes, Holmes, if I may address you in that manner." He chortled. "All is well here. I'm sorry if my cancellation distressed you—a mere precaution, I assure you."

"No, no. Something has just arrived that has disquieted me—something in today's post. It had me think of you. No, not so much think of you . . . bloody hell, Watson, I was concerned for your safety."

"What is it that has you in this disposition?"

"Testes. Human testes."

"What on earth are you babbling about? Testicles arrive in the post . . . and you thought of *me*? Ha! I can assure you, mine are firmly in place, for all the good they are doing me."

"No, it wasn't that, so much as *why* someone would send them to me."

"Yes. Well. Of course, you have acquired many bizarre adversaries over the years, so . . ." Watson's voice trailed off. "Hm-m-mm. There is a chance I may know the former owner."

"You're serious?"

"I am indeed. Just two days ago I received word that an old comrade of mine, John Goodnow died—murdered actually—rather brutally. We served together in the York & Lancs' Regiments of Foot in Afghanistan. Shared lodgings in Kandahar for a time. With his discharge he was appointed as the British consul at Shanghai before I lost track of him. We recently became reacquainted—"

"Watson, please!"

The Doctor's brows rose. He pursed his lips and took a calming breath. "I called on his family and discovered the rather strange nature of his murder. Not only was he killed, but his testicular apparatus had been removed—taken away—missing as it were."

Holmes's body stiffened. "Do you see it? My enigmatic missive is not happenstance. Whoever sent them rightly reasoned that I would call you. Someone is inviting me to investigate this murder."

"That may be so, but to what end? The murderer has already been apprehended—a young woman. She is in custody, if the *Daily Mail* is to be believed."

Holmes shook his head. "But surely, they have the wrong person."

"Doubtful. Caught red-handed. It was his housekeeper."

Holmes glanced at Mrs. Thornton who remained slumped in the doorway, mopping her brow with the hem of her apron.

"Do you think, if I were to bring the testes to you, that you would be able to tell me if they might have belonged to Mr. Goodnow?"

"Only in a general way."

"Can you spare me the time?"

"That is something I have in great abundance. I would love to see you. And please, bring your specimen."

"Tomorrow then. We shall meet at Rules for lunch—noon."

Holmes replaced the handset on the phone box and returned to the kitchen table. As he opened the casket again, his mind turned back thirty years to a cardboard box that contained two severed human ears. He closed the jewelry box and examined the wrapping. Then his hand went to the knot that bound the twine—a common binding or overhand knot. However, the twine itself proved more interesting.

Holmes walked into the light of the window twisting the cord in his fingers. It was three strands of a course hempen weave. Fishermen use it to mend nets—cotton cord being the variety commonly used at mercantile stores. *The package likely originated from a rural locality—possibly coastal*, he surmised.

He returned to the parlor to retrieve his pipe from the mantle. As he filled and lit it, he began making a mental inventory of nefarious persons who were never apprehended.

*****

Aboard the 9:14 from Seaford to London Victoria, Holmes repeatedly turned the enigmatic brass casket over in his hands. The object's mundane rectangular shape was relieved by ornately carved glyphs and symbols. Most were unknown to him and harkened back to a time before history. However, the symbol in the center of the lid was vaguely familiar. It displayed a bird of prey, an eagle or hawk, with two heads.

Holmes knew just the person to decipher this glyph, and the others on the casket. Professor Augustus Stone would be receiving a visit. However, Holmes decided that an interview with the young woman accused of committing the grisly murder would begin his investigation.

The taxi ride from the station to Watson's flat on Sheen Lane allowed Holmes to finalize his itinerary. The Doctor's maid, Nora, explained that his friend had already departed for their promised luncheon. He left his bag, put his specimen in the icebox, and made a brief call to Scotland Yard before setting out for the restaurant.

Watson was undoubtedly perusing the menu at this very moment. However, Holmes knew the Doctor would order the Galloway beef, and he would have the pheasant. Friends and confederates for more than thirty-eight years, their lives coalesced around many legendary adventures, and Holmes hoped that one more might be in the offing.

As the waiter cleared the dishes, Holmes placed the brass casket on the table and lit a cigarette.

"So that's the infamous family jewel box?" Watson remarked, with a smirk.

"Yes. I took the liberty of placing my specimen in your icebox."

"I will examine them in the morning."

"It took a bit of persuading for Mrs. Thornton to allow me to do likewise yesterday . . . and in my own home. I wish you could have seen her face when she opened the casket."

"Ha! I can imagine."

"Oh, and do you know. She *knew* what they were. She . . . somehow . . . knew what they were."

"Women know these things, Holmes."

"Women know these things?

Watson stifled a smile. "She, no doubt, has harbored similar designs herself."

"Your adolescent witticism borders on the obscene, Watson."

"It was more than a mere jest. As the consummate symbol of manhood, I have no doubt that an angry woman is at cause here."

"I cannot believe that," Holmes remarked.

"Had you been in the city in recent times you would have encountered many an angry woman. The suffragette's wartime hiatus has ended, and the People's Act has not diminished the ladies' ardor. I would only admit it to you, but encountering gangs of women in the streets is unsettling.

"I am surprised to learn that you are caught in the masculine hysteria about the suffragettes. They want the right to vote, not castrate."

Watson's brows rose. "Given your conviction that emotions cloud reason, I am surprised to learn that you feel women are able to make rational political choices."

"Murky reasoning knows no gender, Watson. Women simply display their emotions more openly. I've come to believe that they cannot help themselves."

"I must say, Holmes, you do a masterful job of masking yours. Why, one might think you had no emotions at all."

"Thank you," Holmes said, snuffing out his cigarette and signaling for the bill. He reached across the table and tapped Watson's hand.

"Pray tell me what you know of the dreadful murder of friend Goodnow."

"Little more than I have already shared. When I paid my respects, I learned of the mutilation. There was also talk of a threatening message, an omen that came prior to the dreadful event. But, I did not think it appropriate to inquire further."

"Which brings us to the motive. What are your thoughts there?"

"The man had an commendable career in the military, followed by Foreign Service. He held several posts that, I assume, he served honorably. We parted ways long ago, but were reunited at a welcome home celebration two weeks ago, hosted by his club. Your brother was present at the dinner, by the way."

"Mycroft? His presence at Goodnow's celebration suggests that he may be able to share some valuable information. I will pay him a visit while I am in town."

Watson nodded, "Yes, but if you are looking for a motive, you had best talk with his murderer."

"His *accused* murderer," Holmes corrected. "It appears that I remain in the good graces of Scotland Yard. I took the liberty of placing a call to Inspector Walls from your flat."

"So, you're off then?"

Watson leaned back in his chair to fully take in his friend. "It's good to see you in such high spirits, my friend. At the risk of raising a sore subject, I was not certain country life would serve a man of your nature and temperament. I take back what I had said about your move to the Sussex Downs."

"Why not admit it, Watson, you miss me."

"Yes, I can hardly bare up under the strain a good nights sleep, regular mealtimes . . . and am positively despondent that I no longer have a chemical laboratory bubbling away in my parlor."

CHAPTER 3

WITH INSPECTOR LASTRADE GONE, and Gregson retired, Holmes felt like an uninvited ghost as he entered Scotland Yard. His last visit was before the war when he had helped Inspector Walls with a case in which a fellow Inspector, Osborne, had been murdered. Holmes used his tenuous connections within the London underworld to point Walls in a direction that lead to a successful arrest and conviction.

Holmes was directed to an office overlooking the Thames. Joshua Walls was waiting, and rose from his desk as Holmes entered. As the detective explained his interest in the Goodnow murder case, Walls' brow remained bent in scrutiny.

"Mr. Holmes, I appreciate your concern. I am uncertain as to what your involvement is, but I will not prevent you from poking around. However, I can tell you that you are wasting your time if you feel Eva Allsop is innocent. Mr. Goodnow's body was still warm when Miss Allsop was found in her room with bloody hands. Her nightdress was spattered with gore. Her bloody fingerprints were all about, on the stairway and in her attic bedroom."

"Cause of death?" Holmes asked.

"A slit throat and a monumental blood-letting when his organs were removed."

"Miss Allsop's age?"

"Eighteen."

"Holmes repeated: "Eighteen, really. An execution-style murder is not typical for a woman."

"Most women, you mean to say," Walls shot back.

Holmes nodded. "Did anyone witness the murder?"

"No. It occurred after midnight. The household was in bed. All, that is, except for Mr. Goodnow and Miss Allsop."

"Did you find the weapon used to kill and mutilate the murdered fellow?"

"No. She likely hid it after the murder, or later in the commotion that followed the discovery of the body."

Holmes waited.

"We looked for that knife but did not find it. As you seem to know, the victim was disemboweled, to put it politely. This necessitated a large sharp blade. The autopsy told us it was one with saw-like edges."

"Does this not seem strange to you? The accused did not flee. She did not wash the blood from her body, or change her clothing, but rather returned to her room. Add to that, the weapon—a formidable gelding knife—was not found on the scene nor in the room of the accused."

"It is an anomaly, I will admit, but it does not supersede the larger body of evidence."

Holmes smirked. "Dr. Watson inferred that there was a warning of some kind."

"We are uncertain. One of the maids called it 'an omen.' She reported that a day prior to his murder, Goodnow received a package in the post . . . a trinket of some kind. He seemed to be visibly shaken upon receiving it, and took it to his office."

"Curious, is it not?"

"Possibly. But, correlation and relation are not the same thing."

"I understand. Your investigation is still underway."

"Indeed. I have not yet interviewed Mrs. Goodnow."

Inspector Walls retrieved a notebook from his coat pocket. "I also plan to pay a call on a Miss Tessa Wiggins. Her references brought Miss Allsop to the Goodnow home."

Holmes momentarily startled at the mention of Tessa's name, but Walls' eyes were in his notebook as he continued: "I will call on Mrs. Goodnow and Miss Wiggins tomorrow."

"I appreciate your thoroughness, Inspector. I intend to keep 'poking around,' as you say. If I discover anything of interest, I will bring it to your attention."

"Please do, Mr. Holmes. "I am curious as to why you harbor an interest in this investigation. Was Goodnow an acquaintance?"

"No."

"Then, may I ask who your client might be?" Walls followed.

"The client is *me*," Holmes said. "I failed to mention that I received a threatening missive at my home related to this murder.

Walls sat motionless for a moment. "Interesting. So, you believe they are baiting you?

"I do. I might be of assistance in many ways. If nothing else, I may bait the murderer for you."

"Nonsense. In the past, your skill and ability has been invaluable."

"But . . . that was *the past*."

"Nothing of the sort. I simply wish to point out that policing has improved immeasurably in the last couple decades."

"Most assuredly. But one thing has remained the same."

"And that is?"

"Investigations are conducted by human beings . . . who make mistakes."

There was no reply.

"One favor," Holmes continued. "I was wondering if you might allow me to visit the accused woman?"

"If she does not object, I can make that arrangement. She is being held at Bow Street."

Holmes glanced at his watch. "This afternoon? Is that possible?"

"Yes. And, you will share anything that you learn?"

"Have I ever kept anything from Scotland Yard?" Holmes teased.

"How would we know, Mr. Holmes?"

The desk sergeant offered a warm greeting as Holmes arrived at London's first police station.

"Welcome, Mr. Holmes," the policeman said. "The Inspector has alerted us to your visit and request. The accused must agree to see you, and I have not yet secured her permission." He raised his brows. You know, Miss Allsop may not recognize your name."

"Yes, sergeant. I suspect yours may be the last generation to hearken to the name Sherlock Holmes."

"Please take a seat, sir. The accused is with someone at the moment."

Holmes leaned closer. "I would be interested in knowing who is with Miss Allsop at the moment."

"No one of consequence, Mr. Holmes. A street missionary . . . a Salvationist."

Holmes took a seat opposite the front desk and, pulling his pipe from his coat pocket, held it up with a questioning look. The police sergeant nodded his approval.

Holmes was formulating a list of questions when the iron gate to the detention area clanked and opened. A woman in the bleak black dress of a Salvation Army 'slum sister' walked with speed toward the outer door. She was agitated—heavily worked by life's troubles. A bonnet was in hand, and her mane of thick black hair was economized in ornamentation with but a single pink ribbon tightly binding it. About her neck was a tarnished crucifix, the bottom of which had been rubbed to a shine with worried fingers. She was a plain woman, but there was keenness in her manner that was captivating.

The desk sergeant could not see beyond the street grime clinging to the hem of the sister's dress. But, if he had, the penetrating green eyes of this black Irish lassie might have charmed him. Holmes, being unhampered by standards of comparison when it comes to women, saw beyond her garb and manner. It was Tessa.

As she passed the counter, her hands came together in front of her breast, and a broad smile blossomed on her freckled face. "When the just cry for help, the Lord hears and delivers them out of their troubles. Mr. Holmes, I should not be surprised that you are here." She was virtually bouncing with excitement.

"I might say the same of you, Sister Wiggins."

"Please, Mr. Holmes, Tessa. You've known me my entire life," she said in a playful scold.

"So, Tessa, your saintly mission includes the jails of London."

"To think myself a saint would be bad for me. And, it is a rather dreadful business that brings me here this afternoon. I prayed for help, and here you are."

"Yes, well and good, I suppose," Mr. Holmes replied. "However, I suspect another hand is at work here. Nonetheless, I am eager to help if I may. However, it must wait, as I am here to interview an accused murderer."

"Eva. You are here to see Eva Allsop. You see, Mr. Holmes, trust in the Lord," she chided.

"Eva Allsop? Accused of murdering Mr. Goodnow?"

"I know she did not do the dreadful things for which she stands accused."

"On that we concur," Holmes answered. "Well now, I think my inquiries might best begin with you."

19

CHAPTER 4

BENCHLEY'S TEA ROOM evoked a startling simplicity—traditional black enamel façade, rectangular tables with white tablecloths, and hand-colored daguerreotype landscapes adorning pallid walls. It is strictly about tea and conversation.

Holmes smoothed a wrinkle in the starched tablecloth and turned his eyes to Tessa. They had touched one another's heart thirty years ago, and it seemed that they still possessed that capacity.

"I often think of Rory with remorse. I might have . . ." Holmes's words lapsed into silence. A wave of sadness rippled across his features.

"Mr. Holmes, there is no cause for recrimination. My brother was a troubled man. She stretched her hand out across the table. He raised two fingers as if to reach out.

Holmes nodded. "I admire your ability to see and accept the truth in every situation — a rare talent. "

"Not in Spitalfields where wishes are useless and dreams impossible."

One of Holmes's hallmark meditative silences passed before Tessa clanged her teacup on her saucer. Holmes returned to the present moment and smiled. He pulled a penny from his waistcoat pocket and held it out. She opened her palm and he dropped the coin within.

"My penny man." she said.

Thirty years ago, her brother Rory had got himself in a fix and was kidnapped. Tessa was given a ransom note. Holmes gave her a penny when she delivered it. From that day forward, Sherlock Holmes had been her "penny man."

"Three months ago, Eva Allsop sent a note to an acquaintance pleading for help. It miraculously found its way to our headquarters on Queen Victoria Street. She was being housed, against her will, in a warehouse in Southampton. Her letter was given to me, as my mission now includes the recent epidemic of white slavery."

Holmes's eyes widened. "So this deplorable practice is no longer confined to Greece and Eastern Europe?"

"No. It has spread, like a plague, across the continent. Everyday, girls and young women are seduced, abducted, and sent into a life of unspeakable degradation, disease and death."

"An enormous burden for you," Holmes said. "Surely there is help from the authorities . . . or the government."

"The Salvationists provide most of my support . . . although that may not hold true in the future. I falls to me now, to make a report about Eva to Major Dugmore. I fear the news will ignite his recent displeasure with me. Nonetheless, with or without the Salvation Army, I am committed to care for these ill-fated women because the police and government are limited in what they can do. You see, many of them leave the country voluntarily. Their abductors are sly, Mr. Holmes. Young women are led to believe that they are being courted. They are promised marriage or a wonderful job in an exotic foreign land. Such was the case with Eva. She was promised a position as a companion for a wealthy lady in France — irresistible to a young woman from St. Giles whose future could be no better than a life of drudgery in a laundry."

"And, you rescued her?"

Tessa described Eva's liberation in detail. Holmes patted his breast pocket in search of a pen, no doubt thinking that Dr. Watson would already be scribbling in his notebook. She told the story of how, with the help of Scotland Yard, Eva was rescued from her imprisonment in a dingy room near the Southampton wharf.

"It's strange, Mr. Holmes. None of her abductors was apprehended at the time of her rescue. However, the next day, Eva and I were called upon to identify one of the scoundrels who was found brutally murdered near the warehouse. Someone had evidently reckoned with one of her captors."

Holmes's interest peaked at this news. "You said the man was murdered? Do you happen to know the nature of the attack?"

"We only viewed the face of the man. A cover lay over his body. But, if the blood soaked canvas was any indication, it was a rather gruesome attack — one that inflicted large wounds in his belly.

Holmes's eyes glazed over for a moment. "So, you ministered to Eva?"

"Yes. In her state, I could not leave her alone at a shelter. I took her to The Nest. She became very dear to me. She reminds me of myself when . . ." Tessa paused in reflection.

Holmes's brow lowered. "You were saying?"

"It's nothing. I wonder if I did the right thing—bringing Eva to The Nest."

"It's the home for abused girls that you established?"

"Hardly, Mr. Holmes. I am simply a caretaker. Eva was too old to reside there. We only house girls between six and sixteen years of age, so The Nest was always intended as a temporary refuge for Eva. When she arrived, she was traumatized — barely able to hold a thought or manage a conversation." Tessa's eyes glistened. "Eva is a remarkable young woman. Despite all that happened to her, she maintained her innocent nature. And, she seemed to recover quickly. Some women in her circumstance must cope with the ordeal for years, not only with their rage and fear, but also with feelings of shame and self-doubt."

"It's difficult for me to imagine," Holmes interjected.

"For any man!" Tessa spat with a sharpness that startled Holmes. "I'm sorry, Mr. Holmes, people are blind to the pain that the world inflicts upon its women." Her lips trembled.

"What is it, Tessa?"

"I abandoned her. I sent Eva on her way. I was being pressed to remove her from The Nest and I succumbed to that coercion. A suitable job turned up and I urged her to take it. I am responsible for —" Tessa began weeping.

Holmes awkwardly touched Tessa's hand. "Moments ago you asked me not to blame myself for Rory's death. Now, you're doing likewise with Eva."

"Sometimes it appears that a woman is moving beyond her trauma, but the pain merely goes deeper," she said, tapping her breast. "I should have known better. It was wrong to let her leave."

"We all suffer under the most human of all illusions — the illusion that we're responsible for what other people do. Now, I may be an egotistical old man, but I believe we can help Eva. Tell me what you know about her?"

"Little. A hard life, to have her tell it. She claims to be an orphan — adopted when she was eight. However, the loving couple did not so much want a daughter as a drudge to work in their laundry."

"How does something such as that happen?" Holmes wondered aloud.

"It's common, Mr. Holmes. While orphanages are a blessing, they are horribly overcrowded and understaffed. Inquiries into adopting families are superficial. The orphanage does not want to find reasons to refuse an adoption."

"Do you know from which orphanage she came?"

Tessa had a puzzled look. "Why do you ask?"

"I may wish to make a visit."

"I'm sorry. I never thought to ask her."

Tessa seemed dazed.

Holmes tapped her hand. "So, the loving couple put Eva to work in their laundry. I suppose it wasn't hard to coax her away," Holmes surmised.

"She left home two years ago — well before I came upon her. She was on a quest to find her parents — common among orphans. There were but a few items left within her bag on the front steps of the orphanage."

"A weighty endeavor for a young girl. How could she think that she could find her parents after all this time?"

Tessa shrugged. "Hope springs eternal for orphans and their mothers."

"So, where did she search?

"London. Like my mum and me, she sold flowers and picked rags to make her way. That is where she fell in with the villain who tried to enslave her."

"She seems to have pluck," Holmes judged, "like someone else I know."

Tessa bowed to the compliment. "She will need it, as she stands accused of murder."

"What did she tell you about the murder?"

"She seemed confused or . . ."

"What?" Holmes prodded.

"When I asked her what happened that terrible evening, she used the word 'retribution.' She knows more than she is willing to share. Mind you, I believe that she is innocent of the murder. But, she may be involved in some way."

Holmes listened with a keen intensity. "A few nights behind bars will loosen her tongue," he predicted.

"Maybe so. But I must protect her."

"I will be happy to keep you apprised of new developments. By the way, Inspector Walls will be seeking an interview with you."

"He has already contacted our office. I am meeting him at our headquarters tomorrow morning at nine." Tessa paused, pursing her lips. "I'd like to ask a favor, Mr. Holmes."

He waited.

"I wish to join you in your investigation."

"Tessa, you know my ways and methods. I am most effective when I am untethered."

"I know your ways. And on more than one occasion, I helped — if you recall." Tessa grabbed his hand. "I need to do this! Eva was in my care. My responsibility. I put her into service at the Goodnows. We have a special bond. I know her ways . . . how young women reason."

"I'm sorry, Tessa. Two hounds on the scent will frighten our quarry. You have your duties at The Nest, do you not?"

Tessa pushed back and stiffened in her chair. "I will not be put off, Mr. Holmes. If I must, I will go my own way."

"That would be foolish — dangerous. I believe the true murderer has an eye on me, and persons with me will be in danger," Holmes explained. "As I have in the past, I will depend on your help. Presently, I need to interview Eva, and talk with others at The Nest. So, you *will be* assisting with the investigation. Beyond that, I believe Eva's interests will best be served if you remain at your post."

"And out of your way," Tessa remarked.

"I would like to interview Eva tomorrow morning. I will come to your headquarters at nine to be present for the Inspector's interview."

"Why? Are you concerned?"

"The good Inspector believes that he has the murderer in Eva, but he lacks a motive."

Tessa's eyes widened. "Yes, and one would have to have a grievous motive to kill a person in such a horrific manner!"

"Indeed. I believe that he will be looking for evidence of emotional instability in Eva. Did she display such?"

"No. Eva had a natural ease about her. She got on well with the other girls and was well-liked. She spent most of her time in the gardens, and often took long walks with her friend Abigail."

"And what about Abigail?"

"Abigail has an edge to her, but seems harmless," Tessa noted. "She is a local girl who helps us in the garden. Do you think that Abigail might be involved?"

"Human beings are pack-like animals in that they become more dangerous when they group together. And, from what we know of how Mr. Goodnow was murdered, there was likely more than one individual involved."

CHAPTER 5

TESSA WIGGINS STOOD AT ATTENTION before the desk of Major Dugmore.

"Please take a seat," the Major began.

"I am not here for a chat. I have something to report," Tessa responded.

"You are referring to Eva Allsop, I assume?"

Tessa grimaced and her eyes closed. "I should not be surprised that you have heard."

"Heard? The whole city has heard. The newspapers are awash with the grisly details of the young woman who murdered her master — a young woman who was left in your care, and that of the Salvation Army."

"I take full responsibility, and intend—"

"To do what?" the Major asked. "To rectify the besmirched name of the Salvation Army? To still the voices calling for The Nest to close its doors?"

Tessa pointed to the crest on her dress. "I am a Salvationist. I believe the crossed swords signify that we will fight for those who are down — for people like Eva."

"Sister Wiggins, I am well aware of the Army's mission. You have a good heart, but your ways are often antithetical to our cause. Eva is the latest example of your poor judgment."

"To what are you referring?"

"Patricia."

"I understand, but I believe she'll return to The Nest."

The Major smirked. "As she has before."

29

"Exactly. I believe Patricia's behavior —"

"The Nest is not a hotel, Miss Wiggins. This is just another example of your appalling lack of discipline," Dugmore stated. "Patricia should have been punished the first time she ran off. What will do you if she returns now?"

"I will restrict her to her room until I understand where she has been and why she is doing this." Tessa affirmed.

"So, another chance?"

"Yes," Tessa answered.

The Major leaned back in his chair. "And how many chances does Tessa Wiggins deserve?"

"Possibly more than you are willing to give her."

*****

Holmes's and Watson's day usually began with a shared cup in the morning. Today however, there was a small deviation in this ritual. Watson curiously watched Holmes measured the tea into their cups and poured the hot water.

"So, you have abandoned the use of a pot and strainer?" Watson noted.

"Yes, I enjoy the more robust flavor that tea steeped in a cup gives me." He looked up playfully. "Of course, I also enjoy reading the leaves afterwards."

Watson laughed. "You always were a Gypsy at heart. Will you read my leaves?"

"For a shilling."

"I would gladly give thrice that to know my future," Watson answered.

Holmes handed Watson his cup.

The Doctor brought the cup to his nose, letting the flowery aroma tantalize his senses. "Surely, our fortunes are easier to discern these days as our future becomes shorter with each passing day."

Holmes placed his cup down on the saucer with a clank. "It's all well and good to be aware our days are numbered, but you need not dwell upon it, old man."

"I do not dwell. I am simply aware that there is much to do, and frightfully little time in which to do it."

"And what is pressing on your time these days, Watson? I understand that you are writing?"

"I've taken up essays."

Holmes attempted to smother a chuckle by sipping his tea.

"You find that amusing do you? What of that monumental tome you have been scribbling for the last twenty years?"

"I intend it to be a definitive work on crime and criminals. An entirely useful product intended for the benefit of mankind."

"Am I to suppose that my essays would not have a similar impact?"

"I would not presume to say that, but I am curious as to the subject of your essays."

"My latest one makes the case that the telephone has been a boon to human beings."

Holmes's eyes widened. "A boon? Telephones intrude on our tranquility, dehumanize relationships, isolate people, strip the human voice of the subtleties that give the true meaning of another's words, and take up useful wall space. Telephones are only a boon to gossip-mongers."

Watson pursed his lips as he looked away. "I venture this would not be a good time for me to offer my opinion of your masterwork."

"Now, now, Watson. I look forward to reading your essay. I really do."

"Thank you. And, I hope that your manuscript will soon find its way into the world where it will, no doubt, benefit all."

"That is precisely my intention."

"But even the most adroitly written book will not deliver the desired result; for there must be a great mind to absorb what is contained in your book . . . and a strong heart as well. There is but one Sherlock Holmes."

Holmes smiled. "A premature eulogy that has me aware that my methods cannot be solely embodied within a book. They must be expressed within an individual."

"Oh my, the thought of a Sherlock Holmes doppelganger skulking about boggles the mind."

* * * * *

Tessa retreated to her haven on the roof of the Salvation Army headquarters. Gazing over the city streets below, with her diary in her pocket, and a warm cup of coffee in hand, she reflected on Major Dugmore's words. She was thankful that she did not say what was in her heart when his accusations were hurled at her. For, if she had, she might lose the one place that offered refuge when she was nearly swept into the gutters of Spitalfields.

She was left alone when her mother died. Rory had fled the city. She could not sell enough penny bunches of violets to feed herself. Holmes reached out for her help just as she came to the end of her tether. He needed to gain entry to the women-only facility on the third floor where his quarry was hiding, and he asked for her help.

She recalled her first glimpse of this 370-bed facility ten years ago. She thumbed the diary for her entry:

The entrance to the chamber was crowded with women and girls pressing to the front of the line in the hope of retrieving a bed ticket. The beds were nothing more than padded mats lined up head to toe in long rows. Talking ceased when the overhead lights were turned

*off, but the women tossed and groaned silently
until one of them would cry out in the midst of
the nightmare that was her life.*

While the sight of the Sally Army marching and preaching in the streets was ever-present in the slums, Tessa never gave them much notice. She was surprised to learn that the Army offered far more than a good night's sleep and a warm cup of tea. Women and girls were assisted in outer world experiences — the reconciliation of wives and husbands, the restoration of girls to parents, medical care, and midwifery for women who had no means. The girls who most touched Tessa's heart were the sad ones who had been sexually abused, or abandoned when they became pregnant. The mission was ill equipped to deal with this kind of earthly trauma.

Cradling a sobbing twelve-year old girl in her arms one evening, Tessa envisioned a refuge for the girls and women who suffered from the depravity of evil men. Sister Florence Booth, wife of General Bramwell Booth, took up the cause with her. Two years later, The Nest was founded in Upper Clapton, thanks to a donated property.

Now, her headstrong manner threatened to take away the thing that meant the most in her life — her girls. She resolved that she would change, starting today. She would redeem Eva and do whatever was needed to bolster her position at The Nest.

When Tessa returned to the lobby, she found Mr. Holmes waiting. She assumed a confident demeanor, but Holmes noticed a tinge of red in her eyes.

"Don't worry. Walls is a decent sort."

She smiled. "It's not about the interview, Mr. Holmes. I am anxious to meet the Inspector. He must know the truth about Eva. She is not capable of hurting, let alone killing, another person."

"You know little about her," Holmes was quick to note. "You understandably have a soft spot in your heart for street urchins."

Tessa looked stone-faced. "What does that have to do with this? I know my girls. Eva is not capable of killing."

"That is how you feel, but your feelings will not sway Inspector Walls. He believes Eva is guilty and is putting a case against her. He will want to know how she found her position, and why you placed Eva in the Goodnow household."

"The opportunity did not come through any efforts of mine, Mr. Holmes. Eva found the position herself. She asked me to provide a reference, and I was happy to do so."

"Did you not find it odd that she was able to find a suitable position on her own?"

"It was that very fact that led me to believe she was ready to stand on her own feet."

"How long after her rescue did she take employment at the Goodnow home?"

"Five . . . no, six weeks."

"And, she resided at The Nest during that time?"

"Yes. We are at our capacity so she shared a room with another girl — Patricia."

"At some point, I will want to talk with Patricia and any others Eva befriended."

Tessa balked. "Patricia is not presently available. However, Abigail Watterson still comes around. She was Eva's best friend. Abigail was Eva's age, so it is not surprising they became close. As I explained, she is a local girl who helps us in the gardens. Should I mention Abigail to the Inspector?"

"Only if he asks. I think it best if I were the first to talk to Abigail. Remember, Walls will be looking for evidence of mental frailty."

"There was none."

Holmes checked his watch. "It's nine."

Tessa took Mr. Holmes's arm and walked toward the front office.

The front doors banged open. Walls rushed into the lobby. Upon seeing Holmes he held both arms in the air and let them fall to his side in a gesture of despair. "Eva Allsop has escaped!"

CHAPTER 6

"A SALVATIONIST WAS INVOLVED in the escape," the Inspector said.

Before the shock of his accusation could fully register on Tessa's countenance, Walls held up a conciliatory hand. "I am sorry, Sister. I should say that Eva's accomplice was *dressed* in Salvationist garb, black dress, bonnet—a woman though—and a clever one. She timed her entry just before the changing of the guards in the jail. After the relief officers were in place, *two* Salvationists walked out of Bow Street station."

"So, you do not suspect a Salvationist was involved," Holmes confirmed.

"It was a ruse, Walls affirmed. Then, turning to Tessa, he added: "I apologize for any unwarranted alarm, Sister."

Tessa nodded, but her pale face did not regain its color because she knew that her already tarnished reputation was about to suffer another blow.

"Given this event, Miss Wiggins, I wish to postpone our interview."

"Very well. I will take my leave gentleman," Tessa said. And then to the Inspector: "I'll be at The Nest in Clapton if you need me."

Both men acknowledged her with a nod.

As Tessa departed, Walls turned to Holmes: "So Miss Wiggins is an acquaintance?"

"Yes. Did I fail to mention that? One of my irregular army—all grown up now."

"Indeed," Walls replied, raising an eyebrow.

"Her involvement is coincidental," Holmes added.

The Inspector smiled. "Very well. I have an appointment with Mrs. Goodnow at half-past one. I invite you to accompany me if you are able. She may offer something that might put us on the trail of the murderer or murderers."

Holmes was encouraged by Wall's use of the demonstrative pronoun "us," and that he thought the murderer may have had an accomplice.

"Thank you, Inspector," Holmes replied. "I will meet you at the Goodnow home, if I may. I have two engagements before then.

*****

Augustus Stone was generous in proportion and spirit. He ambled about his office in a confident British style, with his hands twitching—eternally grasping for something new and different. He had devoted most of his life to curating the East India Company's Asian collection at the British Museum. With his retirement, the collection was disassembled and sent to far-flung institutions and galleries throughout the empire. However, Augustus remained unrelenting in his probe of mankind's veiled history.

The Professor was at his desk, penning a treatise on what he had tentatively titled: *The Kuang-i chi Gavel*. The mysterious object, an ornamental brass hammer found near the tomb of the first Chinese emperor Qin Shi Huang, lay upon his desk. He put the pen down and ran his fingers over the enigmatic object that had been forged in a time before the historical Jesus. His concentration was such that Holmes resorted to pounding on the door with his fist before he gained the Professor's attention.

"Ah, Holmes. I am pleased to be in your presence. Please come in."

The Detective entered, carrying the brass casket wrapped in an oilcloth. Augustus noticed it immediately. "You have brought something for me, have you?"

"Yes, Professor. Do you have time for me?"

"Time, time, time," the pear-bellied man exclaimed, as he shepherded Holmes into his office. "Time is something I now have too much of, and also too little of, if you catch my meaning?"

"I appreciate your riddle," Holmes answered. "We hear the seconds tick away but the years pass silently."

Augustus motioned for Holmes to take a seat. He retreated behind a prodigious pile of books stacked along the front perimeter of his desk. "My retirement has given me time for those endeavors I have put off for decades. Take this object here. I call it the *Kuang-i chi* gavel because I am led to believe, from the inscriptions, that it was meant to represent the gavel used by the judges in the court of the Underworld — the tribunal of the Ten Kings. In Chinese tradition this court resides in the spirit world. The judges summon mortals, and sometimes even animals, when their time has come. They are then confronted with aggrieved plaintiffs, who bring them to account for political, moral, or ritual offences. On rare occasions, they are released and returned to the world of the living.

"You see, Mr. Holmes, while the ancient Chinese believed in two worlds — physical and spirit, for them the veil that separates the two is thin and fragile. Those in the spirit world can come into our plane of existence, and we can travel into theirs."

"As Dante did," Holmes remarked.

"Yes, but from Dante Alighieri's hell there is no escape. Quite fortunate for you, as you have sent many to that dark dominion."

Holmes gestured toward the gavel. "May I?"

"Please do, Mr. Holmes."

The Detective hefted the mallet in his hands and brought it closer, twisting it in his fingers. "The detail is amazing. To think this object was forged from molten brass."

"Yes, and this one from double stone molds—before the lost-wax method, you know. The finer carving and etching was done after the object was cast."

"I am certain now that I have come to the very man who can help me to uncover a small mystery that recently came to my door."

The Professor's eyes sparkled with blissful expectancy as Holmes unwrapped the casket and placed it atop a pile of books. Augustus Stone's fingers twitched above it as if he were afraid to touch it. He stood over it, twisting his head to capture the various sides. "May I?"

Holmes nodded.

Stone snatched up the jewel case and turned it over in his hands. "Celtic. These symbols have a vague familiarity." He tapped the cover of the casket. "But this one on the lid is different."

"Why does it look familiar?" Holmes pondered.

"Ah, well, it has many origins. The double-headed eagle is a Masonic symbol. Could that be it?

"Possibly. However, I doubt that is its source," Holmes said.

"Very well then, what do you know of heraldry?

"Only what I find in catalogues."

"Well Mr. Holmes, there are many family crests that have some variation of this pictogram."

"I do not wish to impose on your valuable time."

"Tut, tut, Mr. Holmes. Your visits are felicitous. You offer the opportunity to ignite this old brain and get it bubbling again."

The academic's body puffed up, and his voice took on the measured tones of a lecturer: "Let us start with what we can assume is the most important symbol, since it is on the lid. And, as you believe that Masons are not involved, we will look in other directions. This symbol is often referred to as the Eagle of Lagash, after one of the oldest uses of the emblem in the ancient Sumerian city of Lagash. The Emperor Charlemagne popularized the two-faced eagle in Europe. You will find some version of it on flags and banners from the Holy Roman Empire to Albania. However, since the other symbols on the casket are Celtic in origin, I would propose that we might look to coats-of-arms from our own nation. Unfortunately, there may be too many to be of any real help. However . . . ."

The Professor shot up from his chair and bustled out of the room. Holmes wandered the bookshelves behind the Professor's desk and ran his finger across the bindings. As Holmes would expect, there was King's *History of Babylon*, and Budge's *Guide to the Egyptian Rooms* — to which Stone contributed a chapter. But what surprised Holmes were the Professor's more eclectic tastes: Proust, Joyce and Kafka. He blew the dust from his fingertip and returned to his chair, using the time to clean and fill his pipe. But, before he could put a flame to it, Augustus burst back into the room with a splayed book in his hands.

"Here we are, sir, neat and tidy. Arthur Charles Fox-Davies has kindly categorized the coats-of-arms by type for us."

Augustus proffered the massive volume to Holmes: "Here, look over these pages yourself, as there are well over forty Irish, Scottish, Welsh and English coats-of-arms that incorporate a two-headed bird of prey."

Holmes returned his pipe to his pocket and placed the book in his lap. He slowly ran his finger down the pages. After a minute, Holmes's finger paused. "Hm-m-m."

"A possibility, Mr. Holmes?"

"Murtagh. You did say that the other symbols on the casket are Celtic in nature?"

Stone nodded. "Yes, the figures on the four sides are well-documented Celtic warrior tattoos. The Celts were fierce warriors, as you know — and not just the men. In the Celtic culture, women and men were equal in most ways. Women could own property, participate in politics and religious services. Indeed, it is a common misconception that druids — the priests of the Celts, were all male. They were not."

Stone pulled his chair back and walked toward the bookshelves that covered the wall behind his desk. He ran a finger along the spines on the top shelf. He pulled out one of the books, and then wiped the dust from his fingers onto his vest. The leather crackled as he opened it. He motioned for Holmes to come near.

"You will find much more in this book," Stone said. "MacBain has an entire chapter on symbology." He held it out for Holmes. "You may find it useful."

"Thank you, Professor."

Professor Augustus Stone turned back to the casket and pointed to the front panel.

"This symbol on the front is interesting—two crossed swords. It was a tattoo worn by *female* Celtic warriors. We believe they earned the right to wear it after their first battle. These crossed swords denote that women fight side-by side with the men. And trust me, Celtic women were fierce adversaries."

The Professor pulled another volume from the shelf and began thumbing it. "Here we are. The historian Plutarch stated this while describing a battle in 102 B.C. between Romans and Celts—and I quote: 'The fight had been no less fierce with the women then with the men themselves. The women charged with swords and axes and fell upon their opponents uttering a hideous outcry."

Augustus looked up. "I am wondering if this casket might have been fashioned by a woman."

Holmes smiled. "I suspect it was, given what the casket contained."

"Yes, I noticed the sealing wax under the lid," Stone stated.

"It held the remains of human testes."

The Professor's eyes widened, "Remarkable." He cocked his head and, with hesitation, said: "I am sure it has occurred to you that this may have been sent as a warning?"

CHAPTER 7

HOLMES WAS A HARRIER ON THE HUNT upon leaving
Professor Stone, so his luncheon engagement with Watson was akin to
a "going home" call from the huntsman's bugle.

Holmes arrived ten minutes late, and refused to be put off by the
Doctor's dour demeanor. "Apologies, my friend," Holmes said. "I just
left Augustus Stone."

"Yes . . . well then, that explains it. How is the windy old
grandee?"

"Well. The casket delighted him."

"It would, of course. Does he know the former contents?"

"Yes."

"And, speaking of that, "I have examined your specimen,
Holmes.

"And?"

"As I said, I cannot match them to the deceased, but they are
human testes in keeping with those of a man Goodnow's age."

"Thank you. You may dispose of them."

"I have. My maid Nora saw them in my icebox and asked what
they were."

"I thought *women knew these things?*"

"Women of a certain age, Holmes. Nora is not yet twenty."

Holmes laughed. "So, what did you tell little Nora was in the
jar?"

"Pickled kumquats."

"Hah! I may never eat another kumquat again. However, I have a
tooth set for ocean trout."

As the lunch concluded Holmes put his napkin on the table and looked sheepishly at Watson, striking a pose of thoughtful reflection.

"Alright Holmes, you have been champing at the bit all through lunch. What is it you wish to tell me?"

"Stone offered several ideas related to the jewelry box. The symbol on the lid presented the possibility that the sender may be an old acquaintance of ours."

Watson waited.

"Maeve Murtagh."

Watson was dumbfounded. Maeve Murtagh was daughter of Holmes's former archenemy Professor Moriarty. The name change, for a time, protected her from Holmes, but there was nothing to protect him from her retribution.

"I thought she was long gone, or even put to rest by her aggrieved former employer." Watson declared. "Does Tessa know?"

"No. And, as I am not certain my deduction is correct, I think it best if we did not mention that the person responsible for her brother's death may be mixed up in all this."

Holmes was behind his time when lunch concluded, and he hurried to his appointment with Inspector Walls. The detective was gratified to see that the Inspector had waited for him. As Holmes joined him, Walls mounted the stairs to the Goodnow home saying nothing about his tardiness.

The practice of wearing a mourning dress had subsided since the war, but Mrs. Goodnow was observing the tradition. However, the widow gave the appearance of having moved beyond her shock as she put on a smile the moment Holmes and Walls were escorted into the parlor.

Sympathies were offered before the Inspector began: "Mrs. Goodnow, you said earlier that you were asleep in your room when the event occurred and the alarm was given?"

"Yes, Inspector. My bedroom is on the second floor, well away from John's room or his office down here. Emily was awakened."

Walls flipped open his notebook. "Emily reported: 'considerable shouting,' yet it took some time before she came to the office."

"I suppose she did not immediately intrude as it was not uncommon for Mr. Goodnow to elevate his voice."

Holmes leaned forward. "So, Mr. Goodnow had a boisterous nature?"

The widow's eyes widened as if standing guard. "John spent his last years serving in some dreadful places in the colonies. His experiences seemed to have . . . Let me merely say that he could be brusque at times."

Holmes made a mental note to get a peek at Goodnow's official dossier—assuming Mycroft would share it. "Did Mr. Goodnow's harsh temperament show itself to you?" Holmes asked.

She paused. "To *anyone*," she said in a deliberate manner.

Holmes changed direction: "There was mention of an item that arrived in the post the day before the incident—something that angered or disturbed him."

Mrs. Goodnow straightened in her chair, bending her brow in consideration. "Disturbed? Concerned, possibly."

"Can you describe it?" Walls asked.

"No, but it was small enough to fit in the palm of his hand. When it fell from the envelope to the table it made a noise suggesting it was metal or something hard. He snatched it up and went off to his office. After that, he left his study only for meals."

"And you never saw the object again?" Holmes asked.

"No. We don't go into John's office. He is . . . was particular that way."

"Would you mind if the Inspector and I were to look in his study?"

"If you must. No one has been in there since . . . that night."

Walls returned his notebook to his pocket, assured that he had captured everything the widow said, while Holmes was filing away everything she did not say.

When Emily came, Mrs. Goodnow instructed her to show the gentlemen to the office. The maid stiffened at the request. "Very well ma'am," she said, walking ahead to show the way.

As she opened the office door, Holmes noticed that the maid made a concerted effort *not* to look inside. As Holmes passed through, he turned. "Emily, might I ask how Mr. Goodnow treated you and the others in the household?"

"I can't say, sir," she replied, lowering her eyes.

Walls took an interest as Holmes pressed on: "Were you, in any way, mistreated by Mr. Goodnow?"

Emily's eyes became glassy. "Please, sir. I can say no more. I could lose my position."

Holmes nodded. "Very well, Emily. Did you and Eva room together?"

"No. My room is off the kitchen; Eva's is in the attic. There's a service stairway from the kitchen."

The Inspector stepped closer. "Did you happen to notice the bloody hand and footprints on the stairway, that evening?"

"No sir, not at first. It was dark when I went through the kitchen."

"But later, before the policemen arrived, you noticed them."

"Yes, Inspector. I thought Eva might be hurt and I followed the bloody footprints to her room. When I asked her what happened, she said that noises brought her to Mr. Goodnow's office and she found him bleeding on the floor. She was frightened and went back to her room, but not before putting her feet into the blood on the floor."

"What was her demeanor, when you found her?" Holmes followed.

"She was in shock, naturally. Crying."

"Thank you, Emily," Walls said.

When the maid was out of earshot, Walls turned to Holmes. "What was all that about Goodnow's treatment of the help?" Walls asked.

"If we are looking for a motive as to why a housekeeper might resort to an act of violence, then we might seek to know if violence has been done to her."

"Mr. Holmes, you may soil this man's reputation with your innuendo. At this stage, we should keep any suppositions between us."

The rebuke startled Holmes. "As you know, motive is usually the key to solving a murder. A killer would require a strong motive to disembowel their victim. What was Eva's motive?"

"Point taken, Mr. Holmes. Let us see if we can find anything of value in here. My men searched here on the evening of the murder, but we were looking for a weapon. We may have overlooked other objects. However, he may have disposed of it."

"Unlikely," Holmes replied. "If the object made him angry, he would likely keep it. If it frightened or embarrassed him, he would wish to dispose of it. If it was metal, or other hard substance, as Mrs. Goodnow suggested, he couldn't burn it in the hearth. Nor could he put it in the dustbin for fear it might be discovered. You recall that his wife told us that he left his office only for meals. He did not go out. No, Inspector, I will wager he hid it somewhere in this room, biding his time until he might dispose of it away from the house. However, that opportunity did not present itself before he was murdered. Trust me, the object is in this room."

Walls began his hunt—rifling through desk drawers, checking under rugs and inside Asian vases lined up along one shelf.

Holmes surveyed the room—his eyes resting for a moment on a Buhl clock on the mantel. He then went to the far corner of the room, rested on a *settee*, and closed his eyes.

After a few moments, Holmes opened his eyes and scanned the room again. Only after Walls stopped his rummaging and stood in the center of the room shaking his head, did Holmes rise and walk toward the fireplace. The Inspector watched.

Holmes stood on the hearth and pointed to an exquisite Verney-Carron Express rifle hanging on two hooks above the mantel. Its walnut butt was hand-carved and checkered. The two barrels stood apart, large, thick, and menacing. Walls advanced and lifted the rifle from its mount and began inspecting it. He ran his hands over it, opened the breach, and tapped the butt to ascertain if it were solid. He shrugged his shoulders.

Holmes pointed upward.

There, hanging on one of the hooks, was a metal ring.

"I simply asked myself," Holmes said, "What objects in this room would not likely be handled by others in this household. As Goethe said: 'We are best at hiding those things that are in plain sight.'"

Walls smiled. "I wish I had more like you on my force."

Holmes reached up and took the object from the hook. He carried it to the window for a better look. "Crude. Not an item of jewelry. A handle possibly." He took a glass from his pocket and held it over the object. "There is a symbol or letter on it — omega. The Greek letter is followed with stamped numbers 1-3-2. What do you make of that?"

"It may be an identification tag of some kind. I will need that for evidence, Mr. Holmes."

The Detective paused as a pleasant sensation vibrated within. It was the feeling he had when the pieces of a mystery converge—an inner pulsing that told him he is on the scent. "Inspector, would you allow me to keep this object a while longer. I know someone who might shed light upon it origins and purpose. I will return it."

CHAPTER 8

THE FAMILIAR FUSION OF DREAD AND EXHILARATION was a tonic for Holmes, his pace quickening as he returned to Professor Stone's home. His knock was unanswered, so he let himself in. Following the light to the office, he was greeted with an even higher wall of books lining the Professor's writing desk.

"I suppose that somewhere behind this literary fortress I will find my good friend." Holmes surmised.

"You will indeed, sir," Stone answered, as he stood in welcome. "Your earlier visit prompted me to draw upon my library in the attic. I believed that I would never need these volumes again, but I couldn't bear to let them go."

Stone completely disappeared again behind the books as he took his seat. Holmes remained standing. "I have another little trinket that may interest you."

The Professor's rubicund face poked up just above the bookish barricade. "Capital!" His twinkling eyes were ablaze with delight as Holmes handed over the brass ring. The connoisseur of antiquities disappeared again behind his makeshift library. "Hm-m-m-m."

Suddenly, the Professor's hand shot up with the item. "A slave bracelet of recent vintage. The telltale sign is that it is clasped with a rivet. It most likely emanated from pirates or smugglers from the Aegean Islands. Where did you find it?"

"It was hidden in a murdered man's office."

"Hidden, you say. Well then . . . one would have to suspect that this vile object might be connected to his murder."

"I was thinking exactly that, Professor."

"And, this murder is one connected with the casket you brought earlier?"

"Yes."

Stone rose and placed the bracelet in Holmes's hand. "I suppose you noticed the Greek letter stamped here — omega."

"Yes, the last letter in the Greek alphabet," Holmes answered.

"The end. The poor fellow's end to be sure. For the life of me, I cannot see how the Celtic casket, the testes, and this slave bracelet come together."

Twisting the metal band in the light, Holmes rejoined: "I am certain there is a connection. And, when we find the wrist or ankle that bore this horrible ornament, I believe we will be close to finding our murderer. One suspect already stands out."

★ ★ ★ ★ ★

The news of Eva's escape sent Tessa into the basement laundry room at the Salvation Army headquarters. Eva's accomplice had obviously laid hands on two woman's uniforms. Tessa reasoned that there were only three ways this could be managed: taking the uniforms from sisters on the street, stealing them from a room, or from the laundry. The laundry was certainly the most discrete scheme, and not immediately detectable.

The laundry operation was managed by women who needed more than a meal. They worked each day for a few extra shillings in addition to room and board. Tessa batted her way through the maze of canvas bags that hung on hooks from the ceiling. Her inquiries of the busy washerwomen initially bore little fruit, until she noticed a young woman dodging behind a pillar. Tessa followed. When confronted, the woman fidgeted, looking like a chestnut on the coals — ready to pop. Her right hand went to her apron pocket.

"What's in your pocket?" Tessa asked.

"Money."

"Show me." The woman proffered her hand that held two ten-shilling notes. Tessa knew that the laundry staff was paid in coin, and she had but to mention this fact when the woman began weeping, and quickly fell into ruins.

The interview confirmed that a middle-aged woman had bribed the laundress — early forties, buxom, dark skin, and black hair. Tessa promised not to report the theft. As she left, she asked one more question: "Do you recall anything unusual that the woman said?"

"The lady called me 'sister.' I told her as I weren't in the bloomin' Sally Army." She laughed, and said, 'All the more reason to claim you as my sister.'"

Tessa filed this tidbit away. The report of another woman bolstered Tessa's conviction that Eva was not the murderer. However, Eva had obviously joined forces with a cunning older person. She was anxious to share this news with Mr. Holmes, but she had already been too long away from her post at The Nest. She telephoned Watson's flat, left a message with Nora, and departed for Clapton.

* * * * *

Holmes arrived at Watson's flat shortly after Tessa called. He invited his friend to come along with him to The Nest, but Watson begged off, saying that he needed a nap.

The train ride was a short one.

Watson's indolence is worsening. This thought remained *sotto voce* in Holmes's mind as he walked from Clapton Station to The Nest. It was the height of the fall season. Damp brown leaves, and crabapples on the ground, filled the air with a sweet tannic smell. As he strolled, Holmes enjoyed the fading luster of the gardens that were succumbing to cooler breezes. It refreshed him in a manner that reminded him why he had adopted a county life.

As he approached the orphanage, he saw three girls sitting on the steps of the broad stairway, chattering away and plucking petals from daises. Arrayed in simple white pinafores and gay rompers, the girls giggled as they went about their game. As Holmes looked on, he supposed that it would not be difficult to deduce the wishes of little ones such as these. The tallest girl plucked a petal and said, "A home."

As he approached, the littlest one, no more than ten, waved to him. One of the older girls offered a mild rebuke, which only emboldened the youngster. As he put his foot on the last step, the young girl broke away from the others and presented a flower — rather, the remains of a flower. Hearing a faint bell in the distance, the two older girls disappeared into the home.

Holmes accepted the little girl's offering with a slight bow. He pointed to one of the three remaining petals. "What is this wish?"

The little girl's mouth puckered. Her brow tightened in serious deliberation. Plucking the petal, she looked up: "Someone to play with me."

A rare moment of consternation came over Holmes. The little one's imploring eyes disquieted him.

"Mr. Holmes, what a wonderful surprise," Tessa said, from the doorway. "Althea, it's time for your dinner."

The girl bounced up and clutched at Holmes's waist. "Play with me." Frozen in place, he was stupefied by this sudden burst of affection. Tessa was amused by Holmes's reaction, and that evening she wrote a short poem in her diary:

> *The twins: Innocence and Honesty*
> *surprise us.*
> *As when they clutch at our waist*
> *and say: "Play with me."*

"Althea, come along," Tessa beckoned, more sternly.

Holmes took the child's hands in his and came down upon one knee. He retrieved a penny from his vest pocket and held it up. The little girl's eyes riveted upon the coin. He nodded and smiled. Althea grabbed it and scampered into the house.

"Still the 'penny man,'" Tessa said. Would you like to stay for dinner?"

Holmes retrieved his watch and flicked open the cover. "I am afraid my stomach would not know what to do with food at five in the afternoon."

"Of course. The little ones must eat early so they can settle down before bedtime. What brings you here?"

"I am anxious to speak with the girls who befriended Eva Allsop," Holmes said.

"Of course, come in. I've been asking the matrons, and some of the girls, about Eva's time here. Also, I made a discovery in the laundry at headquarters that I am anxious to share. However, Eva's friend, Abigail, will be leaving soon so you will want to talk with her first."

Tessa took Holmes by the arm and led him into the mansion and out to the back porch. "Abigail is over there," Tessa pointed.

Long auburn hair tumbled over Abigail's face, nearly veiling her watery blue eyes. She bolted to attention as Holmes and Tessa walked toward her. She pulled her hair back from her face and looked straight at them as they approached. While only in her late teens, Abigail already possessed an inner strength that was apparent in her sure movements and attentive eyes.

Holmes was introduced as "a friend who is trying to help Eva." Upon the mention of the Eva's name, Abigail shook her head wistfully: "There's a woman who needs true friends."

Tessa noted that Abigail used "woman" to describe Eva. "Why do you say that?" she enquired.

Abigail went on to describe Eva as haunted by memories, and plagued with what Abigail called righteous anger. "I understood what she was going through. I wanted to help her and I'd like to think I have."

"So, would you say Eva has moved beyond her trauma?" Tessa asked.

"Mostly . . .yes."

Holmes held back as Tessa continued: "I understand that Eva took walks into the village."

"She may have. My work was here in the garden."

"You were seen leaving with her," Tessa followed. "You know that the girls must get permission to leave."

"I didn't tell because I wanted us to be friends," Abigail said, mustering up a sad look. "I couldn't see the harm. I'm sorry."

Tessa placed a comforting hand on the teens shoulder. "Where did you go?"

"Just for a walk," the girl answered.

Holmes intervened. "How did Eva find her position? Eva must have gone into the city?"

Abigail took on a blank expression. "Where would she get the fare?"

"Indeed," Tessa said. "How did Eva feel about her new position?"

"She was pleased about it . . . eager," Abigail noted. "I told her that I would like to come by to see her at work." Abigail's face brightened. "She was so looking forward to being in service." Looking up at Tessa and Holmes, Abigail added: "Eva saw it as the beginning of a whole new life." Then, suddenly, the teen ended the interview: "So sorry, but I must be leaving. Goodbye."

As Abigail trotted back into the home, Tessa turned to Holmes: "What do you think, Mr. Holmes?

"She's lying."

CHAPTER 9

AFTER THEIR ESCAPE from the Bow Street jail, Maeve
Murtagh and Eva Allsop took the first train available to Bromley
Cross. "You will be with your sisters before the mid-day meal,"
Maeve promised.

"My sisters," Eva thought. She had always wanted a family,
but this was so much more. Maeve said that the women of the
world must cast off their bonds and forge them into a powerful
chain linking all women together.

Maeve's penetrating brown eyes studied Eva closely. She
was pleased with her newest recruit. Eva, who was deep in
thought, startled as a passenger walked by their compartment.
"Don't worry Eva. I will protect you. You are safe now."

The young woman was captivated by the hazy magic of the
mistress. "I feel so bad about what happened," the teen said. "I
acted cowardly."

"The fault is mine," Maeve said. "I put you in Goodnow's
household, and did not prepare you for what would happen."
Maeve took Eva's hands in hers. "You must remember that you
are now a member of a grand circle — no longer a victim of a
violent patriarchy. Our sisterhood is strong because women are
innately powerful. We are . . ." Maeve paused, holding up one
finger. Eva nodded and, in unison, they quietly intoned: "We are
the givers and takers of life."

Arriving at Bromley Cross, Maeve gave Eva cab fare as they
disembarked. Eva knew the drill from her previous forays from
The Nest: She walked to a cart selling flowers near the station's
entrance and bought a small bouquet. Maeve left alone in a taxi.

Five minutes later, Eva followed, arriving at the Bromley parish church with flowers in hand. She strolled into the church cemetery and stopped at a headstone to be certain no one was following. It read:

Hannah Twynay
October 23rd 1803
Age 21 Years.
In bloom of Life,
And Here she lies in a bed of Clay,
Until the Resurrection Day.

When she was a frightened prisoner in the Southampton warehouse, Eva recalled thinking that she would not live to see her twenty-first birthday. Sister Wiggins liberated her and the other girls. The next day, Maeve punished their captor, and today saved her from the gallows. Two strong women had changed the path of her stars. Her quest was ended . . . she had found her home.

Eva placed the flowers on Hannah Twynay's grave and walked toward a limestone crypt sitting atop a rise in the far corner of the cemetery. The massive blocks of the ancient crypt were blackened with soot. Tall grass shrouded the base of the tomb, belying its true size. While the austere stone structure was but five yards square, it sat high atop a massive undercroft.

Eva move toward the entrance of the crypt, coming to rusty iron gates. The gates were decorated with an elaborate Celtic knot that protectively wrapped itself around the lock. She grasped the cold iron, pushing her face between the bars to let the air inside fill her lungs with sweet, earthy smells. She waited. The veil of darkness parted like a mist as Maeve approached, holding a candle and a ring of keys. Without a word, Maeve twisted a key in the lock and pulled the gate open just wide enough for Eva to slip inside.

The dark mistress silently stood watch for several moments to be certain no one was about. She locked the gate behind them and took Eva in hand.

A faint glow emanated from a narrow stone stairway descending into the undercroft. Nearly two flights brought them to a foyer lit by candles in wrought iron candelabras. At first, the sudden light obscured the labyrinth of hand-hewn tunnels that lay beyond.

Maeve picked up a bulls-eye oil lamp on a nearby table and handed it to Eva. She lit the lantern with her candle and motioned for Eva to proceed.

The passageways were carved from chalk, and wound into an elaborate warren that branched in many directions. Eva found her way by repeating a rhyme she was taught during her initiation into the Sisterhood of Scáthach:

> I am the *right* wind that breathes upon the sea.
> I have the *right* heart that murmurs with the billows.
> I will catch the last salmon *left* in the river.
> I am the point of the battle lance that takes the *middle* path.
> It is *right* to proclaim the age of Scáthach.
> For we are the givers and takers of life.

Eva's pace and heart quickened as she heard the voices of women in the distance. Within the community of twelve, Eva found the family she had sought her entire life.

Just ahead, golden light filled an arched entryway. She could smell the incense that burned on Scáthach's altar in the gathering chamber.

Maeve slowed her pace to let Eva enter the room alone. Patricia was the first to see her. "Sister Eva! We were so very worried."

The women rose from their benches and surrounded Eva, kissing her cheeks in welcome. Brigit, the oldest and strongest of the clan, took her by the shoulders. Eva felt the woman's remarkable strength. "We all wanted to come for you, but Mistress Maeve knew that it would be a mistake," she said in her gravelly voice.

"Not a mistake," Maeve interjected, "but unnecessary. It takes but one confident woman to outwit the London police."

The women laughed and nodded, as Maeve continued: "It fell to me because I did not prepare Eva. I put her in Goodnow's home, in harm's way." Maeve put her arm on Eva's shoulders. Candlelight glimmered on a large iridescent stone pendant that hung around Maeve's neck. She pointed to the talisman.

"This opal came from the hilt of Scáthach's sword. In it you can see her power, and sense her presence."

A soothing calm came over the room as Maeve raised the pendant. They stared at the crystalline blue stone that glistened with specks of red, yellow and green.

Maeve's gaze appeared to go beyond the room. "Eva . . . all of you, are women of a new age — the age of Scáthach. No longer women conditioned against violence, you will not suffer in silence at the cruelty of heartless men. Warriors are defined not by what they say or fail to say, but by what they do or fail to do. We fight violence against women, and punish those who perpetrate that violence. John Goodnow received justice befitting a pimp and rapist."

Maeve paused, relaxing her shoulders. Her eyes returned to the room. She smiled. "Some of you have shared your stories. I will share mine another time. But, you need to know that Goodnow did unspeakable evil to me and many other women. And he was but the henchman of another vile creature — Basil Zaharoff. He deceived me, like all men will if you let them. A year ago, I tried to repay him in kind, but I failed and fled. I feared for my life. Zaharoff's cruelty went beyond anything I could have imagined."

Maeve's face twisted into a terrifying mask. Then, in an instant, an astonishing tranquilly rippled through her body, and a congenial smile spread across her face. "Later, I will tell you more of my time on Skye — the secrets of Scáthach, and the source of her power. All will be revealed."

Eva got up from the table and knelt at Maeve's feet and kissed her hand. Maeve caressed Eva's hair. "I am sorry, Mistress. I ran from Goodnow's office. I acted shamefully."

"No," Maeve said, running her fingers through the cloudlet of Eva's black locks. "You did well. There is no cause for shame. No *place* for shame in our sisterhood. Shame is the instrument of oppression. Becoming a Sister of Scáthach requires that you reject shame."

Maeve took Eva by her hands, raised her to her feet, and scanned the assemblage. "You have been taught from the first day of your birth to feel shame — about the way you look, act, dress, speak . . . and most especially, shame about your bodies. Men will gladly use you as a child might a doll. And when the doll is soiled, it is hidden away in a closet or sent to the rubbish."

Maeve opened her blouse revealing her bare breasts. "A woman's body is a sacred thing. It is to be revered and honored. It is not an object of shame."

"Aye!" The women cried. Some bared their breasts and chanted: "We are the givers and takers of life! We are the givers and takers of life!"

With that, the women dispersed to take their mid-day meal. Meals were ceremonial in the sisterhood: Each morning the food intended for the day's meals was placed on Scáthach's altar, which was located adjacent to the kitchen in the gathering chamber. An imaginative chalk portrait of Scáthach was sketched on the wall above the altar. Lying upon the dais was the *gae bolga*, a barbed battle sword designed to inflict a fatal wound with a single blow. Later, a Gaelic invocation blesses the foodstuffs before they are returned to the kitchen to be prepared.

After the meal is placed upon the table, the twelve women circled around the altar, singing the ancient melody: *Mo Ghile*

Mear. This haunting ayre echoed throughout the chamber and surrounding tunnels. This anthem, which had been written as a lament by the Gaelic goddess Éire for Bonnie Prince Charlie, took on new meaning when sung to a slow marching rhythm.

While dining, the women were allowed to socialize and chat, but during the mid-day meal they were encouraged to discuss their martial arts training that followed.

An incredible fighting force was being forged. Brigit taught hand-to-hand combat using knives, and taught the sisters how to transform canes, hairpins, and umbrellas into weapons. With each new skill mastered, their confidence grew, as did trust in their sisters, and their allegiance to Maeve. However, Maeve knew that training and practice alone were not enough. Her experience in Goodnow's home told her that the Sisters of Scáthach must be "battle hardened," and she planned a challenge for her new squadron. As the dishes were cleared from the table, Maeve asked the community to remain a moment.

"The time has come for us to spread our wings. In the safety and solitude of our hidden retreat, we are healed and nurtured. But now it is time to take flight."

Maeve held a scroll in her hand, and scanned the faces of the young women around her. "One of our band is absent, but she will soon be reunited with us." Maeve closed her eyes and let the silence penetrate the chamber. The only sound was the distant fluttering of the wings of bats taking flight from the maze of tunnels. The beat of their leathery wings sounded like water rushing off a cliff onto rocks below, as they left, *en masse*, to seek their daily meal.

"We will fight many battles together, but our next one has a special meaning for me. That is why I told you about Goodnow's master."

Maeve unrolled a scroll and spread it on the table. "This is a death warrant. Some of you have seen the names on it. You will be able to add names when your training is complete. But for now, there are but five names here. The first name is that of Peter de Neumann." I put his name here because of what he did to Eva, and to other women in Southampton."

Maeve handed a pencil to Eva. "Scratch his name off the list."

Eva took the pencil and stood motionless over the scroll. Then, in a sudden outburst, she stabbed the scroll and obliterated de Neumann's name.

"The next name is John Goodnow." But before Maeve could ask, Eva angrily smudged the letters of his name with her finger. Maeve smiled. "Thank you, Eva."

"And, now we come to Basil Zaharoff. He cast me into the pits of hell, but I have risen out of the ashes to bring him to justice."

The Mistress went to the altar and took the battle saber she called the "belly ripper", and held it overhead. "Zaharoff is coming to London tomorrow. He believes he comes for a liaison with a beautiful woman. He thinks his body will be caressed with warm hands and tender kisses." Maeve drove the point of the saber into the list. "But his cold blood will temper the hot steel of the *gae bolga*."

CHAPTER 10

AN AWE INSPIRING STEAM YACHT cruised up the Thames toward Tower Bridge. The rising sun gilded the city of London, and cast a halo about Basil Zaharoff as he stood at the bow of his two-hundred-and-thirty-foot floating palace. He watched the iconic steel and stone bridge open its maw as the steamer approached. He took it as a personal welcome by the city. A strong breeze tossed his grey hair and billowed his trademark grey cape. His weathered face, flabby belly, and dull eyes showed the ravages of comfortable living. He stroked his beard, bringing it to a point under his chin as his anticipation swelled within him.

The Greek's bastion was on Skorpios, but he spent little time there. His international arms business was sluggish following the war; but he knew it was only a matter of time before the world inevitably flung itself into another conflagration, and he would be there to stoke the fires. For now, he would enjoy the privilege that his millions brought him — his most delectable indulgence being women.

Zaharoff received a tantalizing invitation from Edna Avery to attend her triumphant return as Princess Ida in Gilbert and Sullivan's popular play at London's newly renovated Savoy Theater. He had met Edna at a reception in New York City honoring Sarah Bernhardt, his inamorata at the time. Flirtatious taunts from the vivacious Edna prompted him to extricate himself from his relationship with Bernhardt, who he judged was *aging poorly*.

Avery was an American comic actress who, as the adage goes, was "banned in Boston." Her bawdy language, and breezy sexual independence, hinted at a new era for women. Edna's effervescent personality and sultry singing voice captivated audiences on both shores of the Atlantic. But it was her scandalous interview in *True Story Magazine* that catapulted her into stardom.

She posed for the magazine in a translucent robe, wearing bobbed blond hair in an Elton cut. Large, pointed bangs framed violet eyelids and pouty blood-red lips. When asked why she adopted such a dramatic haircut, she answered: "Long hair is one of the many shackles that women must cast aside in their passage to freedom." Her photograph got Zaharoff's attention. Her words got Maeve Murtagh's.

Maeve reached across the ocean to Edna Avery with a simple acknowledgment. Her cable read: *It's in your power to change the station of women around the world, and I can help you.* She signed it M, followed by a cable address. That was the beginning of a six-month overseas friendship. It was one of many that Maeve was nurturing as part of her plan to internationalize the Sisters of Scáthach. So, when Edna Avery signed a contract to perform in London, she wrote to Maeve proposing a meeting. The timing couldn't have been better, for Maeve had recently located Basil Zaharoff. Edna would bring her former employer, and tormentor, to her. He had cast Maeve into a heathen hell, but now she would rise up like a fearsome phoenix out of the smoldering embers.

Maeve watched the yacht come into harbor from the roof of a warehouse on the Isle of Dogs in east London. Having traveled with Zaharoff in past years, she knew that he would dock at nearby Canary Wharf. His red Daimler limousine, a twin to King George V's, was already waiting to whisk him off to his suite in Brown's Hotel. Waiting for him there was a message, presumably from Edna Avery, but crafted by Maeve Murtagh:

> *Basil darling,*
>
> *So sorry, but the bastard of a director has insisted on a run-through this evening. I was so looking forward to answering*

*Princess Ida's question: "Pray tell us, if you
can, what's the thing that's known as Man?"*

*I would love to hear your answer — possibly
after dinner tomorrow evening on your
yacht? I promise, I will make it up to you.*

Leave word at the theater.

Edna

Being an egotistical lecher, Maeve knew that Zaharoff would
take the incomplete quote from Princess Ida as praise. It was her
little joke. For Lady Psyche's answer to Princess Ida's question
mirrored Maeve's conviction:

> *Man is of no kind of use,*
> *Man's a donkey, Man's a goose*
> *Man is coarse, and Man is plain*
> *Man is more or less insane.*
> *Man's a ribald, Man's a rake*
> *Man is Nature's sole mistake!*

*****

If Holmes had traveled to Whitehall five minutes earlier, he might
have seen his old nemesis cruising up the Thames on the high tide.
He was deep in thought as he made his way to his brother's office.
The five-story edifice of the War Office stood as a white knight in
the center of a bureaucratic battlefield. Turrets on each corner
guarded the pallid building that served as the hub upon which the
country had turned in the previous five years. His brother Mycroft
provided much of the "grease" that kept the wheels of warfare
turning efficiently.

Having been a frequent visitor to the War Office, Holmes passed through the lobby unchallenged and made his way to a receptionist on the fourth floor. Her job was to protect Mycroft from unwanted interruptions — meaning *any* interruptions. However, when Holmes appeared, she nodded a friendly hello. "Good morning, Mr. Holmes. Please let me ring your brother for you."

It took three buzzes, the last one being particularly long, before an answer came over the intercom: "Blast it, Monahan, what's so urgent!"

The receptionist replied calmly: "Your brother, sir."

There was a short pause before an outsized oak door adjoining the reception area swung wide revealing the portly form of Sherlock Holmes's older brother. Mycroft looked wildly discontented with his grey stubble and puffy eyes. Without a word, he turned and motioned toward a sitting area. Holmes did not sit, but followed his brother toward his desk. *En route,* Holmes looked with envy at the two-story gallery that was lined with books and racks of newspapers and magazines, some of which lay scattered about the room on tables and chairs.

His older brother stood before a large map of the world that hung over his desk, spinning a miniature Union Jack in his fingers.

"What is the latest bagatelle of the moment?" Holmes quipped.

Mycroft did not turn. "Our American friends are bent on removing our blockade on the Germans. Nasty business."

"But, the war is over."

Mycroft's jaw tensed. "Is it?"

"What are you going to do, Mycroft?"

"Life is mostly a bluff, and I can play it as well as anyone," he said, stabbing the flag of Britain into center of the North Sea. He stepped back and, with the tip of his index finger, pushed the flag deeper into the map and turned. "And you? I am hesitant to ask what it is that has lured you away from your bucolic domicile."

"Human testes," Holmes answered.

Mycroft was only momentarily puzzled. "Ah yes, Goodnow."

"I supposed you would be familiar with the incident."

"As he was a member of the Foreign Office, his untidy demise naturally came to my attention. However, he came into my purview well before his murder."

Holmes waited.

"It's a bit unseemly, but as you seem to be mixed up in the affair, I will share some details . . . confidential, of course."

Holmes nodded and approached his older brother.

"John Goodnow did not retire. He was recalled, suspended from his post, and deprived of his pension."

"Quite serious then. Treasonable?"

"No, but, rather odious. He was a ringleader in a white-slavery enterprise."

"Oh!" Holmes said. "Your news suggests that I may have made an error in judgment."

Mycroft chortled and wagged his finger in his brother's face. "I believe the phrase is: I was *wrong*."

"I *may* be wrong. Given the nature of the gruesome murder, I assumed that the young woman who was accused of the crime is innocent."

"But now . . . because she may be entangled in white slavery . . ."

"Exactly so," Holmes confirmed.

"I take it someone engaged you to prove her innocence?"

"No. John Goodnow's testes were mailed to my home."

"By the murderer — to challenge you. How marvelous!" Mycroft held out his hands as if he were about to receive a gift. "You seldom fail to entertain me, Sherlock. So, your closing act . .

. the next great Sherlock Holmes escapade, will be: *The Adventure of the Missing Bollocks!*"

Holmes pursed his lips. "If you are going to be silly, we may just as well end this interview."

"And if you do, you will miss a tantalizing tidbit regarding the late Mr. John Goodnow."

Holmes spread his hands apart with an expression that said: *Well?*

"We were tipped off about Mr. Goodnow's dastardly enterprise by a crusading woman writer — Olive Malvery. She was doing an exposé on the white slavery trade. Her article made mention of Goodnow's hidden bank account in Egypt."

"And, the point?" Holmes remarked.

"The point is, when we looked into his bank accounts, here and abroad, it showed him as having far too much money for a civil servant. However, it was his last deposit which rather got my attention." Mycroft paused for effect. "His last deposit was a check for £500 from Mr. Basil Zaharoff."

Adrenaline shot through Holmes's body and bile rose to his mouth. The Fates, once again, brought the duo of Basil Zaharoff and Maeve Murtagh into his life. Their reemergence summoned gruesome memories and fugitive emotions. Four years prior Sherlock Holmes had set out to release seven members of his former irregular army from the clutches of Zaharoff's henchmen led by a Maeve Murtagh. He rescued most of his irregular army, but the dearest of the irregulars, Rory Wiggins, was killed.

"Zaharoff!" Holmes repeated. "So, he is mixed up in white slavery?"

"Not so much now, but he got his start in that business — enticing and abducting Greek maidens. That was thirty years ago — before he moved into the beastly business of international arms."

Holmes's mind was spinning. "But, he still maintains ties to the loathsome enterprise."

"Possibly. His payment to Goodnow may have nothing to do with the slave trade."

"Blackmail?"

"Mr. Goodnow was not the smartest creature, but he was wise enough to avoid tangling with Basil Zaharoff. Unfortunately, with Goodnow's death, it may be impossible to know what that £500 bought, or what it was intended to buy," Mycroft concluded.

"And, we'll not find out from Zaharoff."

"Not directly. But, as luck would have it, the chief harbor master just informed us that Basil Zaharoff's yacht Omega has just sailed into the city."

Holmes lurched upward in this chair. "Zaharoff's yacht is named Omega?"

CHAPTER 11

THE OMEGA WAS ALIGHT from stem to stern. Zaharoff recalled seven of the thirty-two-member crew from shore leave after he received Edna's note. Chef Caréme had remained aboard, and was preparing a special meal for two. It included all of Mr. Zaharoff's favorites: Chicken liver and port wine *paté* with fig chutney, spice roasted Cornish cod with artichoke and chestnut *velouté*, roasted field mushrooms, and *Bombe tutti fruiti*.

Two bottles of Moet & Chandon, 1914, were chilling near a candlelit table on the deck adjoining Zaharoff's upper level suite. The sheets of his bed had been rinsed in lavender water. Basil Zaharoff planned every detail: from the moment Edna Avery would step on board at sunset, to breakfast the next morning.

As the sun plunged into the Thames the *nouveau riche* capitalist paced his cabin. He slammed his empty glass down on the bar. "She is being coy," he mumbled. But underneath this utterance a dark resentment was smoldering: *No one makes Basil Zaharoff wait.* The waiter promptly filled his glass with Scotch.

Then, in the distance, he heard a vehicle pulling onto the wharf. His shook the tension from his shoulders and put on a smile. "Christoffel, tell chef that my guest has arrived," he said to his bodyguard.

He downed the scotch in one quaff and went to his bathroom to rinse his mouth. He was appraising himself in the bathroom mirror, combing his greying beard, when he heard shouts and feet scrambling on the deck below.

He paused to listen.

Quiet.

An inexplicable groan . . . and then whispers.

More footsteps scrambling on the deck below.

He called out: "Christoffel! What's going on down there?"

He walked onto the deck and looked over the railing. His restless eyes settled on a lorry parked near the gangplank. No one was around. *No one!* His body stiffened. *Where are my men?*

Basil Zaharoff had many friends around the world, but he possessed as many enemies. As such, two bodyguards traveled with him everywhere. One was always stationed at the gangplank of the yacht, but there was no one there.

He straightened the lapels on his dinner jacket to quell his trepidation. He returned to his suite and buzzed the main salon where his chauffer and bodyguards usually waited. One buzz . . . two . . . three . . . then, an answer: "Sir?"

The Greek let out a long breath. "What the hell is going on? Why aren't you waiting for my guest?"

"We'll be right up sir," a stilted voice replied.

"Up? Get to the gangplank! And what's that lorry doing out there?"

A pause, then: "Supplies."

Something is wrong. "Raimo, is that you?"

"Run, sir! There's . . ."

The intercom buzzed and went dead.

There was a clattering on the ladder below. Zaharoff ran toward his bedroom to retrieve his pistol, but a hideous cry arising from the stern stopped him in his tracks. Changing course, he ran to the far railing.

The shrieking below became words — a strange tongue: *Faugh a Ballagh! Faugh a Ballagh!*

Zaharoff climbed over the railing and balanced himself on the edge of the deck staring down into the murky water three stories below . . . white knuckles clamped on the rail behind him. Teetering on the edge of the deck, he turned to see an apparition —

a wild-woman leaping from the ladder. The wind twisted the woman's black hair. Her face, painted in indigo and blue, framed the fiery eyes of a madwoman. She leaped onto the deck, landing on one knee, holding a warrior pose — a bloody saber raised overhead.

Zaharoff's mouth went dry: "Who . . . what . . . do you . . ."

A chilling smile spread across the warrior's face. She roared, "*Faugh a Ballagh!*" and ran toward him swinging her blade.

Terrified, Zaharoff released his grip on the railing and tumbled into the dark water below.

* * * * *

Holmes tipped his hat to the coroner as he stepped aboard the steam-yacht Omega. Not since *The Case of Vishnu's Temple Treasure* had Holmes seen such bloody carnage. "Good morning, Peters. It appears you may require more than one wagon."

Dr. Peters nodded. "A lovely mess," the coroner told him. "We have three lovely bodies down here, and I am waiting to see if more lovelies are discovered." He nodded toward the salon door where Inspector Walls was waiting. The detective waved Holmes forward. The rear deck was mottled with blood. Holmes carefully stepped around the bodies draped with canvas tarps.

"Thank you for coming, Mr. Holmes."

"I was planning on making a call on this vessel."

"Then your investigation has yielded something to bring you here?"

"Yes, the pieces are coming together. It appears you know my habits, as your call came to Watson.

"The good Doctor did not accompany you then?"

"Would that he had," Holmes replied, as he gazed upon the blood soaked tarpaulins. "He might have been able to shed some light upon these ghastly murders."

"Yes, well . . . it doesn't take a doctor to know that all three men were brutally murdered with knives and swords, judging from the wounds.

"Weapons not dissimilar to the one that killed Mr. Goodnow. Other similarities?"

"If you are speaking of their genitals, they seem to be intact."

"Would you mind if I looked about?"

"I was hoping you might."

Holmes took a handkerchief from his pocket, removed his topcoat and draped it over the railing.

He went to the gangplank. "Only one point of entry." How did the attackers get aboard unchecked, I wonder?"

"Look in the water," the Inspector said.

Flowers were floating below, trapped between the hull and the dock.

"A flower delivery?"

Inspector Walls picked up a trampled rose on the deck. "Someone knew the ways of the yacht's master. I'm told Basil Zaharoff cascades flowers on women."

"Were any women on board? Holmes asked.

"None at the moment, but he was expecting one according to the chef. Do you know an Edna Avery?" the Inspector asked. "We found a note from her in his suite."

"So, she avoided this calamity?"

"Apparently so," Walls added.

"Do you have a torch?" Holmes inquired.

Walls signaled a policeman who was standing by the door of the salon. The PC handed his torch to Holmes, who took it in hand and began sweeping the light from side to side as he moved along the deck. "There are several sets of footprints. I would estimate eight or more. And, what's this," Holmes exclaimed, bending lower.

The Inspector came closer and bent over Holmes's shoulder. "Bare feet?" the Detective exclaimed. "Strange indeed."

"The blood has not completely dried. I suggest you find some paper and make a print. It may prove helpful."

Walls nodded to the bobby nearby who scampered off into the salon.

As stretchers were brought on board, Holmes held up his hand. "One moment Peters. I would like just a brief look before they are taken away."

Holmes walked to each of the bodies and pulled back the canvas covering, shining the light over the lifeless bodies. Lowering the tarp on the third and last body, he nodded to the coroner's men. He wiped his hands with his handkerchief and walked toward Walls. "Two of the three were brutally slashed with a large blade."

"Like the one that killed Goodnow," the Scotland Yarder noted. "What could Goodnow and Zaharoff have in common?"

Holmes looked at his bloody kerchief. "Not 'what', but 'whom', Inspector."

"So, you do know something, Holmes."

"Let me say that I am entertaining a curious possibility."

"And you will let me know if that possibility materializes, will you not?"

"Of course."

The two men stepped back as Dr. Peters' crew struggled to put the body of a large man on a stretcher. A flash of light, coming from under the body, caught Holmes's eye. He bent lower and picked up a small charm, dangling it before his eyes. "Metal. Two crossed swords, and a broken chain."

"What is it?" Walls asked.

"An ornament that might have been worn by a Celtic women warriors."

Walls raised his eyebrows.

"Just a little late-night reading, Inspector. It matches one of the symbols found on a casket that was sent to my home."

"Do you believe the necklace was left here deliberately?" Walls asked.

"Possibly, but the chain is broken," Holmes noted. "Nonetheless, a pattern is emerging. Basil Zaharoff and I share a history."

"The inspector wagged his finger and grinned. "Miss Wiggins, now Zaharoff. It appears you are more deeply entangled in this business than you care to admit. What was the nature of your relationship with the infamous Greek?"

"Let me simply say that I would not have been disappointed if I had found him among those slain. By the way, have you located him?

"It was a very wet and frightened Mr. Zaharoff who brought the alarm to a constable on patrol near the wharf. He literally begged for our protection."

"We can well see how such a scene might bring a man to his knees. Where is he now?"

"In his suite at Brown's Hotel. I put a man on his door."

"Just one?" Holmes asked, with raised brows.

CHAPTER 12

MORNING'S SUMPTUOUS SUN offered more promise than usual as Tessa watched her girls at work in the sprawling vegetable garden behind The Nest. It was part of the healing process for them. Tessa was testing a theory that vegetarian meals, combined with the nurturing labor required to grow their own food, would aid in healing the girls and young women. They were well into the harvest season, but Tessa saw a new life budding. She said to herself: "The garden of love is always green," and made a mental note to record that thought in her diary.

Today, she came to the garden with a purpose. She watched Abigail, who regularly came to help. With a hoe in hand, the older teen stood apart from the younger girls. Her efforts were perfunctory. She half-heartedly scraped on the ground — watching more than working.

A bell rang from the back porch announcing lunch was being served. The girls obediently picked up their implements and marched off to wash up. Abigail was the last to leave, providing the opportunity Tessa was seeking.

"Abigail, if you have a moment."

The seventeen-year-old did not respond with alarm or concern as she walked toward Tessa. She was poised and self-assured — atypical behavior for someone her age.

"What is it, Sister Tessa?"

"Abigail, I've been meaning to have another chat about Eva."

"I've told you and Mr. Holmes everything I know."

She guided Abigail toward a bench and gestured for her to sit. "Yes, but you must have some insight or ideas about Eva and what she was up to while she was away."

Abigail's eyes narrowed for a moment before she put on a smile. "You're talking about that famed feminine intuition, I suppose. Well, it appeared to me that Eva was in a good place. She was happy to be leaving here. Pleased that she would have a good position." Abigail cocked her head and feigned a frown. "The other girls say that she is involved in a horrible murder. Is that so?"

"We don't know, but she may be. That is why it is important for us to know more about her forays into town?"

"You sound like Mr. Holmes now. Questions . . . questions . . . questions. I don't know where she went. I'm sorry."

"About how long would she be gone?"

"I'm not sure."

"And she never talked with you about where she went, or what she did? I find that difficult to believe."

Abigail's mouth clenched. "I'm not *lying* to you, Sister."

The girl's acerbic tone and demeanor sent chills through Tessa. "You had better run on to lunch."

As she left, the young woman turned. "I can see why Mr. Holmes and you are great friends. You're very much like a detective yourself."

As Tessa watched Abigail stroll toward the dining room, chiseled memories burst forth as she recalled the day she met Sherlock Holmes. She was only six years old, but she could still recall all the details of that fateful day:

> Holmes was in search of a stolen pearl necklace. The thief's poor wife was dispatched to hide the loot. Unfortunately for her, she walked through Exmouth Market — her brother Rory's run. It wasn't until the woman dug a hole for the loot that

she discovered that someone had neatly lifted the pearls from her pocket.

Unfortunately for Rory, Sherlock Holmes was not the only one on his trail. The thieves were as well. And, thinking that Rory had given the necklace to Holmes, they held him for ransom. Tessa was with Rory when the thieves whisked him off in a growler. They tucked a ransom note in her pocket and told her to take it to Holmes. When she found Mr. Holmes, she was frightened. He gave her a penny when she proffered the note.

Mr. Holmes saved Rory, who then presented Holmes to his mates — and the backstreet battalion that would be known as" the irregulars" was born.

Doubts about Abigail smoldered in Tessa's mind and were reignited later that day when a female messenger came to The Nest asking for Abigail. The messenger was directed to the kitchen, where she was helping with the washing-up after lunch.

A female messenger was rare enough, but the fact that the messenger came to The Nest was inexplicable, as Abigail did not live there.

Tessa waited and watched — a skill she had honed as a member of Sherlock Holmes's urchin army.

Shortly after the messenger departed, Abigail hurried down the front steps and up the street. Tessa made her way to the kitchen.

As she was rummaging through the rubbish, one of the cooks made a face. "I'm looking to find the envelope Abigail's message came in," Tessa explained.

The cook's countenance lit up. "Oh, it's not here Sister. She went into the garden."

Tessa searched outside. There, in an empty flowerpot next to the garden wall, she found the charred remains of the message—a pile of ash but for a small corner. The burnt scrap of paper yielded only three words: . . . park boathouse, 4 pm.

Tessa ran out the front door and down the street that Abigail had just travelled. Her pace slowed when she caught sight of her. When Abigail stopped on the corner, Tessa hid herself amid some shrubbery.

A bus came along taking the girl aboard.

As the bus pulled away, Tessa went on to the Rossington Street bus stop to check the schedule posted on a placard. Abigail was on the number twenty-nine bus.

As she walked back, Tessa twirled the scrap of stationary in her fingers . . . *park boathouse, 4 pm.* She paused abruptly. *I know where Abigail is going.*

Hyde Park was on that bus route, and the park had a boathouse. It would just be possible to make it there by four.

Tessa caught the next bus. During the trip, countless questions and fears percolated in her mind. Her mounting anxiety was abated only once when the autobus traveled past Swinton Street where she and Benjie had lived. She could almost picture him now — swaggering down the street with his hands in his pockets.

She got off at Park Lane and entered the park. Her mounting fear had Tessa clutching at her stomach. The dimming afternoon sunlight cast the shadows of surrounding trees across the landscape, making it appear as if huge gnarled hands were creeping across the ground.

Hyde Park covered more than three hundred acres. Serpentine Lake comprised a good chunk of it. The boathouse, which was closed for the season, is situated on the shoreline near the wide end of the lake.

It was nearly four o'clock.

Tessa walked as fast as she could without calling attention to myself. She was panting by the time she saw the boathouse. It looked quiet. No one was about.

A passerby turned to look at her as she approached. Tessa became aware that her iconic black dress might cause undue attention. As she drew nearer, she was pleased to see that the area around the boathouse was devoid of persons. But, approaching the entry, she heard voices within. She put her ear to door.

Suddenly, a hand slammed her head and pinned her body against the door. "Please," Tessa shouted, "please. I mean no harm."

"I doubt that," came a familiar voice.

"Abigail, what are you doing? Let me go!"

"I should have known. You are always sticking your nose into everyone's business. You think because you provide food and shelter, that you own the girls," she hissed. The Mistress will know what to do with you."

Tessa struggled as Abigail rapped on the door. Before Tessa could break free, the door opened and a large woman pulled her inside.

Tessa's eyes were slow to adjust to the candlelight. There she was — the Mistress. Her dark eyes glared and turned on Abigail. "You were followed."

The teenager started to protest, but quickly bowed her head. "I'm sorry, Mistress. I don't know how she found me."

She's been trained by the best. Isn't that right, Tessa? The great Sherlock Holmes taught you his little tricks. But evidently, not all of them, for here you are."

As Tessa shook free of Brigit's grip, she saw Eva. "You're part of all this . . . these . . . these murderers."

Eva threw her shoulders back and raised her chin. "You care for the raped and wounded women of the city, but you do nothing about the men who use us."

"Enough, Eva. I fear your words are falling on deaf ears," the Mistress crooned.

Tessa slowly backed toward the door, but found the exit blocked.

"There is no escape, Tessa, but you will not be harmed. Our code binds us to preserve and protect the lives of women — even ignorant ones like you. I truly wish we could take you with us tonight. You would see how to properly deal with men who abuse, rape, and torture the women you claim to protect." She turned to a large, broad-shouldered blond who towered over everyone in her vicinity. Bind and gag her Brigit."

"Yes, Maeve," Brigit answered.

Tessa shuddered at the mention of the name: *Maeve*.

"You bitch! You killed my brother."

Brigit slapped Tessa hard across the face.

Maeve smirked. "Aren't you going to turn the other cheek?"

The Sisters laughed.

Abigail and two others dragged Tessa to a post, stuffed a foul piece of cloth in her mouth, and bound her tightly with a length of rope.

Maeve approached. "Your brother was a fool, and he died a fool's death. You put your lives in the hands of Sherlock Holmes and the old bungler let your brother slip through his fingers."

Maeve turned to the others who huddled around her. "We each take different routes and rendezvous behind Brown's Hotel," she reminded them. "We will enter through the kitchen door — all except Eva, who will go to the employees' entrance off the lobby." She clutched Eva's shoulders. "This is your chance to show your brave heart. Clean uniforms are stacked on the shelf in the cloakroom. When you are ready, come to room 410. Your sisters and I will be waiting."

The girls departed in pairs, carrying carpetbags and satchels. When the last pair left, Maeve turned to Tessa. "In a way, I am pleased that you found us. I've been dropping clues like breadcrumbs, but the poor old man could barely keep up. You can deliver a message for me, if you will. Tell Mr. Sherlock Holmes that the Sisters of Scáthach are coming for him."

CHAPTER 13

TESSA COULD NOT BREAK HER BONDS, or call out for help. Her futile efforts came to an end when she remembered that the boathouse was closed for the season and passersby would be rare. No one at The Nest knew where she was, or even that she had left. This awareness compounded her mounting fear.

Then, the boathouse door creaked open.

They're back! She thought.

Her bindings kept her from seeing who entered. A musty woody scent punctuated the air as she felt hands untying and removing the gag. "Who is it?" she asked.

"*Tha mi caraid,*" came the answer in what Tessa recognized was Gaelic.

As the last of the bonds loosened and fell to the ground, Tessa twisted to see the genial face of an old woman materialize in the glow of a candle she was lighting. The woman's face was withered, yet her eyes possessed a youthful energy. Her hands were wrinkled and corded with blue veins, and her iron-grey hair was woven into an elaborate plait that fell over her left shoulder. As she brought the candle closer, her azure eyes brightened with delight. "*A bheil Gàidhlig agad?*" she asked.

Tessa's silence evidently gave the answer, as the woman nodded and, in a stilted brogue, said: "I am Ganna. You are injured, my child?"

Tessa stepped back to fully take in what, in the glow of the flickering light, seemed like an antediluvian apparition. Ganna's dress was of a rough mouse-colored weave, and belted with a leather thong. Her green cloak was open, and a large leather satchel lay across one shoulder. Hempen sandals were laced up her ankles.

The old woman's eyes were mesmerizing—burning with memories or specters from long ago. She cupped Tessa's face in her palms. "*Coínín . . . coínín*," she said. Her hands felt warm and smelled of smoke and rich earth. Then, Ganna smiled, cocking her head. "I know you."

"I would have remembered."

"Maybe not," Ganna answered. "I came as quickly as I could. This city is new to me, and I do not know the way of the roads."

Suddenly, Tessa reached out to touch the cheeks of the old woman. "You are an angel," she said, surprised by her own audacity.

The old one chuckled. "I'm no more, and no less than you. I can see that you are a good woman, as I strive to be."

"What brought you here, Ganna?"

"Maeve."

"That horrible woman!"

"I have been as a mother to her, and now she burdens my heart. She was born in the shadow of a blood moon, and those shadows cling to her. When word came of the man Goodnow, I knew Maeve was near. I am sorry it took so long, but I am uneasy using trains and other machines."

"You are too late. Maeve is going to kill a man at—"

"I have stopped her."

"What have you to do with all this?" Tessa asked.

"I am a woman the world has forgotten. I come from the verdant earth that binds people to Creation and reminds us all to honor our true mother. Maeve was raised to take my staff and mantle, but —"

"She is a murderer!"

"The power to bring forth life can also become the fury of the slaughter. Maeve's power is unbridled."

"Unbridled! She's a madwoman. She is responsible for my brother's death."

The old woman closed her eyes.

Tessa paused and took a breath. "How did you stop her?"

Her eyes opened. "She dishonored a *geasa*, and I ordained a tribunal. Maeve is of our tribe. She has no choice but to obey."

"What are you? A sorceress?"

Ganna's mouth clenched and her eyes burned with ire. Then, just as quickly, a winsome look transformed the woman's face into one of munificence. "No," she said, in a measured tone. "Some might use that word . . . or witch, or magician, because they do not understand the ancient arts. I have also been called a *bandrui*. My lineage goes back millennia."

"Before Jesus?

"Yes. Long before the man called Jesus. I am a descendent of Gomer."

"Noah's grandson?"

"You know the Bible. Yes, our tribe existed before the great flood."

Sensing more questions, Ganna put her finger on Tessa's lips. "I must go now. Your friend in black will be coming for you." With that, she turned and left — framed for a moment in the crimson sunlight of the boathouse doorway.

The noises of the city encroached on the green space where Ganna stood. She sensed that Maeve was already far away, somewhere to the southeast. She wasn't sure if she could track Maeve in this city of brick and stone. But, she knew Maeve would seek refuge beneath the earth, a place like the one in which she was raised. She would find her tomorrow.

Ganna walked through the trees along the water's edge, pausing when she came to the border of the park. She looked about with sadness at the dull eyes of the people rushing to and fro on the street, the raucous automobiles belching foul smoke, and putrid water in the gutters. The oppressive labyrinth of brick and stone buildings had usurped her natural world.

*****

"My life was spared by an old witch!" Basil Zaharoff shouted, as he nervously paced his fourth floor suite at Brown's Hotel. "The finest police force in the world, you say. You're a joke." He swore in Greek — which seemed well suited to the moment.

Inspector Walls' lips were pursed. Resentment blazed in his eyes. "My man risked his life for you! And, what of your men? They were useless in the face of a dozen armed — "

"Women — a dozen fanatical *girls* led by a madwoman!"

The moment Holmes reached the top floor he heard Basil Zaharoff bellowing in the distance. As he entered the suite, Walls' greeting was cut off by the Greek's puerile laughter. "Perfect! The great Sherlock Holmes to the rescue," he exclaimed. "We go from useless to incompetent!"

"May I remind you, sir," Walls returned. "You are a guest in this country."

"And fine hosts you are. My yacht is attacked, and three of my people killed. And now you cannot protect me in the middle of Mayfair." The Greek walked to his bar cart and poured a drink.

Walls motioned to Holmes and led him into the hallway.

"Thank you for coming, Mr. Holmes."

The Inspector shared what facts and information he received from his man, Carter, who had been posted at the door of Zaharoff's hotel suite before the melee ensued: "You were right to be concerned about my posting only one man here. Nearly a dozen women came into the hotel through the kitchen. A hotel maid, likely one of the gang, gained admission to the suite as the horde reached this floor. They seemed to have donned disguises after they entered the hotel. Carter reported that their faces were painted and they carried knives, swords and clubs. Carter was caught off guard by a young housekeeper who asked to gain entry."

"Was anyone killed or injured?" Holmes asked.

"No." Walls paused and swallowed hard. "Carter reported that an old woman in strange garb appeared out of nowhere. She put herself between the attackers and Zaharoff, holding up a piece of linen with a symbol on it. She uttered some gibberish. Carter believes it was Gaelic."

"And the attackers stopped?"

"Apparently so. The invaders left. As the old woman departed, she placed the piece of fabric in Zaharoff's hands, and gave Carter a message for you."

"Me?" Holmes was startled.

"Yes. She said: 'Tell Mr. Holmes that the Sister in black is in the park.'"

Holmes eyes narrowed. *But which park?*

He immediately took his leave of Inspector Walls. There were three parks near Brown's Hotel: Hyde Park, Regent's Park and St. James. Holmes went to Hyde Park, the closest of the three. He hurried, knowing that the approaching sundown may make it difficult for him to find Tessa. But his concern vanished when he saw Tessa striding toward him — her black skirts rustling.

"You are well?" he asked, to confirm his quick assessment.

Tessa nodded. "I was told that you were nearby.

"An old woman told you?" Holmes asked.

"Yes. Her name is Ganna. She said that she thwarted the attack on the man in the hotel."

"It was Zaharoff. I don't know how he deserves such good fortune, but he is unharmed. However, the same danger that threatened him, now threatens you. It was foolish for you to —"

"I am not new to danger, Mr. Holmes."

Tessa went on to describe her pursuit of Abigail and the encounters in the boathouse. She provided the small details she knew Mr. Holmes would appreciate. He nodded when Tessa told him that Maeve was the ringleader.

"It all makes sense now, given Zaharoff is involved," he said. "We thought Maeve fled the country to escape his retribution. But she is striking back at him and others."

"And she has three of my girls," Tessa reminded him.

Holmes held up a hand. "I understand, but it was *me*, four years ago, who unraveled her plan to take over Zaharoff's enterprise and frame him as a murderer. Promise me that you will let me handle this affair."

"Maeve is responsible for my brother's death. She has Eva, Patricia and Abigail in her clutches. There is *nothing* you can do that will keep me from bringing this madwoman to justice."

"There is a place for you, but promise me that you will not go after Maeve without me."

"Are you staying with the Doctor?"

"Yes, on Sheen Lane."

"Very well, I will look for you there."

"I will accompany you back to Upper Clapton."

"No. If I may borrow the fare, eight pence, I can find my way."

"Very well," Holmes agreed. "All to the good, as I wish to pay another call on a friend who, I believe, can put us on Maeve's trail."

CHAPTER 14

PROFESSOR AUGUSTUS STONE WAS IN HIS STUDY when Holmes rang at the door. When there was no answer, Holmes showed himself in and found his friend, once again, at his desk.

"I see that I am not keeping you from your bed, Professor."

"No. I work long into the night. So many books, you see. I accumulated a great library in preparation for my retirement. It appears now that I have more books than retirement."

"I quite understand, sir. And I fear I might be contributing to your dilemma, for I would like to coax you out of retirement — for a time anyway."

"Delightful!"

When they were both settled in the Professor's study with a cup of tea, Holmes related the events of the last two days. Stone listened intently, interrupting only once to ask about the old woman's attire.

"So, you see, Professor, that Celtic casket I opened, nigh three days ago is a veritable Pandora's box."

"An apt metaphor, Mr. Holmes, for it has unleashed great evil in the city. But take heart. As you recall, when Pandora finally closed the box, Hope remained inside."

"It is in that hope that I come to you. For somewhere in your head, and in the many books inhabiting your library, we may discover a way to rid ourselves of this evil."

"I believe I can help you there, as it appears that my analysis of the casket was correct. Maeve Murtagh and her band have taken on the part of Celtic warriors."

"And the old woman?" Holmes asked.

"You say that Tessa said that the old woman described herself as a *bandrui* — a druid. The first use of that word can be found in the writings of the Roman historian Tacitus around 100 AD. He recounted the horrible slaughter of the druids on the Island of Mona in Wales. You see the druids, being the priests of the Celts, were powerful and well-respected. The *bandrui* had many functions. They fought alongside the army, enchanting rocks, trees and rivers in support of their warriors. And . . .," the Professor paused and brought his index finger to his temple. Popping up from his chair, he dashed into the adjoining library.

Moments later Stone came back with an open book.

"Yes, yes, I was correct." He stabbed a finger onto the page. "Cassius Dio mentioned a druidess named Ganna."

"The same name," Holmes said.

"Yes. Ganna went on an official trip to Rome, and was received by Domitian, the son of Vespasian. The Romans respected the druids as philosophers. They were particularly intrigued with their doctrine regarding the immortality of the soul, and reincarnation, also known as metempsychosis. This was not a Roman belief, so the idea fascinated them."

Holmes looked askance at Stone. "You're not suggesting that the old woman is an incarnation of the Romans' Ganna?"

The Professor shrugged his shoulders. "She may have just taken the name." Professor Stone sat down, closed the book, and pointed at Holmes. "But admit it, Mr. Holmes, metempsychosis, the soul passing from one body to the next, captures the imagination, does it not. That is why the Celts fought so fiercely in battle. They believed that they were immortal."

Holmes waved his hand to interrupt the Professor. "Let us come to the matter at hand. We must find Ganna. I believe that she is our best hope for stopping Maeve and her band. Where would we look for a druid in London?"

*****

94

Ganna followed the Thames westward, walking more briskly as twilight approached. After several miles she came to a bridge and stopped by the water's edge, waiting and listening.

A boy on a bicycle rode up to her. "Are you lost, ma'am?" he asked.

"I am," she answered. "What place is that across the river?"

"Part of Richmond, ma'am."

"What is there?

"Nothin'. The woods."

"Are there great trees in those woods?"

"Yes. Big ones for climbing."

"You like to climb trees, do you?"

"When you get up in the big ones you can watch and listen to the people below and they don't know you're there. It's great fun." He looked cockeyed at the old woman. "I think you're too old to climb trees."

Ganna smiled. "We are never too old to climb trees."

She waited for the boy's confused pout to twist into a vague smile. "Right, ma'am. I have to go home now. Goodbye."

As the youngster rode off, the *bandrui* made her way onto the bridge. She stood for a time in the center enjoying the rush of the incoming tide vibrating beneath her. The eager pulse of the water throbbed within her body.

She walked on.

Near the end of the bridge she saw rushes growing in the backwater. She took off her sandals, tucked her gown in her belt, and strode into the river. She paused as she felt the mud sliding between her toes. Extending her arms and hands over the coursing water, Ganna closed her eyes and cleared her mind of everything but her deepest intentions. She remained there, trance-like, letting the balsamic air fill her lungs, while her spirit frolicked in the whooshing water. She bade the currents to carry her intentions to the city.

She dipped her hands into the river, aware that it had been cooled by a million winters, and warmed by as many springs. She coaxed the cool water onto her forearms, and then cupped it in her palms and cleansed her face.

Returning to the shore, she plucked some of the taller rushes, and placed them in the leather satchel on her shoulder. She cleaned and dried her feet in the grass, put on her sandals, and headed toward a dirt path that snaked off into the woods. As she was enfolded within the shroud of trees, she held her hands up in thanksgiving.

Ganna gathered her dinner as she walked: wild asparagus, acorns, hickory nuts, lamb's quarters — and, for desert, the last dried mulberries of the season.

Near the middle of the woods she came upon an auspicious sentinel. Like her, while the oak's great boughs swayed in the winds of the world, it was rooted in eternity. Its history was inscribed on its trunk and misshapen limbs — the lush years and the dry ones — the storms endured. It was gnarled, with great hollow spaces where limbs had broken off. Huge portions of the tree were hollow, yet it still burst with life. The last of the season's leaves clung to the great oak's boughs.

Ganna approached the aged tree reverently, placing her hand on its rough bark. She bowed her head and offered a prayer. She tucked her dress under her belt and, in the last of the daylight, climbed upward. About halfway up she found a hollow in a branch that was large enough to cradle her body. She removed her cloak and, pulling herself up to the hollow limb, laid her cloak into the hollow to make a nest. She climbed into the depression and folded the edges of her cloak over her legs. From where she lay, she could see across the Thames to the city's twinkling lights in the distance. She pulled her dinner from her satchel. As she ate, she stared with curiosity at the dusky metropolis.

Calm touched her heart when she saw the waxing moon rising. This was the third night in a new cycle. *Calan gaeaf is approaching*, she thought. Some called this time *Samhain* or *Samonios* — Seed Fall. It was a good time to pray. As her lips moved with the words of the old tongue, Ganna weaved rushes into an ancient design.

*****

"So, you believe Ganna is sleeping by a tree?" Holmes repeated.

"Possibly in one," Professor Stone added. "Somewhere among these many books I recall that Strabo reported that the druids took refuge in trees."

"How many trees do you suppose are in London, Professor?"

"You only need to find the big ones, mind you, most likely oaks."

Holmes nodded. "Do you suppose we can whittle down the options, knowing what you do about the enigmatic Ganna?"

"I pray that we might. In three days time is the festival called *Samhain*. I cannot recall the Gaelic name. We call it All-Hallows-Eve."

Holmes laughed. "So you believe the witches will be coming out, Professor?"

"It is not what I believe that matters. The Celts believe that *Samhain* was the optimal time for settling disputes and vendettas. It is a liminal time, when the boundary between this world and the Otherworld can easily be crossed. Mark my words, Holmes, Ganna, Maeve, and the others will be afoot on All-Hallows-Eve."

CHAPTER 15

ZAHAROFF LEANED BACK IN HIS CHAIR appraising the huge man standing before him. Yesterday's attack at his own hotel room showed that extraordinary measures are required to protect him, and Jaeger Heinrich seemed just the fellow to provide that security. The mere sight of Heinrich spoke of impending calamity. He certainly warranted his reputation as a witch-hunter. Jaeger's face, especially, cast him as a brutish creation from man's primordial past — early Neolithic, or thereabouts. He possessed a receding forehead, broad nose, and jutting lower jaw. Well over six feet tall, he wore the black wool papaha hat of a Russian Cossack atop shoulder-length ebony hair fixed in back. His bushy beard veiled the lower portion of his face, and set off his piercing violet eyes. His knee-length leather coat was stitched at the seams with a thick red cord giving it the appearance of a uniform. A leather pouch set on his right hip. A leash was wound around his left hand to which was fastened a monstrous black hound. The broad-chested beast sat like an ominous black shadow at his feet.

"Mr. Heinrich," Zaharoff began, "You come highly recommended and I am told that you are just the man to put a stop to a madwoman who is trying to kill me." A childish smirk crept into the Greek's face. "And, while I do not believe in such things, I suppose some would call this madwoman a witch."

Zaharoff's blunt remarks did not register on the man's face. "I do not require zat you believe in vitches," he replied in a thick Slavic accent. "*I* know they exist. They employ fell sorcery and consort with the devil. They are cunning and sly, and can make themselves appear to be something benign," Jaeger Heinrich answered.

"I assure you, Mr. Heinrich, this woman is not *benign*; but she appears to be masquerading as a Celtic warrior."

Heinrich's eyes hardened. "A Celtic witch — very treacherous. I sensed her presence, the moment I stepped from the train."

"Well, you will need all your senses, and more. She travels with a dozen or more . . . witches, or what have you."

"A coven," the witch-hunter noted. He canted his head enquiringly: "Do you want all of them dispatched? I get paid by the head."

The Greek pursed his lips in thought. "I suppose it might be best if the worst of them were dealt with. I wouldn't want them coming around after they have lost their leader."

"I think that is wise, sir. You know my fee."

"I do, and, now, I understand that your stated fee is per-head," Zaharoff said. "I am curious though. How does one kill a witch?"

Jaeger reached into his leather pouch and pulled out a bundle of sticks and a small leather pouch. "Palo Santo and salt can be effective."

Basil Zaharoff laughed. "Incense is it. And what, salt on her tail? I am afraid that you will need more than a magic act if you intend to put an end to this fanatical woman and her brood."

"Mabuz," Jaeger ordered. The hound jumped to his feet and bared his teeth. A rumbling growl vibrated in the canine's chest.

"Do you have anything that belonged to the witch?"

"No, not from the leader, but the old woman with her gave me something."

Zaharoff walked to his desk, retrieved the cloth Ganna had given him, and handed it to Heinrich.

Jaeger held it up to the light.

"Ha! A shield knot."

"Do you know its meaning?" Zaharoff asked.

"A symbol of protection — a Celtic knot. The old woman was trying to protect you."

"I doubt that," Zaharoff answered. "They are allies. It appeared that a disagreement ensued and the old woman thankfully won the day."

"The shield worked its magic for you. But it will not protect her or the others from Mabuz."

The witch-hunter put the cloth before the hound's nose. Mabuz sniffed at it, and then Heinrich tucked it in his pocket.

"Yes, I can see that your hound may prove helpful. But what will you do when you find her?"

Heinrich's brows lifted. He raised his right forearm and opened his palm before the Greek's face. He twisted his wrist sharply. An eight-inch metal blade sprang from his sleeve and jutted out beyond his fingertips.

The blade stopped an inch from Zaharoff's nose. The Greek's eyes riveted on the dazzling tip for a moment before they closed in relief. When he opened them again, he was smiling.

"I think we have a deal, Mr. Heinrich. What's the plan?"

"I'm going to stay close to you, sir," Jaeger stated.

"I have bodyguards."

"Maeve has tried to kill you two times, you say."

"Yes, and I don't wish to give her a third opportunity."

"Yes, you do," the witch-hunter countered. "Trust me, she *will* try again, however, this time, Mabuz and I will be waiting."

* * * * *

101

Maeve could not sleep. She thought that she left Ganna behind in Gilmerton when she left for Dún Scáith Castle on the Isle of Skye. The old woman's unexpected appearance troubled her, churning up chiseled memories.

Growing up, Maeve's father, Professor James Moriarty, was absent from the home most of the time, so Ganna fairly raised her. When she was eleven years old her father disappeared, and soon after, Ganna told her that her father had died. Even now she could vividly recall that fateful day:

It was in the late spring, at their old house near the University of Edinburgh. The property was blessed with an extraordinary garden where Ganna had sowed hundreds of herbs, plants, and bushes over the years. She taught Maeve about each of them. Some were medicinal, some edible, others poisonous, and some florae simply beautiful. Maeve would laugh as she watched her nana prancing about, fingering this plant and that — talking to each vegetal in her Gaelic tongue.

On that singular spring day, a letter from her father's solicitor arrived in the post. Later that afternoon Ganna prepared tea, placed the tray on a table in the garden, and called to Maeve to join her. Though Ganna did her best to project no effect, Maeve could see a quiet fear in Ganna's eyes. Tea was offered, but Maeve did not take it. Ganna breathed deeply, and began: "Maeve, do you have fond memories of your father?"

Maeve recounted when her father gave her a copy of *The Country of the Pointed Firs* on her last birthday, and his kiss on her forehead whenever they parted. She lived for those rare moments of tenderness. Ganna listened to Maeve's recollections before taking her hands in her own. "You must never forget those things. That is your inheritance."

Ganna went on to explain that Maeve's father had died in a far off land, but there were few details. Much later, Maeve would learn that her father died in a terrible struggle with Sherlock Holmes, who unjustly cast her father in the role of a criminal, and hounded him mercilessly.

It was not more than a month later that Ganna and Maeve were forced to vacate their home, as it was the property of the university. At the time Maeve thought it strange that their refuge was a hidden cave near Gilmerton, just south of Edinburgh. There were small underground chambers carved from solid rock, complete with tables and chairs. Ganna said it was a sacred place, hundreds of years old. Even as a child, Maeve could feel its power.

It was in those caves near Gilmerton that Ganna revealed her secret to Maeve: "I am a priestess, Maeve, a druid of the Iceni tribe. You are of my tribe, and I came to live with you and your father so that I might teach you our ways, that you might one day carry on my tradition."

Now, Maeve found it hard to believe that she did not find this revelation shocking at the time, but she had not. The mysteries that had always surrounded Ganna suddenly made sense.

Maeve's early years at Gilmerton were spent learning at Ganna's knee—everything from herb-craft to philosophy. She tried to be a good student, but Maeve interests lay elsewhere.

On Maeve's fifteenth birthday, Ganna prepared a ceremony for Maeve's coming of age — an *imbas forosna*. Maeve breathed in the sacred smoke of cojobana seeds. Then, Ganna placed her under a pile of dry oak leaves and branches, and covered the pile with sheepskins as druid aspirants had done for thousands of years. There, in that otherworldly cocoon, Maeve had a vision: A beautiful young woman in a golden toga stood in a misty field, holding a human heart in her hand. The woman extended her arm to offer the heart to Maeve. When Maeve touched it, the heart began to beat. She awoke suddenly, whimpering like a babe, her body shaking.

When Ganna learned of Maeve's vision, and her description of the lovely young woman in a toga, Ganna told her the story of Siora, the daughter of Queen Boudicca:

Millennia ago, Boudicca drove back the black clad — the Romans, at Camulodunum and Londinium. The Romans rallied and returned, crushing the rebellion, executing thousands of Iceni and taking the rest as slaves. Siora's mother, the Queen, took poison to avoid capture. Siora and her sister, Isolda, were raped and sent to Rome as slaves.

Later, when she bided in the ruins of Scáthach's castle on Skye, Maeve reflected on how, like Siora, she had been abducted, raped, and sent east as a slave. But, unlike Siora, she returned to the land of her people with an avenging sword in hand.

Now Ganna had come into her life again — this time uninvited. She cared for the old woman, but what was more, she feared her.

Where is that old woman now? Maeve wondered.

The next morning, Ganna lay within the old oak, letting the soft animal within her relax. She felt the leaves of the tree transpiring. The onrush of moisture cleansed her body and cleared her mind. Once again, abiding within the patient pace of nature, Ganna was at peace. She took herbs from her satchel and chewed them to quell her hunger. She gathered the remaining rushes from her bag and finished the weaving she had begun last night. She hummed, as her fingers recalled an ancient design.

She had decreed to Maeve that there would be a trial by the oath of men, a Taro. Maeve was not pleased with her decision, but she would submit. However, finding a safe and proper place for the Taro and the *calan gaeaf* celebration would not be easy. Maeve's rash actions put many people on her trail — Holmes, the Greek, and the police. And there was Tessa, who found her way to Ganna. The Fates were weaving a strange tapestry. A feeling of foreboding throbbed within Ganna — a forewarning from beyond.

CHAPTER 16

PROFESSOR STONE BUSTLED ABOUT gathering books on Celtic history and lore. His quest took him from his basement to his attic, and places in between. Having no crates, he commandeered two timeworn steamer trunks. The Hartmann traveling wardrobes had accompanied him on his archeological digs around the globe. He dragged the scuffed brass-trimmed trunks into the hallway and began neatly arranging his books within. Stone was positively euphoric at the prospect of joining forces with Sherlock Holmes. In the past, he was merely a source of arcane information, now he was a true ally.

Holmes went on ahead to inform Watson that his flat was soon to be transformed into a command center from which the quest to bring Maeve Murtagh to justice would be planned and carried out. Holmes understood that the Professor's advent may initially seem an imposition; however Holmes rationalized that it was to the Doctor's benefit: *It will be good for the old boy. He's far too isolated and sedentary.*

This was true. Since Watson had taken notice of his irregular heartbeat, his daily outings took the form of mailing letters at the red pillar-box on the corner, and traveling to a tobacco shop on Sheen Lane to purchase the *Daily Mail* or *Illustrated London News*.

Holmes let himself into Watson's flat with the latchkey he had retained after his move to the Sussex Downs six years ago. Watson was napping. Upon discovering his slumbering friend, Holmes quietly put the kettle on and began perusing Watson's considerable collection of teas. He spied a Dianhong, a robust Yunnan red, which was sure to get the Doctor's heart pumping properly.

Noises in the kitchen startled Watson from his slumber. He shook off his malaise and tiptoed to his desk to retrieve a Webley revolver from the drawer. He listened.

Another loud clink in the distance.

He cocked the pistol and slinked toward the kitchen. Hearing footsteps, he pressed himself flat against the wall to one side of the kitchen door and waited.

Holmes's hands full, he pushed the door open with his foot. Watson swung around poking his pistol into the center button of Holmes's vest—neatly between two cups of steaming tea.

"You take one lump, correct?" Holmes asked.

"Indeed, one," Watson confirmed, lowering the pistol and uncocking it.

It required two cups for Holmes to relate recent events, concluding with his invitation to Professor Stone. He was curious how his friend would receive the news as they had exclusively worked in tandem.

"The Professor still has all his marbles, does he?" Watson quipped.

"He does not have your deductive abilities, Watson, but his grasp of ancient history is unparalleled. And his library, why . . ." Holmes paused and set his cup down. "I fear I may be taking advantage of your exceptional hospitality, my friend, but I took it upon myself to ask the Professor to bring his books along."

"Not at all, Holmes." He pointed behind his desk. "You see there . . . just to the right of the Greek amphora . . . he is welcome to put his books there, so they can be at hand."

Holmes starred blankly at the empty space that was little more than a foot wide.

"I have a special task for you, my friend," Holmes continued. "Eva Allsop, the young woman accused of Goodnow's murder, claims to be an orphan. If so, she would have gone to a home as a newborn about seventeen or eighteen years ago. I'd like for us to locate that orphanage and make a visit. Do you think you can manage that?"

"Rather like a needle in the haystack," Watson exclaimed.

"Yes, well, do your best. You have her parent's last name . . . Allsop. They were, or are, in the laundry business," Holmes replied. "She was adopted at about age eight.

"Very well, I will see what I can do. Do you wish another cup?" Watson asked.

Before Holmes could answer, a knock came to the door.

"Too soon for the Professor," Holmes said, as Watson answered the call.

"Sorry to bother you, Doctor, is Mr. Holmes here?" Holmes recognized the voice as that of Inspector Walls and rose to greet their guest.

"It must be urgent, if you felt the need to come to us," Holmes remarked. "What is it?"

Walls removed his hat and looked about nervously. "Just you two, then? Very well. We have a complication with regard to this Celtic warrior business."

Watson offered the Inspector a seat, and he and Holmes settled into theirs.

"I felt it was my duty to warn Mr. Zaharoff, suggesting that he leave the city. I intended to tell him that we suspect Maeve Murtagh is his attacker, but I never had the opportunity."

"You are a glutton for abuse, Inspector," Holmes observed.

"Be that as it may, I arrived at his suite to find a rather barbaric giant in Zaharoff's parlor. I suppose my curiosity showed upon my face, for the old Greek began laughing and, after a number of jibes about the incompetence of the London constabulary, he introduced Mister Jaeger Heinrich and his nasty mongrel. The fellow calls himself a witch-hunter."

Watson guffawed. "The man has gone raving bonkers!"

"It's not a joke, I'm afraid," Walls rejoined. "I informed the brutish fellow that he should not attempt to take the law into his own hands. He laughed and retrieved a crumbling text from a satchel. He held the bound manuscript before me saying that his law superseded mine. He called the book the *Malles Maleficum* . . . or something of that sort.

"*Malleus Maleficarum* is the term you are searching for Inspector. I have something in my files regarding that rare manuscript and the fellow himself. If he is the person in my file, he is a defrocked priest who joined the Order of the Brothers of Jerusalem, a Teutonic branch of the Knights Templar."

"He has the look of a Templar, to be sure," Walls added.

Holmes went to the mantel for his pipe. Filling and lighting it, he continued: "The *Malleus Maleficarum*—the Hammer of Witches in Latin—is the most famous medieval treatises on witches," Holmes expostulated. He took two long drags on his pipe to help him conjure additional facts from archival mind. "It was written in the late fifteenth century, purportedly by two members of the Dominican Order who claimed to be Inquisitors for the Catholic Church. Its main purpose was to challenge all arguments against the existence of witchcraft, and to instruct others on how to identify, judge and dispatch witches."

"The witch in question being Maeve," Watson surmised, rising to open a window to ventilate the room.

"Yes, however, I fear his efforts will not stop with her," Holmes predicted. "The entire band of women is in jeopardy, as is anyone who stands between him and his holy war. We must watch our backs. I wouldn't worry, Inspector. Heinrich has the same problem we do — finding Maeve and the others."

"I believe I know how he plans to do it," Watson declared, sweeping back the curtains. "If I am not mistaken, that is the nefarious witch-hunter across the way with his hound. He seems rather out of his age."

"So, he expects to follow *you*," Walls remarked.

"Wise fellow," Holmes added. However, he's likely not snooping, given his brazen presence. I believe he wishes to chat, and I feel I should oblige him."

The setting sun cast the alleyway across the street in darkness. The avowed witch-hunter and his hound were one within the shadows. Holmes waited on the stoop, pipe in hand. The man remained still, studying Holmes with a dreary eye. His entire manner spoke of imminent violence. Heinrich finally strolled across the street like a legitimate king — his hound at his heel. He stopped at the base of the stairway and gazed at Holmes.

"You wish to chat?" Holmes asked.

"I am the overcomer, Holmes. I put on the whole armor of God to take my stand against the devil's schemes."

Holmes gave a look of surprise. "I fear you may be five centuries too late. There are no witches about. A malicious criminal who happens to be a woman, but certainly no witch."

"What do you think is the source of her malice?"

"A frightfully poor upbringing, I'm afraid. Her father was a horrible criminal."

"You're speaking of the warrior-witch. What of the old woman? What of the other women in the coven? A plague is descending upon your city."

"And you are the cure?" Holmes taunted.

Mabuz snarled. Jaeger reached down and, without looking, stroked the neck of the beast that was reminiscent of another creature from Holmes's past. Mabuz was not a pureblood hound, nor a pure mastiff; but a combination of the two — gaunt and savage.

"I'm told that you are on the witch's trail," Jaeger stated. "You are said to be a clever fellow. I fear that you may be in my way."

"I had the very same thought," Holmes replied. "You see, what is needed here is good police work, not an avenging angel."

"You may mock me, but do not underrate me, sir. And, do not stand between me and God's will."

CHAPTER 17

TESSA'S BEDROOM WINDOW framed the crescent moon as it leisurely retreated behind the clouds. The silvery light flooded through the window and splashed across her bed and body. It sat above the horizon like an empty bowl wanting to be filled.

Her grandmother told her that the Irish of old counted their year in the thirteen cycles of the moon. It coincided with women's cycles — probably why the superstitious ancients associated the moon with fertility. But tonight, as she lay here, a wondrous feeling was budding in her heart — the possibility that she had escaped her dark destiny. Her brother Rory told her that the darkness was their friend. But he was a thief. She was a thief until their thievery inadvertently cost a man his life. Death had stalked her ever since, taking her mother, Rory, and Benjie. People she loved died.

Father O'Malley told her to do penance. But countless years of Hail Marys and Our Fathers did nothing to wash away her guilt. She became a "slum sister," offering up her life to serve the poor and wretched girls and women of London. But, there was one sin that she never brought to the confessional or entered into her diary — a wicked one that could never be forgiven.

Tessa sat up. Her skin prickled in the damp October air. She pulled the blankets tightly about her neck waiting for the moon to reemerge from the clouds. It was a waxing moon, so she knew more would be revealed. Her heart swelled when she thought of the old woman and the sense that something new was waiting for her — something that would wash away narrow beliefs about her ill-fated life — something that will let her trade repentance for destiny.

Her encounter with the old woman was reminiscent of walks in the woods she took with her grandmother when she was little. Her nana instilled in her an appreciation for nature. Tessa recalled one particular afternoon when they came to a branch in the trail. Her grandmother stopped and took Tessa by the shoulders, pointing ahead. She asked Tessa what path they should take. She pointed to the narrower one. "Is that the right one?" she asked. Her grandmother answered: "If that is where your heart tells you to go, you are on the right path."

Tessa decided: Tomorrow morning she would go to the Major's office and request a leave, asking that someone be appointed to manage The Nest while she was away. Major Dugmore would ask how long she would be gone. She would say: "several months." But Tessa suspected that she would never return. She retrieved her diary from the nightstand and made an entry:

> *What changed?*
> *What I thought I was,*
> *or wished my life could be,*
> *are cinders in my sackcloth*
> *which I cast aside.*

Ganna was gazing at the moon as well . . . wondering about Tessa. *Time will tell*, Ganna told herself. She knew that Tessa must come to *calan gaeaf* and be present at the Taro, when Zaharoff would face judgment. She understood that the certain history shared by Maeve and Tessa might be able to play out during that seminal time. *All the more reason*, Ganna thought, *to find a safe place for the Taro.* She would use the olde ways. *I will go to the river in the morning, listen, and follow.*

*****

Holmes awoke in the middle of the night, but the itinerant moon was not what prompted his ill ease. He had left a message for Tessa at The Nest and the Salvation Army headquarters, telling her to make her way to Watson's flat with extreme care, making certain that she was not followed. She had not replied nor come.

When the dawn came, Holmes had tea waiting for Watson and Stone. His two friends seemed to delight in one another's company. The old curmudgeons chuckled and enjoyed toast over their second cup of tea, fully indulging the British privilege of grumbling about workhouses, taxes, and tariff reform.

"I don't wish to intrude on your tea party, gentleman, but I suggest we settle down to the task at hand," Holmes interjected.

Watson held up a finger as he finished chewing. "I suggest we move the kitchen table into the parlor to accommodate our gathering. What do you say to that?"

Holmes's endorsement was cut off by a knock at the door. Stone scurried into the hallway in a flutter. Holmes followed and watched over Stone's shoulders as the door was opened. Stone rubbed his hands together. "My books."

Watson was still in the kitchen preparing the table for its relocation, when rumbling noises emanating from the hall prompted him to poke his head into the parlor. Two outsized trolleys, bearing enormous steamer trunks, were rolling across his Persian carpet, piloted by two burly men with dirty boots. His mouth was agape and his eyes glazed over.

"Right over there, gentleman," the Professor said, pointing to the area in front of Watson's desk. "Please lay them down if you will, and open them."

As porters complied, Watson's hands went on his hips as he stalked into the parlor. The Doctor cocked his body in an attitude of resolve as he saddled up to Stone. "Look here, my good man —"

Stone turned to Watson, extending his palm. "Could I trouble you for the loan of a shilling?"

Holmes stood at a safe distance, chuckling *sotto voce*.

Fortunately, the trauma caused by the appearance of Professor Stone's mobile Celtic library was transitory. Watson retrieved maps of London and vicinity; Stone arranged his books in piles by topic on top of the trunks, while Holmes enjoyed a contemplative smoke.

When the stage was set, Holmes tapped his dottle into an ashtray and called the gathering to order: "We know that Maeve Murtagh and Ganna are in, or near, the city. Let us put on our thinking caps to identify some likely places we might pick up their trail."

"I've been thinking about just that thing," Stone replied. "Of course, it will not be within the city proper — not in a building nor popular thoroughfare, that is. The Celts, and particularly the druids, sought to dwell in natural settings, within woods, and always near water."

Holmes centered himself on the map and poked his finger near the center of the city. "This is where Ganna was last seen. She would need to find shelter before nightfall."

Holmes refilled his pipe as he continued: "The average walking speed of a person is three miles per hour, and Ganna had less than two hours before sundown yesterday." He lit his pipe and took a long draw. Then, with the stem of his pipe, he drew an imaginary circle on the map. "What woodland places lay within this area here?"

Watson ran his finger along the map. "Very well," he said, "there are several large underdeveloped areas, and a few uninhabited ones near the Thames, particularly along the south embankment."

Homes leaned closer.

"I suggest you look for wilderness," the Professor added. "Trees, oak trees in particular."

Holmes squinted and bent lower. "I seem to remember hearing of a great old oak in the area of Richmond just across the river?

"The Richmond Oak," Watson noted, pointing to the map. "I've been there, a wooded area just beyond a bridge."

"Make a note of that Watson?"

His friend happily complied, retrieving a notebook and pencil from his desk. "Like old times, Holmes."

The astute ears of Holmes picked up modest footfalls on the stairs to Watson's flat. He went to the door and opened it to find Tessa Wiggins with her knocking, her hand poised in the air. "Sister . . ," he said, catching himself, as he noted that she was not arrayed in her a drab black dress and bonnet. Sister Tessa had vanished beneath a rather smart hip-length cardigan of tan and green pattern, with a knee-length skirt to match. The clothes awakened the iridescent green of her eyes. Her ebony hair was swept back and covered by a forest green cloche hat.

"Tessa. Please come in," Holmes continued wide-eyed.

"You see. I am true to my word, Mr. Holmes. I did not charge off in search of my girls without you." Raising her brow, she added: "But, I will not be left behind either. I only retrieved your message this morning, it read rather ominously."

"I will explain later. Suffice it to say, that it behooves us to move with caution as there are dangerous persons afoot," he said, inviting her into the hall.

Tessa acknowledged the warning and strolled into the parlor. As she did so, Dr. Watson blinked in surprise — staring wide-eyed at Tessa for a time.

She smiled: "Clothes are strange, are they not Doctor; they seem to open doors to different parts of ourselves."

Watson, displaying modest embarrassment, replied: "Yes, indeed. One would hardly know you are the same woman who has been bottled up in that drab black garb."

Tessa's emergence from her Salvationist cocoon had seemingly disquieted the three men as it took some time for them to arrange themselves around the table of maps.

"Tessa, please tell Professor Stone everything you can remember about your encounter with Ganna."

As she narrated her story, it was apparent from his expression, that Holmes appreciated Tessa's attention to detail. They seemed to share that rare ability to see and note most everything about them in the moment.

"What did Ganna tell you about her confrontation with Maeve," Stone interrupted.

"She said that Maeve violated 'a *geasa*' — that's what she called it. I believe it is some kind of law or prohibition, and . . . Maeve, being from her tribe, must obey."

The Professor clapped his hands eagerly. "It's like going back in time," he said, effervescing with glee. "Did she happen to mention the name of their tribe?"

"She did, but I cannot recall it," Tessa paused.

Stone rifled through a nearby pile of books. "Here we are," the Professor said, opening one of them. "Holmes, you may recall that Cassius Dio reported that a druid priestess named Ganna was received by Emperor Domitian in Rome in ninety *anno domini*. Well, this text goes on to say that Ganna was of the Iceni tribe."

"That's it!" Tessa exclaimed.

"Is that relevant?" Watson asked.

"Why it is famous!" the old man exclaimed. "Queen Boudicca was of the Iceni tribe!"

Watson shrugged his shoulders.

"Surely you know of Queen Boudicca?" Stone continued, looking about in amazement.

"She defeated the Romans at Camulodunum," Tessa said.

"Exactly," Stone answered.

No one seemed to notice that Tessa stood motionless, silent, and stunned by her inexplicable knowledge.

The Professor stirred Tessa from her trance: "What else . . . what else do you recall?"

"I just remembered. When we met in the boathouse, Ganna said, '*Coínín . . . coínín.*' What does that mean?"

The Professor grimaced. "Are you sure that is what she said?"

"I could be wrong."

"*Coínín* is the Gaelic word for rabbit. You would have her saying, *rabbit . . . rabbit*. What could that mean?" Stone paused. "Wait. There is an old Irish superstition about white rabbits bringing good luck. Maybe something related to that. Anything else?"

Tessa closed her eyes: "Ganna said that she ordered . . . no . . . *ordained* was the word she used . . . she ordained a trial."

"A trial?" Watson echoed. "Who is going on trial?"

"Zaharoff," Holmes replied. "They intend to put him on trial. I will get word to Inspector Walls to let him know Maeve and her gang are still in hot pursuit."

"A trial. How marvelous," the Professor replied. "And I would venture that it will happen at the festival of *Samhain*, on All-Hallows-Eve."

"But where?" Holmes asked, again surveying the map.

CHAPTER 18

MAEVE AWOKE HUNGRY and went to the kitchen. She stopped at Scáthach's altar, lit a candle, and offered a short prayer. She knew it was but a matter of time before Ganna found her. The old druid truly had prodigious power, though she never used it to her own profit or, for that matter, to benefit Maeve. When Maeve was left crying at the altar, she begged Ganna to cast a spell on the absconding groom. Ganna refused, saying: "You have your own power. Learn to use it."

Maeve laughed at the thought of those words now: "I have found my power Ganna — power given to me by the 'Warrior Maid' — Scáthach. You may have your Taro, but I will have my revenge."

"What is wrong, Mistress?"

Maeve turned to see her beloved Brigit brooding. She was Maeve's first recruit upon leaving Skye. Until Maeve came along, Brigit expressed her warrior's heart by helping her father fashion swords and claymores at his famed armory in Mallaig. Seeing a newly fashioned claymore in Brigit's strong hand reminded Maeve of Scáthach herself who trained the great warriors of Scotland in ages past.

"Brigit, I am sorry if I woke you. I could not sleep. I was hungry."

Brigit hesitantly approached. "Why did you let that old woman keep us from Zaharoff? Who is she?"

"Ganna is many things, but most of all, she is the last of the druids," Meave said reverently.

"A priestess?"

"Yes. She has ancient knowledge, and the power that comes with it. We are of the Iceni tribe, and now you and the others are fostered with our tribe. We will obey Ganna. There will be a trial by the oath of men."

Brigit was confused. "A trial?"

"Zaharoff's trial. He will make his plea. Witnesses may be brought forward to speak for or against us."

"Who is to judge?"

"Ganna."

"Can you trust her?"

"Yes. But, she has a weakness: She was always hesitant to shed blood."

"And, if she rules against us?"

"Then the reign of the *bandrui* will end, and the reign of Scáthach will commence."

Suddenly the hall was filled with raucous shrieks.

Abigail ran in breathless. "She's here! She saw me!"

Maeve didn't have to ask who "she" was. *The old woman always possessed an uncanny ability to track.* Did you invite her down?"

"Do I need an invitation to come into the household of macushla," Ganna said, from the doorway.

Abigail and Brigit turned — the later drawing her knife.

Maeve stayed Brigit's hand. "You may go sisters," Maeve said. The women hesitated. "Go, and close the curtain."

"Are you going to invite me to tea?" Ganna began. "I've come a long way."

Maeve motioned her toward the table. They measured one another coolly. "You have come far, Ganna. Why?"

"Because you have forgotten our code," Ganna answered. "The Iceni are brave and courageous, but we are not barbarians."

"I am not the barbarian," Maeve rasped. "You know what the Greek did to me."

"I do. And, I taught you the proper way to address your grievances. Listen to my words."

Maeve listened.

By the time Ganna finished, Maeve had regained her composure. Ganna smiled and cupped Maeve's face. "*Coínín . . . coínín*," she said.

Maeve laughed. "Rabbit . . . rabbit. Even after all of this, you still believe it brings good luck?"

"It means I wish *you* good luck. But remember, luck is mostly of our own making."

"The olde ways are enchanting, but we live in a new time, Ganna."

"Some things never change, my child. Good and evil, and the choices we each make with regard to each."

Maeve held up a hand, "Please, Ganna."

Ganna pushed her hand aside, "Choose wisely."

Maeve heard hushed voices in the distance. "Your appearance is causing unease within our community. I must go to my sisters, but I will return, and we can make plans for the Taro."

The old woman nodded.

Ganna did not know what Maeve said to the Sisters of Scáthach, but they greeted her with deference when she walked into the main chamber to break the night's fast. The ritual singing and procession preceding the meal touched her, but Ganna found the notion of a weapon on an altar repugnant.

After the meal, the women began their morning practice with swords, knives and fists. Brigit was adept as a teacher, and the aged priestess could see that the young women were eager students.

"What do you think of my sisters, Ganna?"

"They are bright and beautiful women. They have quick minds and learn fast."

"They are just the beginning," Maeve replied, looking with pride at the young women in mock combat.

"Brigit is a fine warrior, but I am not as certain about the others," Ganna observed.

"Time," Maeve answered. "They simply need time."

Ganna took Maeve by the arm. "With regard to time, we should talk about the Taro. I would like to have it on *calan gaeaf,* one night hence."

"And you need my help."

"You know the ways and places of this city. My senses here are fogged and stifled."

"Very well. I have already begun weaving the web that will snag Basil Zaharoff," Maeve stated.

"And you will bring him to the Taro . . . alive?"

"Yes, my sisters and I have plans in place. We are using his hedonistic appetite to bait him. We leave for the city this afternoon."

"Where will you take him? Is there a suitable place for the Taro?"

"Yes. The energies are strong in this place. It is some distance from here, but we can go now if you will ride on an omnibus."

"Is it as foul smelling as the rest of the city?" Ganna asked, with a grin.

They both laughed.

✱ ✱ ✱ ✱ ✱

The news that Maeve was intending to put Zaharoff on trial prompted the Inspector to release the yacht Omega from custody. He went to Zaharoff's hotel to give him the news. However, the Greek would not forsake the original inspiration for his visit to

London, Edna Avery. While the Greek might enjoy seeing Avery's triumphant return as Princess Ida in Gilbert and Sullivan's play this evening, it was the after-show dinner on his yacht that titillated his imagination. He had no way to know that the young actress was a consort of the very woman who was, even now, planning his trial and execution.

"Just so that we are clear, Mr. Zaharoff, I am formally requesting that you return to your yacht and leave immediately. I will not guarantee your safety if you insist upon attending tonight's opening at the Savoy," Walls warned.

Zaharoff smirked. "I have no illusions about the competency of the London police," Zaharoff chided. "As you know, I have taken steps to upgrade my security. I will not need your help."

"If you are referring to your so-named witch-hunter, I can only wonder why you would put your life in the hands of a lunatic!" The Inspector looked about. "Where is your protector at the moment?"

Zaharoff called out: "Jaeger, come!"

The witch-hunter burst through an adjoining door, a knife in his right hand and a leg of mutton in the other. His dog, Mabuz, stood snarling at his feet. Jaeger halted, mid-stride upon seeing the Inspector. He swallowed his bite. "You need me, sir?"

"Just wanted to see how you are getting on," the Greek answered. Then, turning to Walls: "Goodbye, Inspector."

"Before I go, I thought I should pass on some news about your attacker. Mr. Holmes believes it may be Maeve Murtagh."

The Greek laughed. "Impossible, Inspector. I happen to know that Maeve Murtagh is far, far away — quite probably below ground." He shook his head in mock sympathy. "I feel sorry for you, Inspector. I really do. You are besieged by incompetence on all sides."

Walls stalked from the room leaving Zaharoff's entourage to busy themselves in preparation for their return to the Omega. His valet was laying out evening clothes for the Greek's approval. "I thought the black and red silk cape would be appropriate for an opening night."

"Quite right, Enzo. Be certain that my smoking jacket is at hand when I arrive from the theater this evening. Run ahead to the Omega and make sure that everything is in order. The police made such a mess of it, but it should all be clean now."

Enzo nodded hesitantly, recalling the blood-spattered decks.

"Oh, and Enzo, arrange for a separate limousine to take Miss Avery and me to the yacht immediately after her performance. Tell the driver to come to the stage door. Jaeger and the others will follow in my car. Do you understand?"

"Completely, sir," the valet said.

Zaharoff turned to gaze upon himself in a large gilded mirror on the wardrobe door. He remained there for some time practicing different smiles. As he did, he clutched the note from Miss Avery accepting his invitation to dine on his yacht after this evening's performance. It came in response to the twelve dozen roses he sent to her dressing room with a lengthy note of apology. Edna explained that, when she had arrived late at the Omega the evening of the attack, she found the area mobbed with police. The truth was, she never came at all.

This was Edna's opening night, with many performances to follow, but she knew that Mr. Basil Zaharoff would soon be taking his last bow.

CHAPTER 19

TESSA WOKE LATER THAN USUAL at the Salvation Army
dormitory on Queen Elizabeth Street. She made her way to the
kitchen, nodding 'good morning' to the Salvationist soldiers that
were already at work preparing the breakfast for the hundreds who
would begin to arrive at first light. Less than a week ago, she
would have been stirring porridge on the stove, stacking dishes, or
mopping the floor — part of her ongoing acts of contrition.

She drew a cup of coffee from a samovar and climbed to the
roof.

The edges of the eastern skyline burned with bold golden
promises. Holding her coffee cup in both hands to warm them, she
let the bittersweet bouquet rise to her nose. If she waited on this
very spot, the sun would rise precisely behind the Monument to the
Great Fire, igniting the gilded urn resting on the top. She had
watched this rooftop magic many times, but it seemed different
today.

She retrieved the diary from her pocket and scribbled some
words to capture the moment:

> *Let me keep a patient vigil*
> *upon my heart*
> *as unfamiliar fruit ripens*
> *on slender stems before me.*

Tessa tucked the diary away and sipped the coffee, chuckling
as she thought of Mr. Holmes, Dr. Watson and the Professor

scrambling about the Doctor's flat with a cup of tea in one hand, maps in the other — all chattering away.

They would pick her up here, as it is in the direction of the first place they planned to search for Maeve and Ganna.

Yesterday afternoon the four of them were hunched over an enormous map of London spread out on a table — the Professor ransacked his books and manuscripts, shared tidbits about Celtic and druid rituals. Tessa was especially fascinated to learn about the places and spaces where rituals and rites had taken place in Britain over two thousands years ago.

Holmes's used his deductive and inductive powers to consider, not only where Maeve and Ganna might be hiding now, but also what their next moves would be, given that a trial seemed to be in the offing.

Watson made notes and managed logistics. Tessa plotted areas where Eva and Abigail might have trekked in their walks in the hope that it might provide clues as to their current whereabouts.

The accumulated information pointed to three different locations that Holmes circled on the map. Plans for the next day's search were formalized over a pleasant dinner at Rules in Covent Garden.

When they returned, Holmes found a message from Inspector Walls telling him that that Zaharoff had ignored his final warning, and was returning to his yacht this evening after an engagement at the Savoy Theatre.

The nearby chimes at St. Paul's rang out telling Tessa that the triumvirate would soon be arriving downstairs. She hurried to the lobby. A gleaming grey Crossley was already at the curb. Watson was asked to escort Tessa who intercepted him as he walked through the front door.

"A taxi is much too small," Watson explained, as they went to the auto. "Holmes thought we must all ride together."

When they were curbside, Watson doffed his hat with a flourish. "Where would the lady prefer to sit, front or rear?"

Tessa laughed. "The lady would love to join the two gallant gentlemen in the back, if she may?"

Watson opened the door and Tessa climbed aboard. "I feel like a princess in this posh automobile. It must cost a fortune."

Watson closed the door and poked his head through the window: "It's nothing. The prince can afford it," he quipped, nodding toward Holmes.

The Professor chuckled. "Jolly good. All present and accounted for," he said. "Wither are we bound, Captain?"

Holmes leaned closer to the driver. "Richmond — the park on the south bank, Mr. Peterbrook. Do you know the area?"

The driver turned. Two deep-set eyes blinked just below the brim of a navy blue cap pulled down tightly over his forehead. "Yes, sir. I know the place."

As they drove off, Professor Stone pointed to St. Paul's Cathedral. "In another age, I am certain that's where the druid ritual would be taking place."

Watson lurched around. "St. Paul's! You are jesting, certainly?"

"On the contrary. When the foundation of the present St. Paul's cathedral was excavated in 1675, the architect Christopher Wren discovered remains of the Stag Goddess temple within an underground chamber of the previous Cathedral destroyed in the Great Fire. It is quite common for one temple to be built upon the ruins of another. Without a doubt, certain places on this earth are inherently sacred. The druids were aware of this. Make no mistake, the places we will go today are hallowed ground."

When the auto reached Chiswick Bridge, the driver commented: "Almost there gentlemen . . . and lady."

The paved road gave way to a dirt lane that meandered through a large pastureland dotted with trees that, at one time, marked a fence line. "It should be close by," Stone said, craning his head. "The Richmond oak is said to be on the northern edge of the park."

"There!" Tessa said, pointing over Watson's shoulder.

"I do believe you're right," Watson exclaimed. "Definitely an oak, at any rate."

The driver turned to Holmes. "Do you wish me to drive off the lane, sir? I can take you to the foot of the tree."

"No," Tessa explained. "We should approach on foot . . . don't you think?"

Watson grumbled something indecipherable, Stone harrumphed, and Holmes answered: "I think we shall, Tessa. Mr. Peterbrook, please remain here."

Holmes asked everyone to wait as he walked along the edge of the dirt thoroughfare, first in the direction from which they had come, and then reversing his course and going farther up the road. The others watched curiously as Holmes squatted twenty yards in front of the automobile. He waved them forward. Lining up behind him they made their way toward the great tree thirty yards away. The dew on the grass dampened their shoes, but no one seemed to notice.

"A small person has been on this path recently," Holmes reported. "Given the rains earlier this week, it would have been in the last two days."

Tessa moved slowly, as if in a trance. *There it is.* She moved toward the tree, her obvious excitement mounting as they approached the trunk. She walked past Holmes, who had paused to look more closely at the tracks. The Detective was startled, but remained silent as he watched Tessa reverently leading the way.

As the shade of the tree embraced her, Tessa proceeded more slowly to its base and put her right hand high on the trunk. She looked upward. Following her gaze, the others stood in awe as they noticed the great trunk twisting ever higher toward the sky. The wind rustled the oak's gold and russet leaves, causing the sunlight to dapple Tessa's face. In that moment, Tessa became mindful of the age of this tree, and the wisdom that comes with those years. *What do you have to tell me?* Tessa asked.

The trunk was nearly hollow—in spots cratered. As Tessa reached up with one hand to catch the edge of a crater in preparation to climb, her hand felt something in the void. *A nest,* she thought. She pulled herself high enough to look inside the crevice. There, resting in a depression was an emerald-colored object woven from rushes—a crude cross.

Holmes was waiting below and helped her down. "You have good instincts, Tessa. May I see it?"

Holmes twisted the object in his hand as Watson and the Professor came alongside.

"I know this one," Watson said. "That's Brigid's cross."

Augustus Stone nudged in closer. "Ah, yes. That is so Doctor — in its newest incarnation. It is also an ancient Celtic symbol. It may appear as a cross —"

"But it's not," Tessa said.

"Correct. It is a crude animation of the big dipper rotating in the night skies over the course of a year. It signifies the endless cycle of creation — the grand design. Some *bandrui* wore this *insigne* around their neck as a badge of distinction. It signified that they comprehended and moved within the grand patterns of the cosmos."

"Well, there is certainly a pattern here," Holmes echoed.

Tessa took the object in her hands. "See how soft and green the rushes are. This was woven yesterday — by Ganna."

"I agree," Stone seconded. "It's rather amazing that we were able to find it."

"*We* didn't find it," Holmes noted, "Tessa did."

Watson plucked the entwined rushes from Tessa's hand. "So, is this the place where the trial is to be held?"

"I doubt it," Holmes replied. "Look about. This is a nearly open field with little cover. It rests within eyeshot of a main thoroughfare." What do you think, Tessa?"

"Ganna was here. She spent the night."

"Under a tree?" Watson asked.

"In it," she countered.

"I believe Miss Tessa is correct," Stone said. "We have two more sites to explore, gentlemen. I suggest we move on."

Continuing their reconnaissance, they decided to travel south of the Thames. Watson eyed Battersea Park as they passed it, but it was obviously too small. Their plan was to go east to Greenwich Park, and then, crossing over the Thames, head north to Epping Forest.

As they rode on, Holmes elucidated the reasons he was optimistic regarding the next sites: "Both sites are close to the Isle of Dogs and Canary Wharf, where Zaharoff's yacht is moored. Greenwich Park is on the small side, but it is mostly vacant this time of year, as cricket season is over."

"Does it have a large patch of forest?" Tessa asked.

"Not particularly, Watson answered, but it does have some magnificent trees, some approaching seven hundred years of age."

"Now Epping," Professor Stone said, "is enormous, and is home to *Quercus Robor*, a magnificent species of oak. In the early seventies, when I was a student, I was a member of an expedition which documented an iron-age earthworks within those very woods."

Holmes scratched his chin and took his pipe from his lips. "I'm having a change of heart. The presence of the Royal

Observatory and other museums in Greenwich likely make it too civilized for Ganna's purposes — even at night.

Watson folded the city map, "So, you believe Epping Forest is our best prospect?"

"What would you say, Professor?" Holmes asked.

"Indeed, Epping Forest is over six thousand acres of protected Royal forest — seems ideal for a Celtic ceremony."

"Well then, let's go straight on to Epping," Holmes said.

When they arrived, they piled out and stared blankly at the huge expanse. The size of their challenge immediately became apparent. Stone's mouth hung open. "For the life of me, I cannot see how we might find them among the thousands of acres here. Why, they could be here now and we would not know it."

"Tessa seems to have a sense of these forests," Holmes said. "Between the two of us, I believe we have a fair shot at finding our quarry if they are here."

The Professor turned to them. "If time permits. I need not remind us that *calan gaeaf* is tomorrow evening."

CHAPTER 20

AS THE FINAL CURTAIN FELL on Princess Ida, another curtain was rising on Basil Zaharoff's performance. He had swathed Edna Avery's dressing room with flowers before the show. And now, when Miss Avery's assistant opened the dressing room door, Basil Zaharoff stood like a little boy holding a single red rose in both hands.

Edna turned from her make-up mirror. "Basil you are a darling," she purred. "You are going to spoil me for other men."

"What? There are other men?" He melodramatically clutched his chest. "I am crushed."

Still in full makeup and costume, Edna strutted toward him, cupped his cheek, cocked her head quizzically, and put a finger to the corner of her mouth: "What is this thing that's known as Man?" Again, this tantalizing line from the play rekindled the Greek millionaire's passion.

"You cannot play the coy princess with me, my dear. I have planned an evening that may live up to even your expectations."

"A bold boast, my good man," Edna said, poking a finger into his chest. "Although, I must admit, my heart was yours the moment I saw these magnificent flowers. Thank you."

"They pale in comparison to your beauty my dear. You deserve the world. I may not be able to give the entire world to you, but you will have all of *my world*."

"And you will have all of me . . . I mean mine," Edna replied, leaning forward and putting a soft kiss on his lips.

As Zaharoff's amorous tête-à-tête ensued, Edna's ally, Maeve Murtagh, readied her trap: Zaharoff's rented limousine. The Rolls

Royce Silver Ghost was, just now, rolling into the alley behind the theater, taking a place in front of the Greek's own car next to the stage door. The driver got out and walked toward the door. A smartly dressed young woman rounded the corner of the alley and beckoned to the chauffeur. "Here for Mr. Zaharoff?"

The driver nodded, "Aye."

"He will be along soon, however we need a strong arm with some luggage, if you will follow me," the young woman said, leading the driver to the end of the alley.

No sooner did the driver disappear around the corner than another uniformed person, smaller in stature, appeared from a nearby passageway and climbed into the driver's seat of the Silver Ghost.

Meanwhile, barely containing his anticipation, the Greek playboy was tiring of the romantic cat and mouse: "Our carriage awaits, my lady," Zaharoff said, taking Edna's arm.

Edna pulled back. "Be a dear, Basil, I know All-Hallows-Eve is nearly upon us, but I need to shed this sweltering costume and finish removing my makeup. I must be fresh for what I know will be an unforgettable evening," she said wistfully. "Be patient. We have all evening, do we not? Be a darling and wait for me in the car. I'll be out as soon as I can."

As she kissed him on the cheek, her intoxicating jasmine scent stirred his passion. Zaharoff heaved a sigh and left the dressing room like a pouting schoolboy.

Two bodyguards, along with Heinrich and his hound, were waiting at the rear stage door as Zaharoff walked past. He opened the door and poked his head outside. He was reassured to see the limousine he ordered was waiting.

Jaeger Heinrich was leaning against the wall whistling Mendelssohn's *Lieder Ohne Wörter*. The Greek motioned for him to come. "You will ride with these fellows in my car, but stay close. We are going to my yacht. Does the other driver know our destination?" the Greek asked.

Heinrich shrugged. "He does not come inside. I do not know."

"Very well," Zaharoff said, "I will wait for Miss Avery in the limousine. Watch for her and make certain that she goes to *my* car."

The witch-hunter nodded and opened the door for his master.

Minutes later Edna Avery pranced toward the stage door to give yet another encore performance. Approaching Zaharoff's contingent, she smiled. One of the men tipped his hat. Heinrich snapped to attention and removed his papaha as she drew near.

"Mr. Zaharoff?" she inquired of Heinrich.

He swung the stage door open. "He's vaiting in the limousine in front, Miss Avery — the silver vone."

The actress ducked under his arm, stopped, and peered down the alleyway. She swung around to face the witch-hunter as he was putting his hat on.

"That limousine driving off?" Edna inquired.

Jaeger pushed past Avery and leaped into the alley. "*Hast du ein wahn oder was?* You, devil! Come, Mabuz," the witch-hunter called. The hound leaped out of the door and ran down the alleyway followed by his master as the Silver Ghost disappeared into the night.

Miss Avery turned to the other bodyguards who were, only now, scrambling to attention.

Edna stood behind them. "Your friend and his dog seem rather disturbed."

The Greek's bodyguards watched the witch-hunter and his hound disappear around the corner. "*Vlacas!*" one of them said.

"My sentiments exactly," Edna remarked, as she strolled back toward her dressing room.

Zaharoff ceased struggling against his bonds. The gash on his forehead no longer bled, but he was woozy. His capture at the Savoy happened in a flash. The moment he entered the limousine a young woman with a knife jumped in the Rolls Royce and ordered him to remain still. When his abductor prepared to bind his hands, he struck her and attempted to flee. He shouted . . . then everything went dark.

He now found himself in a cold, damp chamber of hand-hewn stone. The only light flickered through slats in a wooden door. He heard voices in the distance — women's voices.

He was cold and thirsty. He jumped when a bolt on the door was thrown open. A woman in silhouette strode into the room holding a candle. She appeared otherworldly as the candlelight cast jagged shadows across her face.

She squatted down before Zaharoff, bringing the candle closer to her face. "Remember me?"

He shivered. "It can't be! It's —"

"Yes, it's your old Maeve girl come to pay her respects."

If there were any doubt before, Basil Zaharoff knew that his fate was sealed. He sent Maeve Murtagh to perdition, and now she was reaching up from that abyss to drag him down with her.

"You are going on trial tomorrow. If I could offer some advice, Basil darling, I suggest you prepare one hell of a defense."

"Trial?" Zaharoff echoed.

Maeve tucked her finger under his chin, forcing him to look her in the eye. "It's just a formality."

As Maeve rose to leave, two women followed with porridge, water, and a privy bucket. His bindings were removed. They left a candle and closed the door.

The Greek drank deeply from the mug of water, but only twisted the spoon in the bowl of gruel. His body trembled and his mouth was dry. He was certain death would come . . . but only after he begged for it.

CHAPTER 21

ALL-HALLOWS-EVE found Sherlock Holmes pacing the floor pensively as Watson opened yesterday's mail.

"The Professor is simply behind his time," Watson assured. "No doubt, he is dragging another trunk of books."

"Have you gathered the items we talked about?"

"I have. They are in the green carpetbag by the door."

"Thank you." Holmes went to the window and pulled the curtain aside. He was pleased to see Augustus Stone mounting the stairs. No steamer trunk, but his left arm was tightly wound around a dozen books.

When the Professor arrived he had difficulty finding a place to put the latest additions to the Celtic collection that had infested Watson's flat. "I was able to find information about the *Samhain* ritual. The Celts had several names for it, *calan gaeaf* being one. Should I wait for Miss Wiggins?"

"She will join us later," Holmes said. "She is on a small errand that may keep her. I hoped she might stay behind, but she is like a lioness with cubs who fled the den."

"I believe your fears are well taken," Watson added. "I am bringing my Webley, and I have a pistol for you as well."

The Professor lurched, dropping several of his books. "Revolver? What of the police?"

"I dispatched a message to Inspector Walls at Scotland Yard this morning telling him we were on Maeve's trail and that I would contact him if our efforts bore fruit."

"When do we leave?" Watson asked.

Holmes turned to the resident expert. "Professor?"

"We know little of the actual rituals and ceremonies of the Celts and druids. But it would be reasonable to assume that the event climaxes at midnight tonight, November first being the start of the Celtic New Year. However, I believe that the festivities will begin several hours before that seminal moment."

"Very well," Holmes said. "We will leave at seven to have the cover of darkness."

The Professor continued: "Gentleman, I have no idea how the trial will unfold. There is nothing in my books about trials on *Samhain*. However, we do know something of Celtic justice."

The Professor looked at Holmes and Watson to poll their interest. Holmes nodded. Stone picked up one of the books and assumed a professorial stance: "The druid priests, or priestesses, functioned as judges. Their decisions were inviolate. No one dared to countermand them, neither king nor chief. Their process was a simple one. Indeed, the druids may be the true inspiration for our current system of justice. They called it a 'trial by the oaths of men.' Men and women were called to testify on the guilt or innocence of a person being charged. It has been called a trial by adjuration, but it is not. It is a trial by jury, and a good one."

"And if someone is judged guilty, Professor," Watson asked, "Do they become fodder for sacrifice?"

"There are those that attributed human sacrifice to the druids, but those accounts come from the Roman and Greek historians who wish to justify their efforts to exterminate them." Stone patted the book he was holding: "In the Gaelic language, customs and traditions you will find accounts of sacrifices to be sure, and even executions of enemies, but I have found little that speaks specifically about human sacrifice."

"Somehow, I am not consoled by that fact," Watson grumbled. "However, it seems that there can be no trial without Zaharoff. So, let us not go all to pot unnecessarily."

"Maeve will snag Basil Zaharoff, if she has not already done so," Holmes predicted.

Then, waving a just opened letter, Watson beckoned: Holmes . . . Holmes, I have received a reply to my inquiries about the orphanage where Eva Allsop resided."

A dull knocking was heard coming from the street below.

"Can you see who that is, Professor?"

"It's a messenger," Stone reported from the window.

The knocking continued.

"It's important," Holmes said, "Please excuse me." Watson tucked the letter away and followed Holmes as he went down the stairs.

When the door was opened a young lad proffered a message: "For Mr. Sherlock Holmes. I'm ta wait fer a reply, sir."

Watson looked over Holmes's shoulder as he opened the message and read:

Zaharoff went missing last night.
Shall we join forces?

Walls

"Hah! You were right, Holmes!" Watson exclaimed.

"It was a reasonable deduction. Maeve is determined and creative — a potent mix. However, Walls' confirmation does suggest urgency. We should find our way to Epping Forest as soon as possible, as we will require more daylight and time to rescue the wayward Greek. We will leave the moment Tessa arrives. She should have returned by now. We cannot wait much longer, but we can give her another hour. And Watson, call Mr. Peterbrook and ask him to come as soon as he can."

Holmes scribbled a reply to Inspector Walls and gave it to the messenger with a coin. As the courier rushed off, Watson nudged Holmes, nodding toward the far side of the street. Jaeger Heinrich and his hound were waiting in the shadows of a snickleway.

"Another chat" Watson asked. "He could throw a spanner into the works."

"Heinrich has lost his employer and is in the hope that we might point the way. Keep an eye on him, Watson. Make sure he does not try to intercept the messenger."

"Did you tell Walls we are off to Epping?"

"No. I am not certain that Epping Forest is the correct location. And, if it is, I don't wish to have the police, or that rascal there, tramping through the woods before we can get the lay of the land," Holmes said.

"Tessa was rather keen on Epping Forest," Watson noted. "Did you notice her reaction when we entered there yesterday?"

"She is on the scent to be sure," Holmes agreed.

"Her female perspectives are proving helpful, Watson said."

"Indeed," Holmes agreed. "She went straight for that tree were the old woman slept. Amazing."

"That renowned woman's intuition seems to be augmenting her surprising investigative skills."

"I agree. Tessa has a rare eye for detail. However, I fear her emotions may cloud her judgment. Her singular focus on her girls, Eva in particular, may lend her to recklessness. Nonetheless, I hope she will be able to help us navigate the preserve at Epping."

The sun, which fought against a hazy gloom all day, was finally resting on the rooftops along Sheen Lane when Tessa arrived. Holmes asked Watson and Stone to gather their equipment as he ushered Tessa into the parlor.

"Were you able to find Eva's orphanage?" Holmes asked.

Tessa remained mute and wide-eyed.

"Tessa," Holmes prodded. "What did you learn?"

"Oh . . . it was the London Orphan Asylum. That's where Eva resided until she was eight."

"Were you able to see her file?"

"No, but I was told there was little in her file — a gold cross around the baby's neck they told me."

"Not that unusual, I would say," Holmes remarked, still puzzled by Tessa's dull demeanor. "Thank you. This may prove helpful."

Tessa tugged on Holmes's sleeve as he turned. "I fear Eva has made a choice that will haunt her for the rest of her life."

"That may be so. It could be a nasty evening. Do you wish to stay behind?"

"Eva should never have been abandoned, and I will *never* forsake her, Mr. Holmes."

"Nor I. But, at the moment, it is Zaharoff who is in imminent danger."

"Zaharoff? What is the life of that despicable man compared to Eva, and the others?"

Holmes did not reply. "I have moved up our departure time. We are leaving now."

Watson waved from the open doorway: "We are keeping Mr. Peterbrook waiting. Hurry along."

The drive to Epping Forest was initially passed in silence until Watson remembered the letter in his pocket.

"Holmes, in all our preparations, I did not share the letter I received regarding Eva Allsop's orphanage."

Tessa snatched the letter from Watson's hand as he was passing it to Holmes.

"What did you learn, Watson?" Holmes inquired.

"The London Orphan . . . School. It used to be the Orphan Asylum" Tessa mumbled. She handed the letter to Holmes.

141

Holmes glanced at the letter. "This confirms what you learned, Tessa. That is good, is it not?"

"Yes," Tessa agreed. "I just hoped the letter would offer more information," she said.

The sound of the purring engine intensified as an uncomfortable silence ensued and the foursome girded themselves for what promised to be a perilous evening. They had reconnoitered the general area the previous day, so the driver needed no direction until they arrived at the southern border of the preserve.

"Tessa," Holmes said, "Yesterday your inclination was to enter from this side of the forest."

"The forest is thickest here," she answered. There are trails that invite deeper penetration along this lane."

"It is certainly the best place to enter if you are coming from the city," Holmes added. "Tessa, let's you and I walk ahead and look for signs."

Watson made a grumbling noise.

Tessa and Holmes walked along the gravel road for fifty yards before they saw tracks. "Look there," Tessa said, squatting lower. "If you bend lower, you can see where the grass was trampled."

"It's not animal tracks," Holmes confirmed. Scampering ahead, he went to one knee as he approached the point of ingress on the perimeter of the forest. "Yes, several people —" He stopped and snatched something from the grass — a small leather pouch tied with a leather thong. He opened it and sniffed, then handed it to Tessa.

"Nutmeg," Tessa said. "It smells like nutmeg."

"Whatever it is, it is wrapped in dry leather, so it would have been dropped here yesterday or today, given the rain earlier this week."

Holmes signaled the driver to come forward. When the automobile came to a stop, Watson and Stone disembarked and formed a circle around Holmes.

"Tessa and I believe that we have found Maeve's trail," Holmes began: "It would be prudent for us to reach out to Walls and his men. Tessa, please go back with Mr. Peterbrook to fetch the Inspector and show him the way. We will move ahead and mark our trail as we go."

"If this is your way of trying to protect me, I won't have it," Tessa stated. "The driver can deliver a message to Scotland Yard. I must look to Eva and the others."

Holmes moved closer and lowered his voice: "Please. Bringing help is the best thing you can do for your girls."

"It's because I am a woman, isn't it?"

"It's because you're my friend. I want to do what is best for *everyone* concerned. Please . . . bring Walls and his men as soon as possible," Holmes repeated.

Tessa did not resist.

As the three men marched into the shadows of Epping Forest the driver turned back toward the auto. "We'd best hurry to Scotland Yard."

"Mr. Peterbrook, *you* are off to Scotland Yard. I'm staying here."

CHAPTER 22

THE SISTERS OF SCÁTHACH were making ready. This was their first *Samhain* celebration, and the young women's excitement was mounting. They collected stones, and Ganna counted and blessed them, placing them in a circle in the center of a lea. The druidess offered a hasty lesson in herb-craft as she prepared the ritual vessel and the herbal potions that would be used during the ceremony.

The Taro demanded that all parties must be free to see and hear the accusers, so when a dazed and shackled Zaharoff was escorted into the lea by three of the women, Ganna ordered that he be bound hand and foot and shackled to a tree at the edge of the circle. There was uneasy talk among the sisters about Ganna's seeming power over Maeve. However, knowing what the Greek did to their Mistress, none of them could imagine that Maeve would let anyone avert her vengeance.

The Greek looked like a madman at the moment — wide eyes flitting from side to side, his body jerking with each sound or movement. The druidess had doubts as to his ability to defend himself. She opened her satchel and poked into a leather pouch for a handful of dried plants. She beckoned to Eva. When the young woman came, the priestess cupped Eva's face and said "*Coínín . . . coínín.*" Eva smiled. Ganna placed dried grasses and roots in the palm of the girl's hand. "Make a strong tea and bring it to the man. Encourage him to partake of it."

Eva was hesitant.

Ganna closed the girl's hand over the herbs. "You may tell Mistress Maeve that I have asked you to do this when she returns."

Ganna appreciated loyalty, but the blind loyalty of these young women was worrisome.

As the sun dropped behind the tree line, the old woman stopped to locate the spectral moon. The ancient silver orb was Ganna's old friend, but like an old friend, there was a side that never showed itself. She was aware that the destinies of many swung in the balance this evening. Her thoughts took her back to the great battles in the past, when she was stooped under the weight of responsibility that came with her authority. She had always been her tribe's fragile connection with justice and providence. On nights such as this, she could feel the hearts of every member of the tribe beating within her. So keen was her awareness that she would know the moment one of those hearts ceased to beat. She would experience that sorrow tonight.

Holmes hurried as the last of the sunlight gilded the edges of leaves in the forest. They had lost the trail several times, and he realized that it would be nearly impossible to find his way in the darkness. He stopped frequently to listen—the only sound was the crush of the underbrush beneath Watson's and Stone's boots. The Professor walked behind Holmes holding a compass. Watson took up the rear.

"What use is your compass here? Watson asked. "We're following a trail . . . or attempting to. What do you hope to see?"

"Sh-h-h!" the Professor warned. "I am watching the compass for signs of movement. Sacred sites often possess erratic magnetic energy."

Ganna went to the west end of the circle and began praying as the nighttime descended upon them. Within her prayerful reverie, she sensed a familiar presence in the distant woods, suggesting her prayers might be answered. Tessa's essence was clear and strong, but it was moving away. There were other presences as well—less distinct — an animal possibly. Concerned that Tessa might be lost, Ganna closed her eyes, took a breath, and spread her arms in preparation for a *fonn* — an ancient chant. Her voice started low in her chest, then rumbling and rising in pitch until it spilled from her lips:

Sir . . . eadh Th . . . all

In the depths of her belly a long-drawn plea blossomed into a plaintiff decree:

Sireadh Thall.

Louder and louder she sung, as her unbridled longing rushed from her heart twisting into a primeval descant:

Sireadh Thall.

The words of this, the oldest of the *fuinns,* mean: "seek beyond." It echoes the essence of the druid beliefs. It was more than an edict; it was the embodiment of their deepest desire, and intoning those words transformed their state of being.

Holmes was the first to hear the chant. He stopped, held his breath, canting his head. Then, they all heard it: *Sireadh Thall.*

Holmes pointed and they moved in a new direction at a hurried and quiet, pace — the incantation becoming louder with every footstep.

Tessa heard the *fonn* also. It took on a strange familiarity that quelled the mild panic that was growing in her belly as she struggled through the thick underbrush. The moonlight was painting a patchwork of shadows amid the foliage, obscuring her sense of direction. She paused and sat on a fallen tree trunk to collect her breath. She swept the hair from her damp brow and breathed in the cool air.

"Are you lost, my child," a voice said.

Tessa jumped, squinting into the shadows. "Ganna? Is that you?"

Appearing like a steel blue phantom in the moonlight, Ganna stepped closer.

"You are looking for your girls?"

"Yes. Mr. Holmes and the others . . ."

"Yes, I thought so."

"They come for Zaharoff. I come for Eva and the other girls."

When Ganna did not reply, Tessa confronted the priestess: "I will not let you harm *any* of them!"

Ganna nodded. "I will do all I can to protect the innocent. But, justice must be served. There are powerful currents at work. The Fates are weaving furiously tonight. If you want to protect Eva and the others, you must understand that there is a larger pattern working here. Put aside your enmity for Maeve. She will not harm you. Trust your caring intentions to guide and protect you on this sacred night." She turned and beckoned to Tessa: "Come. When we get to the circle, wait in the trees."

Following the priestess into the underbrush, Tessa no longer struggled to move ahead. It was as if the limbs and branches parted, allowing her to pass. She felt the leaves stroking her arms and legs — the moist earth softening her footsteps. As she walked, the anxious heartbeats that had been pounding in her head vanished. She could hear the crooning of the crickets and the muted wing-beats of an owl high above her. The moon took on a comforting glow. Her mind played with ancient images of ghosts, gods, and demons. *Fantasies*, she wondered . . . *or recollections.*

Maeve was covering Zaharoff's limousine with brush when Ganna's chant came, she stopped and walked toward the clearing. Upon entering, Maeve saw Zaharoff. He was squatting under a tree, his arms wrapped about him to stave off the cool night air. He seemed calm. He no longer tugged at the chain binding him to the tree trunk. Then Maeve saw Ganna emerging from the forest and walking along the circle of stones, blessing them — transmuting them into fatal stones.

Maeve went to priestess. "My sisters do not know the ways of *calan gaeaf.* What is the purpose . . ." Maeve looked askance at the circle. "There are too many stones."

Ganna lengthened her stature and stepped closer to Maeve. "The life of that sad man over there hangs on a thread. We must judge fairly. I told you, others may come."

Maeve's gaze intensified.

Ganna continued: "To judge the guilt or innocence of a man, we must know the *source* of a person's actions. The Taro must cast a broad net."

Maeve grabbed Ganna's arm: "Who . . . Holmes?"

Ganna nodded. "Yes . . . and others."

Maeve smiled. "Holmes is coming." She cackled. "The Gods are good."

"Remember, it is justice we seek here, Maeve. Prepare your sisters for *calan gaeaf.* If the others get close I will tell you. I suggest you place a guard and gather your sisters."

"What if it's the police?"

"If they try to disturb the ceremony, I will hold them at bay. You will have time to escape."

Maeve leaned into Ganna. "I may choose to fight."

"You have many adversaries. You cannot prevail against them all."

"There's not a man who can prevail against me," Maeve boasted.

But, neither Maeve, nor the Druid, foresaw their newest nemesis. Mabuz had Ganna's scent, and Jaeger Heinrich was trotting through the woods to keep pace with the brute.

CHAPTER 23

A DISHEVELED INSPECTOR WALLS STRODE into Bow Street Station. The sergeant at the front desk handed him a note and pointed to the limousine driver who had been waiting for nearly a half-hour. He approached the driver extending his hand: "Inspector Joshua Walls, sir. Thank you for waiting."

The driver touched the brim of his cap, rose and shook the detective's hand. "Daniel Peterbrook, sir. I've told your sergeant what I know. I assume the note speaks for itself."

"Are you aware of what the note says?"

"Yes, it is from a young woman, one of Mr. Holmes's confederates. I am to take you to where I left Mr. Holmes and the others."

"How many in Mr. Holmes's party?"

"Three sir: Dr. Watson, Professor Stone and Miss Wiggins."

"Wiggins, you say," the Inspector noted with surprise.

"A nice lady, but highly stressed," Peterbrook said. "Mr. Holmes asked her to come with me. I think he believes there may be trouble."

"Exactly so, Mr. Peterbrook. They may all be in danger."

"Mr. Holmes seemed to have things well in hand, sir."

"Yes, Mr. Holmes is a capable man. However, they may be outnumbered."

"Aye, but I believe Mr. Holmes may have other associates coming to his aid."

The Inspector's face twisted quizzically. "What others?"

"A rather large fellow with a dog who stood guard at Dr. Watson's flat earlier this evening. The chap said he would be joining in the hunt. He did not ride with us. I was led to believe that he would come later." The chauffeur laughed. "Strange he was, but we know Mr. Holmes consorts with some rather colorful persons do we not?"

* * * * *

Maeve became more anxious as the logs and brush were piled on the fire inside the circle. It was dreadfully dark now and the moon was weaving in and out behind the clouds. Ganna had gone off into the trees heightening the Mistress's apprehension.

Zaharoff was strangely relaxed now, sitting against the tree — mesmerized by the swelling flames. He rocked slowly mumbling to himself. Maeve approached, straining to hear.

"How was I to know?" he mumbled.

Maeve laughed: "Preparing your defense?"

He caught her gaze. "Please."

Maeve guffawed. "Please? Those were the very words I said to your jailer in Port Said. I begged the vile Greek — pleaded with him — to let me go — to stop beating me. I pleaded for a drink of water. 'Please, please," I said. Maeve extended her hands in mock supplication.

Zaharoff reached out: "I beg of you."

Her body trembled. A low growl quivered in her gut and turned into a horrible roar that burst from her mouth, splintering the crisp night air.

The sisters froze in place, turning toward their mistress who was wailing like a banshee. Her guttural roar seemed to twist inside her before it burst into a manic cry — angry and strangely sorrowful.

Ganna rushed back to the circle. Her face, painted crimson by the firelight, took on the look of sudden awareness as she watched Maeve and the sisters who gathered around her. *The spirits are at hand.* As she marched toward the crowd of women, Ganna held one hand out to gather the fire's energy. Maeve's shrieking ceased by the time she arrived. As she regained her composure, Maeve locked eyes with Ganna. The crowd parted.

"What is happening to me?" Maeve shouted. "What are you doing old woman?" Then, Maeve spied Tessa at the edge of the circle. "What is she doing here?"

"Tessa is under my protection."

"What are you plotting, old woman? Have you put a spell on me?"

"Not I. Siora."

"No! It is Scáthach's power within me."

"It is Siora. From the start is has been Siora's pain and hatred you have felt."

Maeve called out: "Brigit, bring me the belly ripper!" Maeve stalked toward Zaharoff and grabbed the Greek by his collar, jerking him to his knees.

Brigit came with Maeve's *gae bolga.*

Ganna snatched the blade as Brigit tried to pass. Maeve's *aide-de-camp* turned on the old woman, seizing her neck in both of her hands. The priestess gagged and buckled under Brigit's grip. The old woman's face was red — her eyes bulging. She raised an arm and cupped her attacker's face.

Brigit's body jolted — her hands fell away and she slumped to the ground.

Ganna picked up the battle sword, stabbed it into the earth. "The Taro will decide this man's fate." Then, turning to the women: "Prepare!"

Brigit came to her senses, struggled to her feet, and wobbled. Ganna raised a finger as if she were about to scold Brigit — then lowered it. "Save your strength Brigit; you will need it."

Holmes halted the entourage when he heard the howls and shouts nearby. The Professor's face electrified: "Holmes . . . it has begun. *Calan gaeaf* is upon us. We are about to see what no modern man has ever witnessed."

"Professor, your research must come after our mission."

Stone nodded. "Of course."

Holmes pulled the pistol from his pocket and held it up. Watson mirrored him. They moved more quickly now, using the voices in the distance to guide them.

When the firelight pierced through the leaves, Holmes signaled for Watson and Stone to stay back. Crouching, he made his way to the edge of the lea. As Holmes turned to signal the others, he caught sight of Tessa. He closed his eyes and dropped his head.

Returning to his colleagues, Holmes announced: "Tessa's with them."

"Bloody hell," Watson rasped.

"We must assume that Tessa sent Peterbrook on, and Scotland Yard is on the way. Walls may get lost, or could endanger Tessa and Zaharoff if he blunders in. Professor, go back, wait, and bring the Inspector here?"

Stone's eyes became saucers. "I will surely get lost. I fear I am not the man for your commission."

Holmes turned to his old friend: "Then, it must be you, Watson."

"Holmes. It's too dangerous to go it alone."

"I will wait as long as I can. Hurry now."

Watson reluctantly agreed.

"Take the torch, Watson . . . and move with haste," Holmes ordered.

The Doctor looked lost, glancing dejectedly over his shoulder as he trotted back into the foliage. Holmes waited until his friend completely disappeared into the darkness.

Again the plaintive mantra echoed in the forest: *'Síreadh Thall.'*

Professor Augustus Stone edged closer to the circle in a childlike state of delight. He was about to witness the primordial Celtic ceremony. Holmes hurried to catch Stone, tugging on the Professor's sleeve. Holmes lowered himself to his hands and knees — motioning for Stone to do likewise. The golden glow of the bonfire's amber light flickered through the branches as Holmes and the Professor crawled to the edge of the trees.

Ganna's call brought the women to their places around the ring. Tessa stood on Ganna's right, Maeve on her left. Eva stood behind Ganna with a clay pot in her hands. Smoke arose from a small Y-shaped tube on the side of the pot. The Druid took the pot and, starting with Maeve, walked from woman to woman. Each of the sisters of Scáthach lowered their heads, putting the tubes in their nostrils. They breathed in a draft from the smoldering vessel and closed their eyes.

Holmes leaned closer to Stone. "Professor, what is Ganna dispensing from the pot?"

"It is a burning herb. See . . . she is replenishing it now," Stone whispered. "The vessel is reminiscent of one that the Taíno natives of the Caribbean use. Notice that vapor is taken in directly into the nose. I have witnessed similar ceremonial practices in Egypt and Turkey. It has a familiar aroma — possibly seeds from cojóbana tree."

"And the purpose?" Holmes inquired.

"If it is cojóbana, it opens the mind to other realms and states of being. We might simply say it causes hallucinations."

"Is it similar to opium?" Holmes asked.

"No," Stone answered. "Opium creates a feeling of relaxation and euphoria. Cojóbana intensifies physical energy and heightens the senses."

This may work to our advantage, Holmes thought.

The Sisters of Scáthach began moving clockwise around the circle — slowly at first, then faster. Some twisted and turned with whoops of delight as they processed around the fire-ring. The heat radiated from the bonfire, warping the air, blurring the edges of the silhouetted bodies moving in unison to a soundless beat. Maeve capered in bold moves with forceful twists and turns. One could imagine she was on a battlefield with her barbed saber in hand. Her eyes were alive, open and unfocused.

Tessa stood like a statue at the edge of the ring. She tried to signal to Eva and Abigail as they went by. Neither noticed her.

Ganna stepped out of the procession and stood at the edge of the procession. She held out the pot as an offering to the women as they paraded around the fire. Many of the women took another draft from the pot.

The bright flames set against inky blackness made it difficult for Holmes to see, but he was eventually able to spot Basil Zaharoff. The Greek was on his knees under a tree. He seemed enthralled by the frolicking young women.

"I think we may soon have the opportunity we desire," Holmes told Stone. "Be ready."

Ganna beckoned to Eva who dutifully came to her side. She handed the young woman the clay pot with instructions, then approached Tessa.

"Why have you brought me here?" Tessa asked Ganna.

"For the Taro. Your testimony is needed."

"I do not know the man."

"You know of him, and you know Maeve," Ganna explained.

"She is the one who should be on trial."

Ganna took Tessa's shoulders in her hands. "You are here because it is your heritage, and your destiny." Tessa was perspiring from the ever-increasing heat of the fire. She did not resist as Ganna removed her sweater, loosened her blouse, and pulled the ribbon from her hair. "Come Tessa, join us in the ring."

The priestess beckoned to Eva. Ganna took the pot as Eva grasped Tessa's hand. They walked toward the ring of dancers. Tessa tried to speak to Eva, but the young woman was hypnotized by the dance. Suddenly — Eva dashed into the procession, pulling Tessa with her.

The old druid walked along the edge of the dancers, moving in the opposite direction. She delighted in seeing the joyful faces of maidens, tinted bronze by the firelight. The beatific images of these youthful women mingled with myriad others faces from the priestess's distant past. Tears trickled down Ganna's cheeks — salty water fusing with crystalized memories of joy and sadness, triumph and failure, fear and love.

Professor Stone's body stiffened. He tugged on Holmes's sleeve and pointed when he saw Ganna moving away from the circle. She was retrieving a bulging leather satchel that was hanging on limb at the edge of the clearing. As the old priestess loosened the straps of her satchel, Stone pronounced: "Something's going to happen now."

The consolidated attention of Holmes and Stone came to bear on the druid as she flung the satchel into the center of the fire. Within seconds, amber smoke billowed up and outward, sweeping over the dancers who now spun and pranced in a mist that spread across the ground like a dense tawny fog.

"Yes, yes, cojóbana," Stone said as the vivid vapor titillated his nose.

"Wait here, Professor." Holmes said. "I'm going to circle around to release Zaharoff. When you see that he is free, you *must* make your way back to the road. I will get Tessa and be close behind. They will give chase, so hurry along."

CHAPTER 24

THE SMOKE OFFERED GOOD COVER, but, at the same time, obstructed Holmes's vision. He became lightheaded and unsteady as the yellow vapor worked its way into his lungs. It was not an unpleasant feeling.

As he circumnavigated the perimeter, he caught sight of Tessa pirouetting from step to step in unison with the others. She moved with abandon, dancing close to the flames that twisted like long silk scarves on a warm breeze.

Ganna continued chanting: "*Sireadh Thall.*" The women submitted, and echoed her plea: "*Seek Beyond . . . Seek Beyond . . . Seek Beyond . . .*"

As Ganna's invocation slowed and ended the women stopped, becoming still, their backs to the darkness, faces to the light. The only movement now was the fire, but even it seemed lethargic. In the calm, all eyes became transfixed on the twirling amber and amethyst flames. It was the blessed hour of sight.

Calan gaeaf is the quintessence of life, the bittersweet mingling of sadness and gladness, of phantom joys and shattered dreams. An unsettling quiet settled on the gathering. Softly at first, the silence became punctuated with tiny cries, whispered names, and soft sobs emanating from the women. Tears streamed from Maeve's eyes. Tessa reached toward the flames with a sad plea.

Holmes, who was momentarily caught in the magic of the moment, shook the malaise from his brain and continued pulling himself along, more quickly now, through the brush skirting the circle. Finally, he reached the tree where Basil Zaharoff was chained. The prisoner seemed oblivious to his presence. Holmes began working the Greek's bindings and quickly freed the man's hands and feet. Retrieving a pick from under the lapel of his coat, he turned to the lock.

Suddenly, Ganna's body stiffened and her eyes froze in a trance. She stared into the surrounding trees and walked up behind Maeve, leaning closer: "They're close." she whispered. Maeve stepped back from the ring and beckoned to Brigit. The Mistress retrieved her *gae bolga* and the two women slipped from the circle and ducked into the trees.

Holmes's attention had remained on the lock, which finally yielded to his ministrations. He shook the Greek's shoulder: "Zaharoff, get down. Come."

The Greek mumbled, but did not move. Whether it was the intoxicating smoke, or muscle atrophy, Holmes realized that he might have to drag the man away. He pulled Zaharoff to the ground. As he prepared to drag him into the trees, he saw Brigit and Maeve enter the ring escorting a terrified Professor Stone between them.

Holmes was stunned.

As the captive was brought forward, Ganna spread her arms wide. "Where is Mr. Holmes?" she asked Stone. He did not register her question. The Professor stood inert, intoxicated by ancient mysteries and the cojóbana—or just frightened dumb.

Then, a black streak shot out of the forest. Mabuz leaped into the air onto Ganna, smashing her to the ground.

The women shrieked. Maeve ran, with blade in hand, to Ganna's aid. The savage hound snapped and snarled over Ganna face. The priestess was barely keeping the fangs from her neck. Maeve swung her saber. The beast's side split and it crumpled and fell away. As Ganna rolled away, Maeve dealt Mabuz a second mighty blow that severed his head and sent it skittering across the ground.

Tessa ran to Ganna's side and helped her to her feet. The druidess pushed her away. "Go! Hurry!" Ganna shouted. She got to her feet and began swirling her arms above her head. Her body writhed and swayed as she reached her hands to the ground and then swept them upward violently. A cold wind rushed in, scattering sparks and embers from the fire, filling the air like a thousand radiant fireflies. The wind blew outward into the surrounding forest, twisting the branches and scattering leaves and dust in a plume. Then the rain came.

Professor Stone, his face agog, watched as Ganna invoked the elemental swarm. Flashes of lightning fractured the night sky. Thunder quaked the earth. The rain splashed in the dirt and sizzled on the burning embers. The acerbic scent of lye accosted the nose and burned the eyes.

Tessa braced herself against the onslaught, frantically searching for Eva. She slipped and fell, finding it impossible to find her feet, in the mounting storm. The cold rain splashed on her face as she called: "Eva! Abigail! Eva!"

Maeve raised her saber and called to the sisters: "This way!" As she ran to take the Professor in hand, something slammed into her body, casting her to the ground. Struggling to focus, she saw a dark form towering over her. It was immense. The witch-hunter raised his metal gauntlet and twisted his wrist to release the blade. Then . . . he caught sight of Mabuz's head and froze. That was all Maeve needed. With a kick, she leaped to her feet, brought her *gae bolga* around and raised it overhead.

The thunder boomed and a torrent of water beat down. Spirals of steam hissed and billowed from the bonfire.

Maeve swung her saber in wide arcs, driving the witch-hunter back. When she briefly lost her footing, Jaeger saw his chance. He lunged at her. She bellowed as his blade cut into her thigh. Her leg folded. A ruthless grin fixed on Jaeger's face. *"Sterben sie hexe!"* he bellowed. But before he could finish the Mistress, Brigit leaped onto his back. Jaeger twisted sharply, casting Maeve's lieutenant to the ground. He swung around and plunged his blade into Brigit's belly. She shrieked and cried out to her Mistress.

The Maeve got to one knee and called out: *"Faugh a Ballagh!"*

CRACK! CRACK! The circle vanished in a brilliant burst of lightning.

Seeing Tessa on the ground, Holmes abandoned Zaharoff and ran to her side.

CRACK! CRACK!

Tessa rubbed her eyes, struggling to find her feet as Abigail, Eva and the sisters rushed toward Maeve's call. When they saw their Mistress on the ground, some snatched sticks from a faggot of wood, others grabbed stones from the circle. They surrounded Jaeger. He thrust again at Maeve and his blade slashed her side. As he moved in to deliver the fatal blow, a huge stone hit his head and knocked him senseless for a moment. The Sisters of Scáthach were closing in with cudgels and rocks in hand. As they encircled him, Jaeger moved away from Maeve and crouched lower.

Ganna's arms continued to sway — her cries barely audible above the howling wind and thunder.

Maeve rose on one knee, but collapsed again into the mud. The witch-hunter turned his eyes again on Maeve. As he did the women pounced. He swung his blade to halt the attackers. "Witches back!" he bellowed. Then, lowering his head, he ran full out — knocking two of the women to the ground, and dashing into the woods.

The Sisters tried to lift the Mistress to her feet. She screamed in pain. "Go!" she ordered. They hesitated. "Go with Ganna!"

CRACK! The meadow vanished again in a burst of light.

Holmes rubbed his eyes. He was swaying like a man on a pitching ship, caught in the uncertainty of this maelstrom.

CRACK! Lightning, like a great spear, pierced a gigantic oak that loomed over the circle. The trunk fractured and burst into flames. Gigantic limbs careened through surrounding trees into the circle.

Tessa's eyes met Holmes's as he reached out for her.

The great tree crashed to the ground with a horrendous thud.

"Please God, no!" "Tessa screamed.

CHAPTER 25

"WILL YOU BE ABLE TO FIND THEM in this maelstrom?" Inspector Walls asked Peterbrook, as the Crossley slipped and slid along the muddy road. A parade of police autos wallowed in the mud, moving at a crawl. Thunder boomed and lightning ricocheted above, cutting a jagged line across the horizon with each blinding flash.

"You're certain this is the way?" Walls added.

"Yes sir, as I told you, the south entrance to Epping Forest was our destination. Mr. Holmes was rather confident that they would find the gentleman and women they were seeking," the driver noted.

"That logic escapes me at the moment, but if you are —"

"Beg pardon, sir. I believe the place I'm looking for is just ahead. I recall that Mr. Holmes said something about this area being closest to the Thames and the Isle of Dogs."

"Ah, of course."

As they came to the edge of the forest, the driver stopped. "I will have to move more slowly from here as I'm losing the road. We are close now."

As they entered the trees, the rain slackened, and the lightning moved off into distant skies.

"Somewhere in here, Inspector," Peterbrook said, coasting to a stop.

The Scotland Yard Inspector pulled up the collar of his coat and stepped out of the vehicle. He waved his torch side to side to halt the autos coming up behind. The motors turned off. A dozen uniformed bobbies jogged toward him, their torchlights slicing through the blackness.

The rain was coming in spits now.

Walls poked his head back into the Crossley. "Thank you, Mr. Peterbrook. One more question and you're free to go: Can you point out the direction that Holmes and the others went?"

The chauffeur pointed to the east. "That way, sir."

The Scotland Yard safari moved single-file behind Inspector Walls as he led the way into the boggy forest. More than a few "bloody hells" echoed as the underbrush thickened. What had been a cloudburst twenty minutes ago dissolved into a drizzle as the clouds dissipated and moonlight filtered through the trees.

"Do you smell that?" Walls asked the constable behind him.

The astringent smell of wet ash permeated the air. "There's been a fire, sir."

"Aye," the Inspector answered. "Let's follow our noses."

"Walls, Walls!" came a call from the gloom ahead. "Watson here."

The Inspector's torchlight settled on a sodden John Watson. His face was mud-spattered and his clothing was soaked. He bent over his knees, struggling for breath.

"Holmes?"

"This . . . this way," Watson huffed. "Zaharoff here. Tessa's in trouble. Hurry."

Walls motioned the men to close ranks behind him and Watson, who was already pushing back into the woods. "I'm sorry, Inspector," Watson huffed over his shoulder. "I lost my way and then my breath. Bloody old age!"

As the troops pushed on, the faint glow from the coming dawn offered a counterpoint to the feeling of dread that was overtaking the rescuers moving with increasing haste.

"There." Watson whispered, pointing to an opening in the trees ahead.

Walls signaled for the party to wait.

He and the Doctor crouched and crept ahead.

An eerie quiet greeted Walls as he pushed aside the last bit of brush to peer into the clearing.

"Keep his face up. Hurry, dig!" came a voice in the distance.

"Stone, is that you?" Watson called.

"Doctor, over here!"

Watson ran toward the plea to find a sad tableau: Stone and Tessa on their knees, hovering over an unconscious Holmes lying in the mud.

"He's pinned under the tree!" Stone exclaimed.

Watson came to one knee and put his fingers on Holmes's neck. "We must hurry. He will go into shock."

Walls called out to the policemen who began pouring into the meadow, their torchlights combing the shadows that were already dimming in the pre-dawn glow.

Several constables shouldered their way passed Watson and the others and began working with hands and sticks to free Holmes. Walls sent one of the men back to fetch ambulances.

As the Inspector looked around, he caught sight of a figure on the far side of the clearing. "Keep digging!" Walls ordered, turning his attention to the solitary person in the distance. As the Inspector moved toward the personage, it sprang to life: "Who's there?"

"Zaharoff, is that you?" Walls asked. His tone was incredulous as the Greek was swathed in mud. Walls threw his coat over the man's shoulders and ordered one of the bobbies to take him back to a car. "Check him for injuries."

Several members of the Scotland Yard brigade returned from a survey of the surrounding forest and watched the diggers. The Inspector barked: "This is not a picnic. Keeping searching. People are missing, hurt or worse. Spread out!"

An unconscious Holmes was pulled out from under massive tree limbs. Walls looked over Watson's shoulder. "How is he?"

Watson echoed the Inspector's fears: "In dreadful shape. We must get him to hospital immediately."

As they waited for more help, Inspector Walls pulled Tessa aside. "The others! Where are the others?"

"Gone, except for Maeve and Brigit — somewhere over there. I think they're dead . . . a dog . . . someone attacked us."

One of the bobbies moved in the direction Tessa pointed. He called out: "Over here!"

Walls hurried to the far edge of the lea where he found a motionless body. The policemen knelt and lifted the limp arm of a bulky woman from the muck, feeling for a pulse. "Dead, sir."

Walls pointed his torchlight at the other body. As the glare from the light struck Maeve's face, her eyes fluttered.

"She's alive! Get a blanket or coat on her," the Inspector ordered. "The ambulances will take some time. Keep her warm."

A policeman in the distance waved his torch: "Over here, sir."

The Inspector slogged through the mud to find the officer standing over the severed head of a dog. "The rest of the beast is over there, sir. Some kind of execution, it appears."

"No," the Inspector replied. "The witch-hunter has been here."

"Witch-hunter!" the policeman echoed. "We're in the bloody Dark Ages, we are."

"We are indeed, Watkins," Walls agreed. "Please see that the remains of this animal are collected by the coroner and brought to the morgue along with body of the woman over there."

When the ambulances arrived, Holmes was hurriedly carried aboard. Tessa climbed in behind. As Watson moved toward the ambulance, Walls pulled him to one side. "His condition?"

"Serious. There is a severe trauma to his back and legs. The tree has staved him in. Internal bleeding."

The Inspector nodded.

As Holmes's ambulance departed, a second arrived to receive Maeve. Walls signaled a policeman and called him near.

"Constable, go to hospital with this woman. Keep her under guard until you are relieved. She is not to be left alone at any time."

"Yes, sir."

"Be watchful for a large, long-haired man in dark clothing. He is dangerous."

McKinney gave a perfunctory salute and climbed into the ambulance with Maeve and the attendant.

The skyline was tinted in yellow as the coroner's van pulled up. Dr. Peters approached with two men and a stretcher in tow. "What a lovely morning," Peters remarked. "Where are the bodies?"

Walls pointed. "A woman — one of the brood who attacked the yacht."

The two attendants grimaced when they saw the muddy trail. "Go on now, my lovelies," the coroner ordered. The attendants trudged onward.

"There is a headless black hound in the clearing," Walls noted. "I would appreciate it if you would also take the beast's body and head and keep it on ice for a photographer."

"Lovely! Warrior women and headless hounds," Peters exclaimed. "You have your work cut out with this one, Walls."

"You'll find the body on the far side of the circle. I fear she may not be the only casualty tonight, but that's all for the moment."

CHAPTER 26

ONE BODY IN THE MORGUE, two witnesses in the hospital, and three suffering from shock and muddled memories: Inspector Walls' initial investigation was proving fruitless.

The newspapers had already got wind of the astonishing events at Epping Forest. *The Morning Post* sensationalized the events: "Witches' Coven Descends on City" the headline read. The city was abuzz about satanic rites in the woodlands. So, Inspector Walls was not surprised to find a message from the Deputy Commissioner waiting for him when he arrived at his office.

The Scotland Yarder had not slept, but fortified with a bath, clean clothing, and two cups of coffee, he knocked on his governor's office door.

"Ah, Walls, come in and have a seat," Deputy Commissioner Brinley James Blakelock said, gesturing toward the chair centered before his desk. He pushed The *Morning Post* toward the Inspector. "I understand that it is early in your investigation, but with mad women prancing about the city, the spotlight is upon us . . . and consequently on you. Additionally, Mr. Zaharoff has filed a formal complaint, and —"

"He's fortunate to be alive!" Walls exclaimed. "I warned him to leave the city."

"Our job is to *protect* the people in the city," Commissioner Blakelock interrupted, "not advise them to leave. Can we assume Mr. Zaharoff is presently safe?"

Walls' jaw set. "Zaharoff showed no sign of injury, so he was placed in the care of his valet at Brown's Hotel. I called his room this morning to check on his condition but he would not take my call. The woman responsible for his abduction was badly wounded and is at St. Bart's under guard. The limousine that carried Zaharoff away was not found in the woods, so we assume that is how the other women escaped from the forest." Walls pushed the newspaper back toward Blakelock. "The reports about a gang of women . . ."

"Coven, the *Post* said."

"The *gang* is led by a fanatical woman who may have committed the murders on Zaharoff's yacht, but last night's murder was the work of a deranged man who believes himself to be a witch-hunter — a man, I would add, who is in the employ of Mr. Basil Zaharoff."

The Deputy Commander stared with his mouth partially open as Walls continued: "While Mr. Zaharoff's eminence seems to merit so much attention, I would remind you that several young women have been lured into this gang, and as a result of trying to rescue them, Mr. Sherlock Holmes is now fighting for his life."

The Deputy Commissioner slumped in his chair. "Do the papers know about Holmes?"

"It is only a matter of time."

Blakelock rubbed his forehead. "Did you know of Mr. Holmes involvement?"

Walls' eyes bounced about the room.

"Out with it, Inspector."

"This case is rather complicated . . .

"And . . ."

"Well, it seems it also involves the Goodnow murder."

"Another unresolved case. How is Holmes involved?"

"Goodnow's dismembered parts were sent to Holmes —"

"My god! I thought things could not get worse. I want to be kept informed of Mr. Holmes's condition — daily reports."

"Yes, sir. I hope to have something more to report after I have spoken with the witnesses involved. One of them is waiting downstairs at this moment."

Professor Stone was bent over a map in the interrogation room when the Inspector found him. He was scribbling along the margins of an atlas. What the Professor intended as an account of the *calan gaeaf* ceremony presently looked like chicken-scratches.

Stone's customarily quixotic nature was absent. His long white hair was tossed about his head in a shaggy halo. His bare midriff poked out from under his waistcoat that bunched up across his belly. His suit was caked with dried mud that was scaling on the floor around him. A mounting frustration showed as he incessantly tapped the tabletop with his pencil. Walls felt pity for the old gentleman.

"Professor, thank you for waiting."

Stone twisted around as if to reconnoiter his surroundings. "I have much work to do, Inspector, but I am pleased to help if I may."

"Thank you. I was told by the constable who escorted you here . . ." Walls opened his notebook—"that you mentioned something about *the otherworld*."

"Yes, yes, the door to the Otherworld the druids called it." He shook with a renewed energy. "I thought it a euphemism or myth. But, I saw it, sir. I saw the door to the other side open within the bonfire."

"Well and good, Professor. Tell me what you can about Mr. Holmes, Mr. Zaharoff, and what transpired last night. A woman was killed, you know."

"Yes, of course. I'm afraid I was not in a position . . . a condition to provide an accurate account. The cojóbana, I believe . . . a rather powerful intoxicant—"

"A drug."

"Yes. It was part of the ceremony. It allows access to the spirit world. It has its origins in —"

Walls put up his hands in a subtle symbol of restraint. "Please, Professor, do you recall what happened to the two women we found on the ground?"

"That devil of a man came out of the forest, led by his black hound." Stone looked up sheepishly. "You think I am pixilated, don't you?"

"I wish you were, " Walls answered. "The witch-hunter's dog was killed, but he evidently got away. Heinrich is still on the loose."

"Sorry to hear that. Is there any word about Mr. Holmes?"

"He has undergone surgery to stop the bleeding, but I know little more."

*****

Basil Zaharoff shook the tiny brass bell on his dinner tray. Enzo entered his bedroom and stood at the foot of the bed with a diminutive bow. "Something more, sir?"

"The champagne has warmed. Fetch a fresh bottle?"

"Of course, sir.

"And Enzo, did you put in a call to Miss Avery at the theater?"

"I left a message sir, but there has been no reply."

"When she calls back, put her through. The poor lady must think me rude, having vanished twice now. Roses will not suffice this time, Enzo. Call Parsons Jewelry and ask them to come by with some suggestions for Miss Avery . . . something special."

As Enzo departed he passed one of the Greek's bodyguards who poked his head inside the bedroom door. "You have a visitor, sir."

"That oaf from Scotland Yard?"

The bodyguard smirked. "No sir, the Germanic oaf."

"He's here? The man has a nerve, I'll grant him that. I suppose there is no avoiding him. Christoffel, make certain he is unarmed, check his right forearm in particular, and accompany him. Stay close."

"Yes, sir."

The witch-hunter stalked into the bedroom with Christoffel in his shadow. Jaeger's leather coat was torn at the shoulder. Dried blood was crusted on his left hand, which hung loosely at his side. His Cossack hat was absent and his hair was untied and splayed across his shoulders. A defiant look burned in his indigo eyes.

"I am trying to recall your precise words," the Greek began in a sugared tone. Then, putting his finger to his temple in a mock gesture. "Oh, yes: *She will try again; but this time Mabuz and I will be waiting.* Wasn't that it?"

Jaeger did not respond. His jaw was clenched.

Zaharoff twisted the stem of his champagne glass in his fingers. Lowering his brows, he screamed: "WHERE THE HELL WERE YOU?"

"You told me to stay back . . . ride in a different car and —"

"Stop! Mr. Heinrich. Here in the civilized world, doing something, and making an excuse . . . ARE NOT THE SAME THING!"

Enzo entered with a cold bottle of wine. He stepped daintily around the German. The Greek held his glass up. Enzo poured.

The millionaire took a sip of champagne, and put on a smile. "Why are you here?"

"You owe me for two heads."

"Two? I was told that Maeve is alive at St. Bart's. Oh, and as for the other, I would say she was but a vague threat at best."

The color rose to Heinrich's face. "They killed Mabuz," he snarled.

"Oh-o-o, the pooch. Sorry to hear that. So, I owe you a dog?"

Jaeger lunged for the bed. Christoffel's arm lashed out around the witch-hunter's neck and pulled him backward.

"You owe me, and you vill pay . . . one way or another."

"Ah, so it's comes to this. Thuggish threats. Well, I'll tell you what. If you put an end to Maeve, I will throw in the reward for the other witch as well. You will be paid for both—and fifty pounds more for poor Mabuz."

Jaeger relaxed. Christoffel released his grip.

"I will be relocating to my yacht. We sail in two days. I suggest you stock up on Palo Santo and salt. Oh, and avoid the constabulary. Inspector Walls is anxious to chat with you."

When the witch-hunter was gone, Zaharoff raised his glass in a toast: "To Maeve Murtagh. Poor thing, she does seem to attract the wrong kind of men. I swear it will be the death of her."

CHAPTER 27

WITH ASSURANCES THAT HOLMES WAS STABLE and would not soon regain consciousness, Tessa made her way to the Salvation Army dormitory to avail herself of a bath and change of clothes.

Her tousled and mud-spattered appearance received odd looks that she greeted with a perfunctory, "Long story," as she moved on. Her former co-workers were busy preparing food, but she knew that one or more of them would report her condition to Major Dugmore who was unhappy that she was still rooming there. She was too tired and worried to concern herself with such matters now.

Once refreshed, Tessa fortified herself with a cup of tea and a moment for reflection and prayer. She wanted to be at St. Bart's when Mr. Holmes regained consciousness. *What will I say?* she wondered. The doctor in attendance did not appear optimistic. When pressed by Watson about Holmes's condition, the physician noted that additional operations would be needed, and a definitive diagnosis was not be possible until after those procedures.

Tessa took her tea to her rooftop perch and gazed out over the people racing about in the labyrinth of streets below. Yesterday morning's excitement seemed a sad farce now. Mr. Holmes did not want her to come, but she had insisted. Once again, her pigheadedness hurt someone she loved. It was that same stubbornness that forced Rory to leave his battalion in Swords in the heat of the Easter rebellion. Like Holmes, he was trying to protect her. Her brother ended up being crushed under an avalanche of guilt that ultimately drove him to his death.

"Forgive me, Father!" she said, dropping to her knees. Prayer had been habitual for Tessa, but now she doubted its power. Rory's death, she told herself, was God's will and way. But now, she felt a fool. *How could injuring Sherlock Holmes be God's will?*

She peered at St. Bartholomew's Hospital nestled on the hazy horizon. Holding back tears she waited for her chest to stop throbbing. The next day she would make an entry in her journal:

> *Regret taps me on the shoulder.*
> *Pokes me,*
> *smiles,*
> *wags a finger*
> *and bids me take my customary place*
> *beside.*

* * * * *

The deputy commissioner's admonitions prompted Walls to forsake his lunch hour and go instead to Saint Bartholomew's Hospital. It was a two-mile walk from Scotland Yard to the hospital, and he used it to clear his mind. The sky, which was a shade of brown all too familiar in London, reflected his mood. He passed a newsboy waving the *Police News*, screaming headlines: "Witch Murdered in Richmond."

There is something bestial and cruel at work in the human race, Walls reflected. *As if murder weren't bad enough, it must be a murdered witch.* Living dreary, predictable lives, many people are quick to embrace the bizarre. His world, on the other hand, was one of unabridged realism—his 'bible' written in the last words of dying people.

With badge in hand, the Inspector's query at the hospital desk yielded the two room numbers he sought. He climbed to the second floor. A constable waiting at the end of the hallway told him he had found Maeve Murtagh's room. As he approached, Constable

McKinney nodded and put a finger to his lips: "A nurse is inside." The CP was still damp and mud-splattered from the previous evening.

Walls waited at the door.

The nurse showed alarm as she exited.

"Inspector Walls, sister, what is the patient's condition?"

"She is stable, if that's what you want to know," the nurse said, in a dour tone.

"Is she ambulatory?"

"She has severe wounds in her chest and thigh, and a fractured ankle. It will be some time before she can move unassisted. I suggest that you talk to the doctor if you require anything further." She took a sideling glance at the constable. "Is this policeman really necessary?"

"This woman is a fugitive."

"Really?" the nurse shot back.

Walls wanted to say: She cut a man's balls off and put them in a jewelry box, but he simply replied: "She is a suspected murderer."

The nurse's deportment softened. "I see."

Walls turned to McKinney: "I apologize for the long evening McKinney. I have yet to send for relief. I will do so now. When it comes, get some rest and a good meal before you report back."

The constable nodded.

Walls walked to the stairway. Two floors up brought him to Holmes's floor and the policeman guarding him. "How's our patient, constable?"

"No change, sir," the guard answered. The man rose and opened the door for the Inspector.

Holmes lay motionless, swathed in white bedclothes. His grey-flecked hair framed an ashen-white face. The bed-blanket was tented above his lower body. Slumped in a nearby chair, Watson was holding his face in his hands. He started as Walls entered.

"Anything new to report, Doctor?"

Watson rose and went to the bedside. "He is under the effects of morphine and anesthesia at the moment — surgery to stop the internal bleeding."

The Inspector waited for something more, but it was not forthcoming.

"I should have stayed with him," Watson muttered.

Walls patted Watson's shoulder. "If there is any blame, we can lay it at Maeve Murtagh's feet." The Inspector pressed on: "I need an accurate account as to what happened last night. Zaharoff's people have —"

"The vile man is fortunate to be alive," Watson shot back. "Holmes saved him and it may have cost him his life!" Watson's pain showed in his wild eyes. Then, he sighed and led Walls away from the bed. "I am sorry. I will come around to your office later. I must stay with Holmes. You would do better to question Tessa, she was on the scene during the attack — when the tree came down."

"I intend to. I will leave a man on the door, if you don't mind."

"A little late for that," Watson grumbled contemptuously.

As Walls left, he noticed Tessa coming up the hallway. She passed without a glance. The Detective called out: "Miss Wiggins."

Tessa turned.

"I need to talk with you as soon as possible."

"I must first see to Mr. Holmes," she answered.

The Inspector nodded. "Very well. I'll come back after I interview Miss Murtagh."

Tessa stiffened. "She's here?"

"Until she is well enough to be moved." Responding to Tessa's troubled expression he added: "She's under guard."

Tessa nodded and walked on toward Holmes's room. She paused and glanced at the constable whose attention seemed to be riveted on the opposite wall. She pushed on the door and tiptoed in. Watson was slumped in a chair, his eyes closed.

"I'm back," she said in a whisper.

He shook himself to attention and wobbled to his feet for a moment before sitting again.

"Doctor, you must get some rest . . . something to eat. I will remain here. If there is a change I will call."

Watson nodded. "Very well, it will be some time before he comes around. I will be back before he goes into surgery again."

As the Doctor got to his feet, Tessa picked up his coat from the nearby table. A loud clunk on the tabletop startled Tessa. Watson took his coat and pulled his Webley out. "Useless," he mumbled. He placed the pistol back in his coat and shuffled out.

Tessa watched Holmes's chest rise and fall. She went to his bedside and brushed the hair from his forehead. *My penny man.*

Seeing the crucifix above the bed would have customarily brought her to her knees at a time like this. But instead, she pulled a chair closer and laid her head on the edge of the bed where she succumbed to her fatigue.

The creaking of the door brought her to her senses. A young woman wearing the stripped apron of a student nurse stood in the doorway holding a tray. A white-tented lace-trimmed hat was pinned to the back of her head, and she wore a mask over her nose and mouth.

Tessa sat up, trying to focus her eyes in the dim light. The young nurse placed a tray on the side-table. "For you ma'am," she said in a hoarse whisper. Thought you might enjoy a spot of tea."

"Thank you, Tessa responded. She pointed to her own mouth with a questioning look.

"A cold ma'am," the nurse rasped.

Tessa nodded. "Thank you."

Tessa went to the tray. The steaming pot brought a welcome aroma to her nose. A white linen napkin covered a plate. "What have we here?" She pulled the napkin away.

There, in the center of a plate rested the insigne of the *bandrui*. Under it a note:

> *Please look after Brigit's remains. Arrangements have been made at Golder's Green. Do not worry, your girls are well.*

CHAPTER 28

TESSA TWISTED THE DRUID CROSS in her fingers. *'I know you'—that's what Ganna had said in the boathouse.* And somehow, Tessa knew her. It was more than the similarity to her grandmother. This message told her that Ganna trusted her, and this strange connection with the old woman would lead her to Eva and the others. She would play along and look after Brigit's remains . . . if she could.

Inspector Walls knocked on the door and, not hearing an answer, poked his head in.

"Miss Wiggins, do you have some time for me now?"

Tessa rose, tucked the woven cross and note back under the napkin, and went to the door. "Not here. Can we go elsewhere?"

As the door closed behind them, the Inspector put a gentle hand on Tessa's elbow and guided her down the hallway. He opened the door of a nearby wardroom and turned the light on. Three empty beds showed the room was vacant.

He motioned toward two straight-backed oak chairs poised on either side of a small round table. He took off his hat, unbuttoned his coat, and sat down. He retrieved his notebook from his coat pocket and waited, pencil in hand. Walls knew that Tessa did not trust him. On the East End, the police patrols were called "the blue wall" — bobbies circle the neighborhoods to remind the poor where they belonged — as if they needed reminding.

"I understand you have known Mr. Holmes for a long while," Walls began.

"Since I was six. We parted ways for some time before being reunited. In a way he was responsible for my becoming a Salvationist."

"Really?"

"It's been more than ten years now. Mr. Holmes was hired by some London jewelers to apprehend a clever female thief who made off with over a quarter million pounds in jewels."

Walls straightened up. "Are you talking about Sonya Golden-Hand?"

"Yes. As you may recall, the thief posed as a wealthy aristocrat. At Parsons Jewelry it was a superbly dressed Russian lady seeking to buy rare blue diamonds. Holmes found traces of beeswax and surmised that the woman used sticky wax under her nails to filch them.

"Bentley and Skinner reported an Indian Princess, with a monkey on her shoulder, was looking for a diamond ring. When she departed, three rings were missing—swallowed by the dutiful monkey, as it turned out. However, Sonya's cleverest scheme was at the House of Gerard.

"A 'woman of noble birth' entered their store on Albemarle and purchased a necklace, asking that it be delivered to her home, where her husband would pay for it. When the storeowner himself made the delivery, a doctor and policeman unceremoniously carted him off to a mental hospital. Sonya had concocted a story about her husband's obsession with buying and stealing diamonds. By the time the affair was sorted out, the woman had disappeared with the necklace. However, the thief left a clue — a receipt from the Salvation Army shelter on Hanbury Street. Mr. Holmes found himself unable to gain entry to the women-only shelter."

"So he turned to you," the Inspector said.

"He dressed me in rags and gave me the receipt the thief had received for some clothes the mission had washed for her. As you know, Sonya was apprehended. And that whole business brought me to the Salvationists."

"Holmes must have been pleased."

"On the contrary, when Mr. Holmes learned that I joined William Booth's army, he was disappointed. I tried to make him see that we were fighting the same battle — each in our own way."

Walls grimaced.

"You think I'm silly? Well Inspector, you deal with those who dwell in the devil's agency by the earnings of vice, and the proceeds of crime. While it is not true in all cases, many of these supposed denizens of the dark have no other recourse but to starve. The Salvation Army offers food and clothing which opens the door to better ways of making a living."

"You make it too simple, Tessa."

"The solution is, at its heart, a simple one. For it is what comes along with that food and clothing: hope."

Walls raised his brows. "Do you think the Salvation Army can save Maeve Murtagh?"

"Maybe not. But I am confident that God's justice will find its own accord."

"It already has," Walls explained. "When she is healed, Maeve Murtagh will meet her justice."

"It may be too late for Maeve, but not for Eva, Abigail and Patricia. We must find them."

"Of course," Walls said. "But, I need your help — a statement about what happened last night . . . how the woman was killed."

"Brigit — *that* was her name."

Walls scribbled in his book and prompted Tessa to continue.

"I believe the fellow they call the witch-hunter killed her, but I could not see well in the dark and rain. I heard the screams and shouts from the melee, but I stayed with Mr. Holmes. Ganna and the others vanished in the night." Tessa rubbed her eyes. "I'm sorry. I am tired and confused. Maybe we could talk again, after Mr. Holmes is out of surgery," Tessa paused and looked inquiringly at the Inspector. "If I may, I have a favor to ask?"

Walls waited.

"I would like to see that the poor woman who was killed receives a decent burial."

"You know this woman?"

"No. But I know what brings women to desperate measures. Sinner or not, she deserves a proper burial."

"Very well. If no one claims the body—and I doubt they will — you make whatever arrangements you desire."

* * * * *

Ganna waited near the altar in the subterranean gathering chamber on the outskirts of Bromley Cross. A meal had been prepared and served, but the sisters did not have an appetite. Abigail, who was serving, brought a cup of tea to Ganna.

"Not a happy new year, Mistress."

"Ganna, my child. Please call me Ganna." The old druidess led Abigail back to the table where they sat. "Last night, we harvested seeds of vengeance that had been planted ages ago. But *Samhain* brings a new year, and new seeds lay in wait for you and the others."

"Is one of those seeds Miss Wiggins?"

Ganna nodded.

"Why do you seek after Tessa Wiggins? She is with Holmes and the others who wish us harm."

"She is part of a larger pattern. Tessa may hold the key to bringing us out of these caves and into the sunlight. She is your sister. When the time is right, she will come of her own accord. Until then, we must reach out to her."

"That is why you sent Eva to hospital?" Abigail asked.

"Yes. She was to inquire about Mistress Maeve's condition, and deliver a message to Miss Wiggins. I pray that I have not endangered Eva by asking her to do this."

"You needn't worry. Eva is clever. She has a gift for melding with people and places around her."

"Agreed, but she is prone to recklessness."

"It is her lack of fear that allows her to move unnoticed."

Ganna smiled. "You like Eva, don't you. You see her . . . you respect her — which is more important. As women we must admire and love other women. When we do this, we not only change them as individual beings, but elevate all women in the world."

Abigail shifted on the bench to confront Ganna. "Mistress Maeve believed this too. We must save her. Brigit's gone, but we have all that she taught us. We fought well on the Greek's ship."

"This is your heart speaking, Abigail. You had the element of surprise on the boat. They will be waiting for us. We must bide our time."

"My blood boils when I think of that horrible Greek and Sherlock Holmes. They both deserve death!"

"It was not the detective that killed Brigit or wounded Maeve. It was another."

"It was a man!" Abigail cried.

"An *evil* man," Ganna added. "I know his kind. The deep-rooted fear that men have for women can fester and grow violent in some."

"He called us witches."

Ganna nodded. "Yes — witches. The churches tortured and killed thousands of our sisters over many centuries. Germany was the worst because it was a battleground for Protestants and Catholics. These religions demonstrated their promise of protection and salvation by executing poor unfortunate women who were accused of everything from a barren cow to the Black Death. And yes, these churches are led by men."

Two of the sisters clearing the table were listening and grew curious. They wiped their hands on their aprons and joined the conversation.

Beth came closer. "So, men fear *us*?

"Yes," Ganna answered. "We have power that they fear."

"What's that?" Beth asked.

"We can reject them, and our rejection evokes a primal fear for survival because, as babes, abandonment means death. Existence requires the attention of a mother . . . a woman."

"I never thought on this," Abigail said.

Ganna smiled. "So, a man's fear is not a thinking one, but one buried deep within them. In some men their fear becomes twisted into distrust or cruelty."

Patricia shook her head. "Why do we fear them?" Patricia asked.

"Patricia is right," Abigail said. "We live with a fear that dictates how we live, what we wear, where we walk, where we sleep, eat and travel. I don't feel that fear here with my sisters — only in a man's world."

"And they can use your fear against you," Ganna said. "They offer protection, but their protection comes with a price."

Other sisters began to gather around the druidess. Patricia then asked the question that was, no doubt, on the mind of all the young women. "Have you had a man Ganna?"

The priestess noticed the rapt attention of the women around her. She was being honored with their trust, and felt the weight of that responsibility. "Of course. The animal part of me seeks to be with a man. It's natural. I've been with men . . . but in *my way*."

Ganna saw the eagerness in the eyes of the young women, their hunger for knowledge and wisdom.

"What way is that? Patricia asked.

The echoes in the distant passageway told Ganna that Eva was returning. "We can talk more about these things later. There are other matters that require our attention now."

Eva bustled into the gathering chamber holding her arms wide, twirling around to display her nurse's costume. The women laughed and applauded.

Eva held the mask over her face and batted her eyelids.

"Look at her," Beth said. "Sister Eva, you make a lovely nurse!"

Abigail popped up from the bench. "Eva, you've given me an idea!"

CHAPTER 29

HOLMES WAS IN SURGERY. Tessa paced the hallways of the hospital in an attempt to drive the fusillade of worries, regrets and anger from her mind. Her excursion, however, was not completely aimless. When she saw the dozing constable at the far end of the second floor hallway, she knew she had found Maeve's room. Just ahead lay a cart parked to one side of the hall — linens stacked beneath, and on top metal instruments lined up like glittering soldiers on a snow-covered parade ground. Tessa snatched a pair of scissors as she went by, concealing them close to her side as she continued toward Maeve's room.

She recognized the napping constable as one that was at Epping Forest on that ill-fated night. Tessa tapped the policeman's shoulder. He lurched, sending the helmet on his lap to the floor. "Miss . . . Miss Wiggins . . ." he stammered as he retrieved his headgear.

"Sorry to disturb you, constable. You deserve a rest."

"Relief is coming, I'm told. How is Mr. Holmes?"

"He's in surgery now," she answered. "And, Miss Murtagh?"

"Her wounds have been attended to and her ankle is in a cast. She is confined to bed, but we will soon find a new home for her at Bow Street," PC McKinney predicted.

"That is good."

McKinney leaned closer. "She asked about the other one . . . the woman that was killed."

"Brigit? What did you tell her?"

"The truth. She's dead." He looked about and, lowering his voice, added: "Do you know how she greeted the news? She said she was grateful that she died a warrior's death. If that doesn't send chills up your spine, what will?" He stood, uncoiling his lanky body, and stretching his arms. "Do you happen to know where I might fetch a cup of tea?"

"The nurse down the way may know. I can stay here until you return."

"Oh, I don't think —"

"She's confined, as you say. If I there is any trouble, I will call out."

The policeman looked about furtively. "I'll return in two shakes."

When he was well down the hall, Tessa opened the door. A spike of light cut through the darkness and fell across Maeve's bed. Her raven hair was tossed upon her pillow framing her waxen face. Her brows were broad and lush — her eyes moved under their lids.

When the door closed, the room was plunged into shadows again, with only a wedge of light slithering along the border of the drapes.

Walking toward the bed, Tessa noticed Maeve's bandaged thigh and cast. She continued toward the bed clutching the scissors tightly. Regulating her breathing, Tessa moved toward the bedside.

Maeve's eyes flashed open. There was no fear in them. She did not move. "What do you want?"

Tessa did not answer.

Seeing the scissors, Maeve sneered. "You came to kill me."

Tessa's hand relaxed and the scissors fell to the floor. "No. I just want Eva. I want all of them home with me."

"Home?" Maeve spat. "The Nest is not their home. You can't heal their wounds with new clothes and regular meals."

"How would you know?"

Maeve's eyes narrowed. "I know their pain."

"We all have pain," Tessa replied.

"Yes, we all have our painful little stories. We need our stories, don't we, Tessa? They excuse our sins."

Tessa flinched. There was something familiar in Maeve's dead eyes. They were the eyes of a deeply wounded woman. "Yes, we all our have stories, but how does yours justify killing people . . . and so brutally?"

"Those men were not people. They were not human. You know, don't you? You've heard their stories — your little girls' stories. Didn't you want to kill the men that ravished those innocent little girls?" She laughed. "We are more alike than you want to believe."

Tessa turned away, trying to avoid Maeve's gaze.

"If you wish to know what brought me here, then listen to *my* story." She motioned toward the chair by her bed.

Tessa hesitated, before she sat.

Maeve began: "Some of my story you know. I tried to rid myself of Basil Zaharoff when I discovered he was planning my permanent retirement. I fought back like he taught me — viciously, and to the death." She shrugged and pursed her lips. "I failed only because of Sherlock Holmes's meddling."

"What of my brother! What did he do to you?"

"Rory owed money for guns he bought from me. I showed him a way to steal that money from Zaharoff. Your brother was not a saint."

"And he paid dearly for his sins. What of you?"

"Oh, I paid with my *life*. Maeve Murtagh died in Port Said." She leaned back. "Do you know it?"

Tessa shook her head.

"Your Bible teaches that Damascus was the original Garden of Eden," she began. "If so, then Port Said, to the south, is certainly the devil's resting ground."

Maeve's eyes closed. "Built from the rubble from the Tower of Babble, Port Said is inhabited by Arabs, Turks, Afrikaners, Greeks, and bloodthirsty islanders from the Aegean who mingle in an unholy megalopolis of lawlessness. At the mouth of the Suez Canal, it is the gateway to the East, and stands at the hub of white slavery in the world."

Tessa's eyes widened.

"Yes, Sister Wiggins, white slavery! That's where Eva was headed. And, it is there in Port Said that I awoke, a year ago, to find myself chained to a bed. The last thing I recalled was eating dinner on the Orient Express, and then I woke up on a filthy mattress.

"I lay there for nearly a day. My hunger and thirst mounting, I must have drifted off, because a rough hand awakened me. My eyes focused on a sweaty brown face starring at me. 'Get up!' he ordered in broken English. I was paralyzed with shock and fear. The man, who was known as 'the persuader,' grabbed my hair and dragged me onto the floor. I slapped and clawed with my free hand, catching his face. He dropped me. Blood dripped from his nose, and ran down his lips. He licked the blood, and his eyes widened in a chilling eagerness. 'So, you want to play,' he said.

"He reached out with one hand and caressed my cheek. Then with the other, he punched me with such a force that I lost consciousness.

"I do not know how much time had passed before I came to my senses. My first sensations were of pain. This time, I lay naked on the bed. The chains were gone, but in their place was a crude brass bracelet riveted on my wrist. It bore the Greek letter omega with numbers stamped upon it.

"I could barely move. My face was swollen and bruised. My body ached. I heard voices in a room beyond and dragged myself to the door. I heard two men quarreling. One I recognized as the vile Greek who beat me. The other was an Englishman, prim and proper. He told the Greek that he was a stupid man, and that they would be lucky to get five pounds for me."

"I'll never forget that voice. It belonged to John Goodnow."

Tessa's mouth gaped. "Goodnow!"

"Yes, Goodnow was the attaché to the British consul in Egypt. He should have been my savior, but he became my torturer. He said, 'Who will want to . . . bed her if she looks like an old corpse?'"

Maeve looked up. "It was then my fate became clear. And, his next sentence told me who dealt me this destiny. 'Zaharoff wants her to be broken,' Goodnow explained. He told the Greek that I was to be used here for a time before I was sent east."

"So, you see," Maeve said, as Tessa lowered her head. "Zaharoff was responsible for my capture, and Goodnow was his minion. I was condemned to death — and it was Goodnow's task to see that I died a death of despair and depravity."

Tessa rose to leave.

Maeve lurched up in bed. "Sit down! That's not the end of my story."

Tessa turned around, revealing her glassy eyes and tear-stained cheeks.

"I was broken. I was starved, deprived of drink, and forced to beg for morsels of food, and sips of water.

Maeve Murtagh died there, and another creature was born."

Her eyes became fixed and vacant. "I heard the vulgar young French and English 'gentlemen' take their pleasure with a woman in the rooms near mine — all the while knowing that my time was coming. And it did."

Maeve was trembling. "My body was sold to inebriated aristocrats and horrible drunks alike — all seeking to satisfy their insatiable male lust." Her hands clutched at her gown. She began wiping them across her chest as if she were brushing dirt from her clothing. Her eyes closed for a moment and she shivered. Then, an eerie calm came over her and her eyes opened, revealing a blank stare. "I do not know why I was spared the more hideous fate of being sent to the opium dens in China. But, one morning I awoke to a clattering coming from the street below. Through my barred window I saw a man raising a ladder to the roof — a Polish plumber hired to clear the drains. I banged on the window. It must have seemed like a wounded animal in the woods. He did not speak English, but there was something in his eyes that told me he understood.

"I lost hope for a time after he left, but he returned many hours later with the authorities. They found me, and the other women; but the Greek got away.

"I regained my senses and strength at the Magdalene House, a Christian mission at the edge of Port Said. When I could travel, I was given passage to London, and from there, to Edinburgh, the place of my birth. The woman who reared me when I was young, nursed me back to health."

Tessa straightened in her chair. "Ganna?"

Maeve smiled: "Yes, Ganna. She is steeped in the olde ways — the last of her kind."

"But she . . . she. . ." Tessa stuttered.

"You think she will help *you*," Maeve said. "She may, if you can live with Ganna's code. I warn you though; she has prodigious power . . . and will use to get what she wants. She used her power to heal my body and spirit. But . . . my heart burned with hatred for Goodnow and Zaharoff. This troubled Ganna. She told me to bide on the ancient ground of my ancestors — in the ruins of Dún Scáith Castle on the Isle of Skye. And so, I dwelt within that crumbling fortress on the island of the mist. It was there that I came to see that most of the suffering in my life could be traced to men — a despicable father who sent me away when I was most vulnerable, a man who promised marriage but only wanted my maidenhead, a lascivious minister, and thereafter, other men trampling through my life — men like Zaharoff and Holmes.

"But, while the cause of my suffering was clear, the means to end it was not. Then, ten months ago, on the sixth night of a waxing moon, I had a vision: Scáthach rose from the waters of *Ob Gausca Vaig* and offered me her battle sword. In the hilt was the sacred *naofa* stone. When I saw her, I knew why I was sparred death."

Maeve's eyes opened. "That's *my* story. Now, Sister Tessa . . . put yourself on that filthy mattress in Port Said . . . imagine drunken men using your body night after night . . . what you would do!"

Tessa ran from the room, passing a confused CP McKinney in the hall.

CHAPTER 30

INSPECTOR WALLS ARRANGED for McKinney's relief and was returning to Maeve's room to report the news. Panic momentarily gripped him when he did not see the constable at his station. He dashed to Maeve's room and kicked open the door.

Empty.

He rushed to the nurse's desk. "Murtagh, Sister! Where are Miss Murtagh and the constable?"

"And you are?"

Walls tore his identification from his pocket and held it before the nurse's eyes. "Inspector Joshua Walls, Scotland Yard, where are they?"

"There's no cause for concern, Inspector. The patient was taken to x-ray. Your man went with her."

Walls let out a long sigh. "Thank you. When will they return?"

The nurse looked at the watch pinned to the top of her apron. "Ten minutes, no more, I should think."

"And, x-ray is . . . ?"

"First floor, east wing."

The Inspector shuffled down the stairs. When he reached the main floor he oriented himself and hurried ahead. When he saw the constable in the hallway, his shoulders relaxed, and his pace slowed.

"X-rays, is it, McKinney?"

The policeman put his forefingers to the brim of his helmet. "Sir."

"She is already in a cast. Why x-rays now?"

McKinney shrugged.

"Is there another exit from the x-ray room?"

"Excuse me, sir?"

Walls knocked on the door and entered. Except for the hulking grey machine bolted to the ceiling and wall, the room was empty. There were doorways on either side of the room. One was half open.

"Hurry," the Scotland Yarder called, running into the main corridor leading outside. As he exited the hospital, he saw two nurses pushing a wheeled chair toward the curb. A large man was running across the street toward them. *Heinrich!*

Jaeger stopped ten feet from the trio of women, blocking their way. Extending his right arm with a twist, a long blade shot from his sleeve. "You stand at the doorway to hell, witches!"

"Go sisters," Maeve shouted.

The two escorts separated and circled to opposite sides of the witch hunter.

"No, Eva . . . Abigail. Get out of here!" Maeve ordered.

Jaeger shifted his weight from foot to foot, moving to keep all three women in sight as they came closer. He slashed out wildly to push them back. Then, seeing the Inspector coming toward him, Jaeger turned toward Eva.

"No you don't, you bastard!" Maeve shouted, wildly thrusting the wheels on her chair. Walls shot past the chair as Maeve careened toward the witch-hunter crying: "*Faugh a Balla . . .*"

Jaeger crouched and pointed his blade at Maeve. McKinney dove and knocked him to the ground.

Walls seized the witch-hunter's weaponized hand and slammed his free fist into the man's face. Heinrich twisted and threw a punch at Walls, catching him in the throat. Just as the blade turned on Walls, McKinney leaped onto Jaeger. The inspector got to his knees and pinned Jaeger's wrists to the ground and removed the gauntlet. The two policemen turned Jaeger onto his stomach and cuffed his wrists. Walls stood, put a foot on the witch-hunter's back, and looked about.

An empty wheeled chair sat at the curb, and a Rolls-Royce Silver Ghost was speeding away in the distance. He plucked his notebook from his pocket and wrote. Then he turned and, picking up his hat, walked back toward McKinney and Heinrich. The policeman grimaced. "Made a pig's ear of it. Sorry sir."

"Yes, but you saved my life. Thank you." Walls tore off a page in his notebook and handed it to the officer. "This is the plate number of the auto. Wait here for help. When you get to Bow Street, put the word out on the vehicle. I'll be along later, but you can start on a report."

The Inspector brushed off his trousers and headed back into the hospital. As he climbed the stairs he imagined the *Deputy Commissioner's response: A new record, Walls: two escaped murderers*, or something of the sort. The papers would have a field day. He called the station from the front desk with his report, and headed upstairs.

It was small consolation to see that the sentry outside of Holmes room was still in place. As he approached, the constable waved him closer, and in hushed tones reported: "Mr. Holmes is still in surgery, sir. Dr. Watson and the lady are inside. There are many long faces. It's quite serious, I believe."

"When did he go under the knife?"

The officer pulled his watch from his coat pocket and flipped it open. "Near two hours ago."

"Take a break. I'll be here a while."

Walls knocked but did not wait for a reply. The only light in the cave-like room emanated from the translucent curtains drawn over the window. A somber gloom surrounded Watson and Tessa who sat motionless on either side of a small table. They simultaneously brought their gaze to Walls. Neither spoke.

"I understand Mr. Holmes is still in surgery." A faint anxiety underplayed Walls' tone.

Watson nodded. "Yes. With the bleeding stopped, they are seeing to his back and legs."

"Did he come around?"

"No," Watson answered. "Some delirium, but he was never conscious. Just as well."

"Do you mind? I would like to wait with you."

Walls removed his hat. He noticed Tessa sat in a trance-like state.

"I have some . . . some bad news," Walls said. "Maeve Murtagh has escaped."

Tessa's head jerked around. "How?"

"Two of her clan, dressed as nurses, carted her off."

Tessa eyes closed. She shook her head.

"This *is* bad news," Watson said. "Back to square one."

"When you go after her," Tessa said, "remember the girls are innocent."

A knock came to the door.

It swung open.

A dark shape was silhouetted in the doorway. A doctor paused, loosely holding a surgical mask at his side. His solemn face forecast his report.

Watson rose to his feet. "Dr. Guthrie."

The surgeon came into the room, and began: "Mr. Holmes came through the surgery well." The gravity of the doctor's face stood in contrast to the seeming good news. "We did what we could."

Tessa burst into tears and slumped back into her chair.

Dr. Guthrie continued in a bland monotone: "His right thigh bone was fractured. His right hip dislocated. And . . . he has considerable damage to some of his vertebrae."

"Which vertebrae?" Watson asked.

"L-two and three." The surgeon swallowed hard . . . "and acute damage to S-one and S-two."

"No!" Watson exclaimed.

"Tessa grabbed Watson's arm and pulled him around. "What does that mean?"

Watson's eyes filled with tears. "Holmes is crippled."

PART TWO

JANUARY 15, 1919

CHAPTER 31

WRITING HAS BECOME MY REFUGE and confessional. Making my way to my rooftop sanctuary with journal in hand, I am aware that, in daily choices, I labor to build a wall between my past and me; but when I take pen to hand, my nagging history, like some iniquitous fury, reminds me that many poems have their genesis in secrets, and the most famous stories are built upon the wreckage of a human heart. If there is any consolation, it is that writing squeezes pain from the past, leaving brazen truth.

As I open my journal I see a note tucked in the pages and reread it:

Dear Tessa,

I appeal for your help. As you know, I insisted Holmes take up residence with me upon his release from hospital. A nurse — the third this month — manages his medical needs. But, I have been unable to alleviate the wretchedness he feels at being confined to a wheeled-chair. Nothing I say or do penetrates his malaise.

I want to hope that he may walk again. But it has been two months since his last operation and that prospect lessens with each day.

You have worked with those who harbor little hope, and you have a special place in his heart. I ask your help in whatever form you can give it. He may reject your attention, but I beg you to try.

Respectfully,

J W

There's a story here, I think, but not one Dr. Watson will recount.

I was already resolved to assist Holmes during his convalescence, so the Doctor's appeal served to bolster that commitment. I had visited my friend in the course of his three surgeries. I wanted to do more, but the need to find and to prepare a new supervisor for The Nest had consumed much of my time during the last two months. With that obligation met, I now felt the seeds of anxiety about my new life sprouting in my belly. I leaped before I looked. A capricious heart can make you do that.

Watson's relief was apparent when I appeared at his door. He took both of my hands in his. "Thank you, thank you," he whispered.

I offered an embrace and pecked him on the cheek. "I should have come sooner, but —"

"No need for apologies, my dear," he said in hushed tones, ushering me along. "I pray that he may listen to you. It's just that —" Watson choked up, pulled a handkerchief from his pocket, wiped his nose and quickly tucked it away.

"Who's at the door!" a hoarse voice bellowed from the next room.

"An old friend," Watson said, leading me into the parlor.

Holmes was silhouetted in the window — sitting like an immutable Sphinx in his wheeled-chair. He did not turn to us.

Watson prodded me forward and stepped back.

"It's me, Mr. Holmes."

His head hung low.

"I thought I might stop by to see how you are getting on."

He feigned a laugh. "Getting on?" Grabbing the wheels, he swung the chair around. His face was unshaven, his eyes sunken and dark. The ashes from a cigarette clasped in his fingers lay scattered about on the carpet. "How do you suppose I am *getting on*, married to this chair?"

I could not answer.

He laughed. "I never thought I should see the day Tessa Wiggins was tongue-tied."

A terrible sadness came over me. My hands trembled. "I'm so sorry —"

He held up a hand. "Please — not in the best of moods, you see."

"Understandable."

He swung back toward the window, peering into to the street below. "So, how are things at The Nest?"

"I have mustered out of Booth's Army."

His head rocked back. "Long overdue, I would say. One would like to think that there is some way to hide from the world, but we find it is impossible, don't we."

"That's a rather harsh statement, but . . . it rings as right and true."

"I take no solace in being correct. I have always appreciated that you are able to look reality in the eye — an admirable trait. I must admit," he said, holding his arms out to present his lifeless legs. "I am struggling to accept my own situation."

"Your current one, but —"

"But . . . but you will walk again, Holmes. How unoriginal. You might have said: Holmes, you have your agile brain. Imagine the books you could write."

"You shock me, Mr. Holmes."

He clutched the wheels to turn away, but I held the chair in place. "Do you recall what you said to me at Benjie's funeral?"

He grimaced.

"You said, we get angry when terrible things happen to us because we find ourselves still breathing, conscious, and alive. You told me that I have a choice: either to let the anger burn itself out, or let it smolder in everlasting bitterness."

"Did I say that? Very clever of me." He patted my hand. "It is a terrible breach of etiquette to use a man's own words against him."

Watson appeared at my side. "I, for one, welcome those words in our home."

Holmes smiled. "I'll tell you what," he said to Watson, "my condition and mood, with which you claim to be concerned, would improve measurably with medicinal therapy."

"Blast it, Holmes!" Watson spat. "Drugs are not the answer."

The Detective's eyes blazed with a momentary ferocity. Then . . . "Apologies, Watson. I know better than to ask you. Now, if you will, I would like to chat with my friend."

Watson stomped off.

"Let us make a deal, Tessa. I will put my great and agile mind to work by helping you find Eva, if you will indulge me with the tiniest quantity of cocaine." He held his fingers barely apart. "Just the tiniest bit."

"It's a devil's bargain, Mr. Holmes."

He pushed himself up onto his arms. "We each wrestle with our own devils. Mine is cocaine. And yours is . . .?"

"You are acting beastly."

He turned away. "I will find others who will assist me, if you will not."

He waited.

"One time. And, I will be here to ensure that it is but one time."

He smiled.

"Mr. Holmes, you are praying on my frailties, and I am exploiting yours. Why do you smile?"

"My dear, using another's addictions and weaknesses to one's benefit is the basis for most human dealings."

"When did cynicism get the best of you?"

He did not respond, but retrieved a crown from his pocket. Holding up the coin, he said: "I will need a syringe and needle as well."

I hesitated.

"It's simple. You want Eva; I wish a brief escape from this wood and wicker prison. Cocaine, if you please."

I opened my hand to receive the money, and then clutched the cold coin in my palm.

Dr. Watson waylaid my departure. He was curious about my conversation, though he never asked if Mr. Holmes bade me procure drugs. Later, I realized that he might want Holmes to have his drugs — wished him to be out of pain.

"Tessa, you cannot imagine what it is like to be here, day after day. Nora tries to help, but she has limited skills and is intimidated by him."

"I thought you engaged a nurse?"

"As I said in my letter, he drove the third one away yesterday."

"Well, I'm here now. I will help out as much as I can. However, I must find another position which may limit my time in the future."

"Thank you. Do you have a place to stay?"

"The Sally Army agreed to give me shelter for the time being. I will return here tomorrow."

I rubbed Holmes's coin in my fingers as I left Watson's flat.

While the Doctor and I shunned the use of drugs, we were in the minority. Holmes was *en vogue*. Cocaine, in particular, was the *demi-monde* of London society. Initially confined to the literary and artistic scene, the drug had become a fashionable pastime for theater people, army officers, aristocrats, and businessmen alike.

Drug dealing was openly conducted at Beak Street clubs on London's West End, as well as the Café Royal. A night on the town often included a stop at Limehouse. Fortunately, I did not have to seek entry to any exotic establishments. I went to Harrods.

There, in a stylish display on a downstairs counter, in Harrods signature tin canister, was a small quantity of cocaine and morphine along with a syringe and spare needles. During the war, I recalled their advertisement read: "A useful present for friends at the front." It later became the refuge for those whose loved ones never returned from the front. The kit was two shillings and four pence.

A chic lady in a tailored silk dress reached around me and procured two tins. "Let the good times roll," she commented, raising her brows and smiling.

I took a kit from the display and handed the clerk the crown.

CHAPTER 32

I'VE COME TO LEARN that there is no middle ground with me, you either like me or you don't. I'm not certain why that is, but I have long since ceased to question the phenomenon. Sister Angela, the Major's assistant, liked me. Upon my resignation from the corps she arranged a cot for me in a quiet corner of the shelter near a window and the loo.

I pulled the blanket over me when the room lights flashed, signaling five minutes until 'lights out.' I cradled the tin of drugs in my lap, and removed the top. There were two corked glass vials: the red-labeled ampoule held powdered cocaine, and the blue held morphine. A cardboard cylinder inside held two needles and a syringe. There was also a cotton ball stuffed into the cavity of the cap. *All very neat.*

I've never taken drugs, but watched Rory inject himself. I wondered what the fascination was, and what it felt like. An older woman on the next cot looked sidelong at me.

"It's not for me," I blurted.

"Of course not," she replied with a wink.

I closed the lid on the canister and cleared my throat. "Excuse me . . . a rather personal question . . . do you have any experience with morphine?"

She shrugged. "Some."

"Why did you —"

"Use it?" Her eyes flashed upward in recollection. "It helped me forget where I was." She laughed. "Sometimes, who I was — for a little while anyway."

I nodded and pulled the blanket up around my neck, knowing most of the women and girls in this loft would echo the words of my bunkmate.

A bell rang — one minute until lights out.

I propped myself up against the wall, opened the tin, and fitted a needle on the syringe. *He only requested cocaine,* I told myself, uncorking the blue vial. I drew out the contents, watching the clear liquid oozing into the glass-lined plunger. I pumped my hand until a violet vein surfaced in the crook of my arm. I pushed the needle in and slowly lowered the plunger. Lights out.

My body became warm. I was floating. It felt as though my arms and legs were falling away. I must have lain down, because I was looking up at the ceiling where tiny specks of light danced with shadows. I rolled over and curled into a ball. Sensation— that's all there was . . . no thought . . . no emotions . . . no fear or regret . . . all my thoughts and feelings disappeared into a void.

Drifting. Can't keep eyes . . . fading . . .

I'm on my knees in a dark mansion scrubbing
a cold stone floor with a dirty rag.
I can hear a dog barking in the distance. I scrub —
wringing the grimy water into a wooden bucket.
I can't see well. People are walking by. They have posh
leather shoes. I only see their feet — just their feet and
ankles. I can't get the floor clean because they are
tramping in dirt and mud
— but I scrub away.
My hands and knees are raw and bleeding.
Then . . . my rag slops onto a pair of bare feet.
I cringe because I expect a scolding or thrashing.
Nothing happens. The woman's tanned feet do not move.
I feel her hands take me under my arms and pull me up.
"Get up," her voice says. "You are a princess, not
a scrubwoman."

I break away and scramble on my knees to escape.
I turn a corner into a long corridor. I struggled
to get to my feet, but
I keep slipping back onto the floor.
I don't see the woman, she's gone.
I continue rubbing, scrubbing and cleaning.
There's a horrible black dog in the corridor.
He's chained to the wall. My body jolts with each of his
terrible barks. He watches me and growls.
My heart is beating fast.
"You can't get me," I say. The hound lunges,
straining the chain.
I grab my bucket and scramble past the brute.
His eyes are mesmerizing — green. His saliva
splattering, dripping,
pooling on the floor.
I go on.
Then . . . a child's cry.
It echoes in the passage. I can see a small bed at the
end of the hallway — just the bed. Nothing else.
No one else.
The child screams. She is very ill.
Her cries become louder
but no one comes.
I get to my feet and look about. Just the great black
hound, so I go to the child. My steps, slow at first,
become more rapid. Just as I can see the child's face,
I hear a loud crunch and a clang of metal
behind me.
The hound has broken his bonds.
I hear his feet thumping on the floor
— becoming louder—closer.
I run. I can hear the breath of the beast now.
It stops.
I turn.

*It's the woman again. It's Ganna. She has the beast
by the collar, lifting him off his front feet
and dangling him in the air
as if he were a bouquet of flowers.
His eyes are still on me.
Ganna smiles: "Now, see to the child."*

I awake with a start. Heart pounding. Short, sharp breaths. I'm in my cot. I hear the wheezing, groans, and snores of the women rumbling in the gloomy hall. A hazy glow radiating from the window tells me the breakfast is already being prepared for the many poor souls who will come clamoring into the downstairs dining room at first light. I dress and follow the scintillating scent of brewing coffee to the kitchen. I'm still shaky from my dream. William Booth's army is setting up chairs and tables. They do not notice me. I am invisible . . . as I was on the floor of that dark mansion.

A Gypsy is not required to interpret my nightmare. The haunting memory of Evangeline again raided my dreams. *The curious aspect of last night's nightmare was Ganna. Her appearance was astonishing in its realism. It was as if she walked into my dream. I had been thinking about the old woman, but still . . ."* I sipped my coffee, wondering what kinds of dreams Mr. Holmes finds at the end of his needle.

These conjurations faded as the new day encroached. Sister Angela appeared, nodding good morning. "This came for you early this morning." She handed me a note.

Letters were a rarity, and most bore bad news. It was Mr. Holmes's training that had me notice the rich stationery. No return address or stamp — just an embossed crest on the rear flap of the envelope.

Angela had noticed the stylish letter as well and was not hiding her curiosity. "Looks rather important," the she said, peering over my shoulder.

216

"Let's open it, shall we."

Using my finger to slit the envelope, I took the missive in hand:

> Dear Miss Wiggins,
> Your marvelous work at The Nest has not gone unnoticed. My sister Gwendoline and I were saddened to learn of your departure. If there is interest on your part, we would like to offer you a position as our secrétaire de direction.
> We beg you to consider our offer, as I am certain that we can come to some arrangement to our mutual benefits.
> We will send a car around for you this morning at eight, si cela vous convient.
>
> Yours respectfully,
> Margaret Davis

"What does it say?" Angela asked.

"My meager French aside, it appears I am being offered a position." I turned to her. "Do you recall the Davis Sisters?"

"That odd, old couple! Their generosity blankets the entire city. They donated the property for The Nest."

"Yes, and it now appears their *largesse* has extended to me."

"Aren't you the lucky one?"

"Luck is not a familiar *confrère*," I replied, practicing my French. I folded the letter and tucked it back into the envelope. "I best ready myself," I exclaimed with mock flare, "a car comes for me in less than an hour!"

Dressing for my interview was simple, for I owned but one smart outfit: my tan and green cardigan with skirt to match. As a Salvationist, I never wondered what to wear — basic black, long and leaden.

Approaching the front entrance, I noticed several of my former sisters lurking about, doing a poor imitation of people at work. Angela had spread the word. I wondered if the little tattletale told Major Dugmore too. Indeed, that is why this offer was so puzzling. I would expect that the Davis sisters would have sought a reference from the Major. If they had, his assessment would have come with a not-so-veiled warning. This was like a fairytale. I am nearly drummed out of the Salvation Army and, unbidden, comes employment two days later. If there is one thing the East End teaches you, you can't believe in magic. And, I didn't . . . until I saw a glistening burgundy colored Daimler limousine pull up to the curb at 101 Queen Victoria Street.

CHAPTER 33

"WELCOME ABOARD, MISS WIGGINS. Clark Button's the name."

The driver carried himself with confidence. His plain grey uniform did not hide his broad shoulders. His auburn hair was barely contained under his cap, and frayed out along his forehead. When he caught my eyes, he paused for a moment as if there were some recognition.

He opened the rear door for me. I stepped inside the posh automobile. As he closed the door, I stopped him: "Mr. Button, if it is all the same to you, I'd prefer to ride in the front. I am uncomfortable back here. I wouldn't want people to mistake me for one of the Davises."

"Hah! Little chance of that Miss Wiggins. They are lovely ladies, mind you, but they carry themselves in a manner that clearly puts them in their class — if ya catch my meaning."

"Then, I don't strike you as the posh type?" I asked.

"If you don't mind my saying so, you have the look of a hands-on woman with grit."

I was stunned by the man's brazenness. "Am I to take that as a compliment, Mr. Button?"

'Aye," he answered.

"And to think, you've known me for less than one minute. You must be a singular judge of character."

"I am that, ma'am."

I walked around to the front and climbed in — closing my own door. When he took his seat, I made a request: "If we are not expected at the residence immediately, I would like to make a stop along the way — a brief visit to a convalescing friend on Sheen Lane — number thirty-nine."

"At your service, ma'am," Button said, putting his fingers to the brim of his cap.

After his cheeky introduction, I rather expected Mr. Button to be bubbling over with conversation as we drove to Dr. Watson's flat. But once behind the steering wheel, he was all business. Indeed, his silence became unsettling.

"Mr. Button, I am curious about the Davis household. I know little of the sisters and I would welcome any advice you are able to share that might serve me in my new capacities."

"They are not in residence at the moment. The mansion has recently been refurbished, following modest damage from a German incendiary. So, they have been spending more time than usual at their ancestral estate in Wales. I was told that they would soon be arriving to take you in hand. You see, we never know when the sisters might appear. Rather keeps us on our toes."

"So, your advice is to be prepared at all times?"

"Do your best," that is all they seem to expect. Even when I come up short, they display a forgiving nature."

"Thank you. I always do my —"

"Oh," he interrupted. "There is one thing you should know."

I shifted in my seat to face him. His eyes never left the road, but his cheery face took on a troubled look as he continued: "There is a small stone cottage well behind the big house. Doors locked and windows shuttered at all times. We are asked to avoid that building. To enter, we've been admonished, may be grounds for dismissal."

"Very curious," I replied.

"Indeed, Miss Wiggins. I can say for myself, that small construction is a constant source of curiosity."

"And, you have no idea why it merits such singular treatment?"

"No." he said, his eyes flashed between the road and me, "I believe it is a chapel of some kind."

"That would not be unusual."

"Of course . . . but if it is a chapel, it's like none I have ever known." He paused.

"Go on."

"The carriage house where I sleep is nearby, you see." He took a deep breath. "I heard strange music . . . singing . . . on last All-Hallows Eve."

"It seems that you believe that there is something unnatural about the place."

"Your words, not mine. That's enough said. The point is, stay clear of the stone cottage." With that, his lips tightened and a smile, once again, visited his face.

We went on silently again. Mr. Button did not seem the kind of man who would be prone to hysteria, but he was obviously superstitious. I understood, more than many that All-Hallows-Eve can conjure up dark suspicions. Two months ago I was dancing around a bonfire and, before the night had ended, Holmes would be crippled and Eva snatched away.

"It's just ahead," Button said. "Number thirty-nine." He maneuvered to the curb.

"Thank you. I may be a few minutes. Do you mind waiting?"

"Waiting is one of the many things I do well," he answered.

I stepped from the car and made my way to the door, collecting my thoughts as I went. As I raised a hand to knock, Nora answered.

"Good day, Miss Wiggins. I was told to watch for you."

"By whom?"

"Mr. Holmes."

As I entered, Watson arose from his chair, a book in hand, to greet me. "Welcome, my dear. We eagerly awaited your return — Holmes most especially. Will you join us for tea? Holmes and I would welcome a second cup."

"Thank you just the same, but I cannot stay long." Harkening to my voice, Mr. Holmes wheeled into the parlor.

"Your raiment tells me that you are expecting to conduct important business," the Detective said.

"Are you insinuating, sir, that I do not consider a visit here important?"

Holmes canted his head and put a finger to his chin. "If I did not know better, I might be inclined to think that a gentleman was involved, but that aside, your attire suggests a new prospect . . . a meeting with person or persons you wish to impress."

"As always, Mr. Holmes, your suppositions are correct. I have been offered a position with the Davis sisters."

Watson popped to attention. "The Davis Sisters you say — the very soul of generosity and benevolence. Most recently, they have been using their great wealth to establish rest homes for wounded soldiers," he said, rubbing his shoulder.

"Keep massaging that shoulder. Watson. That Jezail bullet may be your ticket to your next abode," Holmes joked.

Watson huffed. "You are being silly Holmes."

"Well, I saw you rubbing your shoulder." Holmes put on a puzzled expression, "or was it your leg that was wounded? I can't recall."

Watson harrumphed. "I believe I will assist Nora with the tea."

When the Doctor left, I whispered: "You ought to be ashamed of yourself. You said those things to drive him off."

"We have business to transact, I believe." He swung his chair around and wheeled into the parlor.

I followed him to his desk, and looking to be certain we were alone, I took the tin of drugs from my purse and handed it over. He removed the lid to peruse the contents, replaced the lid, and tucked the tin into the desk drawer. "Thank you, my dear."

"As I say, a devil's bargain." I reached into my purse again, "I have —"

"You may keep the change," he said. "I will not forget my part. I have already put in a call to Inspector Walls. It appears there are some threads upon which we might pull to find Eva and the others. He promised to come by with a report. Do come back . . . as often as you can."

"Our agreement was *one* time."

"You don't understand, do you? It's not merely the pain in my back and legs, for which I seek relief. I've lost much of what gives meaning to life."

"Mr. Holmes. I wish I could put my heart in your chest so you might know that my sympathies are entirely with you, but there are limits."

I surprised him. Not my words so much as my bearing. I saw something in his eye that resembled respect.

I bid farewell to Mr. Holmes and offered my apologies to the good doctor and Nora, who were on their way to the parlor with a tray.

"How's your friend?" Mr. Button asked, as I climbed back into the auto. He had a book splayed on the steering wheel.

"Not well," I answered. I pointed to the book to change the subject. "What are you reading?"

He held it up, "Ten Days That Shook the World."

"What ten days was that?"

"The Russian Revolution."

I must have showed an incredulous expression for Mr. Button added: "So, my reading habits surprise you. What should a man such as I be reading?"

"Nothing of the sort, Mr. Button. I'm certain the book is interesting, if not inspiring."

"It's from the Davis library. They allow staff to borrow books. What do you like to read?"

"I have never had much time for reading, but I like a good story — you know, an adventure, a mystery or romance."

"I like a good tale myself. I read Doyle's books when I could get them. I particularly liked *The Lost World*, and that one about that mummy in the museum."

"*The Ring of Thoth*?"

"You've read it then Miss Wiggins — a rather bizarre version of Romeo and Juliet, that, or *Tristan* and *Isolde*.

"I never made that association. Have you ever read the Sherlock Holmes tales?"

"Beyond the *Ring of Thoth*, one or two others. Are you a fan?" I grinned. "More than I might admit."

His face twisted into a puzzled look. I seemed to pose a mystery to Mr. Button. And, I might say the same of him.

The moment the motor started his casual manner transformed: hands on the wheel, head up, eyes forward.

Arriving at 310 Stratton Street, I was aware that my life, as I have known it, was about to change. The white stone portico was propped upon six Romanesque pillars. The creamy edifice, in the Regency style, rose in three levels above the street with, no doubt, another level below.

"Grey House," Button declared. "We will go 'round the back, but I thought you might like to see the old place at its best. Are you ready to meet your colleagues?"

"Yes," I said— though in that moment, I wished I were still on my cozy cot at the shelter.

CHAPTER 34

GREY HOUSE WAS INCREDIBLE. The drive to the back revealed an edifice of gigantic proportions.

"Rooms?' I asked.

"For all purposes we say twenty-one . . . but that does not include the servants' quarters, or our hall below stairs. As this is not a full time residence, we are able to manage by doing double-duty, and bringing in extra help when the sisters entertain. I am the gardener as well. As you will learn, it will keep the five of us busy." He turned to me in a matter-of-fact manner. "Am I to understand that you have not been in service before?"

"Domestic service is not something I aspired to — although it might have been my only choice if I had not found a place in the Salvation Army. And you?"

"All my life. My father was the head gardener at Godinton House in Kent. I worked with him."

"Do you like it?"

"I disliked having to grovel at the foot of the social ladder. That is, I did until I came to work for the Davis sisters. They treat you like you're a flesh and blood human being. I think you will enjoy working for them."

"So, you are contented?"

He pursed his lips. "Contented? A decent job is one thing, but a good woman and a family is every man's dream. Sharing life is what gives it meaning."

His words were heavy with truth, and his frankness was refreshing. "And, the others?" I inquired. "What of our co-workers?"

"It's best that you judge for yourself. There are five of us now."

The 'five of us' I would learn, included a housekeeper, cook, parlor maid, Button and me — whom the Davis sisters referred to as a secretary. As it would turn out, my position defied a one-word description.

A woman was waiting as the auto pulled up to the carriage house. She wore a somber grey dress and had a great mass of russet hair bound up behind her neck. Her earnest composure suggested she was a force with which to reckon. I looked to Mr. Button. "Emma . . . Emma Moss," he told me. "She is the housekeeper." Adding, in hushed tones: "She fears you may be usurping some of her duties."

As I approached, the woman stood with her hands clutched in front of her. She was about fifty, stoop shouldered and, as noted earlier, carried a suggestion of power. A purple, white and green flag pinned on her collar declared: *Votes for Women* in clear block letters. Evidently, Parliament's recent effort to extend suffrage to some women did not gratify this female — which told me that she was not married, and was not a householder.

She extended her hand as I disembarked. "Miss Wiggins, Emma Moss, welcome to Grey House," she said, before Mr. Button could introduce us.

"I'm so pleased to meet you . . . is it *Miss* Moss?" I replied.

"Mrs. Moss will due." Older single woman often bear the appellation of a married person as a form of respect, and because miss can be indelicate after a certain age — as I am coming to understand.

"I'm told you keep an impeccable house," I lied.

"Really? The sisters were never clear about your duties, but I take it they have to do with their substantial social and business life," she replied.

"I believe you are correct. But, as we are a small crew, I expect to pitch in as needed."

Emma's tight expression relaxed into an almost pleasant smile. "The others are anxious to meet you. Come along." As she turned toward the house, Mr. Button gestured as if to tip his hat.

We walked through the large back porch, through an open door, and down a few steps into the servant's hall. The unmistakable odor of boiled chicken greeted me. A middle-aged woman, solid and dependable, was stirring a pot on the stove. Her brown hair was pinned up in a funny knob atop her head, and one bang fell across her sweaty brow. She went straight for me with both hands held out in greeting. When I offered mine, she grasped them tightly.

Emma leaned forward. Miss Wiggins, this is Hedy Bell, our cook.

"Wonderful!" Hedy exclaimed. "What a fit lass you are, Miss Wiggins."

"Tessa," I replied. I turned to Emma and Mr. Button. "Please, I would like everyone to call me Tessa."

"Very well, but not above stairs," Emma Moss chided.

In a clatter, a good-looking young woman burst into the kitchen, brought her arms to her side and calmed herself.

"Is Miss Wiggins' room prepared?" the housekeeper asked.

With an almost imperceptible curtsey, the young woman answered: "Yes, ma'am."

There was an awkward silence until Mr. Button chimed in: "This is Jeddie, the parlor maid. Jeddie, this is Miss Wiggins."

Jeddie wore a straight cream-colored dress with a white apron and horn-rimmed glasses. Her hair was drawn back and exquisitely braided around her head. She was the embodiment of all that is lovely and innocent. "So pleased to meet you," she said, in a cheerful manner. "I believe you will love your room. It has a window."

Emma Moss stood silent and straight-lipped.

The alert teenage maid adjusted her glasses with nervous fingers. "I have much to do," she said.

The housekeeper suddenly animated. "Yes, we all do. I have just received word that the sisters have departed from their ancestral acres and will arrive this afternoon." She turned to Mr. Button: "Euston, 1:40." Then, she turned to me. "Grey House must be ready at *all* times." She continued with her stentorian pronouncements, obviously for my benefit: "We never know when the sisters will take up residence. I suggest you settle yourself in your room and . . . do . . . whatever it is you are expected to do." Then, she turned to the others and clapped her hands. "Let's move along now."

Button immediately popped to attention: "I'll bring your bag up."

"This way," Jeddie said. With Mrs. Moss's injunction ringing in my ears, I was whisked out of the servant's hall and up the back stairs.

My room was on the third floor at the far end of a long corridor. Jeddie led the way pointing out the rooms of the other staff members. "Mr. Button sleeps in the carriage house," she added. She paused at my room, swung the door open, and let me pass. "Gwendoline — Miss Davis — chose this room for you herself and had it refurnished," she stated, "and not with cast-offs."

"My own room," I said sotto voce. It was grand — with a walnut wardrobe, matching dresser, a matrimonial bed, and best of all — a window. I spread the curtains and peered out on the grounds behind the house.

"You'll have the morning sun," Jeddie said.

We heard Mr. Button's heavy step in the hallway and turned as he entered. The look in Jeddie's eyes told me she fancied him, which was not surprising as Clark Button was not unhandsome.

"Over there, please," I said, pointing to the wardrobe.

The chauffeur put my bag down and checked his watch. "Just enough time to water the garden and wipe down the limo," he noted. "Cheerio." He left with Jeddie in tow. I closed the door and leaned against it, appraising the room. Having shared a small and sparsely furnished room with two other women for the last ten years, I paused to say a prayer of thanksgiving for both the privacy and beauty of my new quarters.

I opened the wardrobe that smelled of cedar. Nearly a dozen wooden hangers were waiting. If only I possessed as many dresses! I ran my hand over the polished top of the dresser and sat down on the edge of the bed, sinking into a luxurious down comforter. A small table near the head of the bed held an electric lamp sporting a multi-colored glass shade. The drawer in the table was ajar. Something lay inside. Curiosity prompted me to open it. My mouth gaped in amazement.

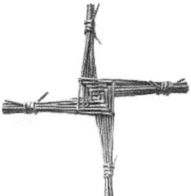

Lying in the drawer, woven in straw, was the insigne of the *bandrui*. I touched it as if to assure myself it was real.

A message from Ganna? Such a notion was too incredible to consider. My first impulse was to confront members of the household. But, as it was obviously intended as a furtive message, the perpetrator would not likely come forward. My inquiry called for a guarded approach.

CHAPTER 35

THIS IS A GOOD THING," I told myself to rein in my mounting anxiety. *Ganna will lead me to Eva.*

I put my few belongings away and went down to help with preparations for the sisters' arrival. Emma showed me to the library and pointed to a large mahogany desk near the corner. Arched above it was a stained glass window depicting a fair-haired lad pulling a sword from an anvil—the right wise king of England, Arthur.

"I would assume the library is your primary domain. The mail is in the tray on the corner of the desk," the housekeeper said. "I will put it there myself each day."

"Very well, Mrs. Moss," I said. "I believe I will wait for the sisters before I open the mail. However, I can help with other arrangements."

"Thank you, Miss Wiggins, but everything is well in hand." She strode out of the library, her shoes skipping along the marble floors of the hallway.

I sorted the envelopes in the tray. Most seemed to be common enough, but one letter stood out: A red envelope with an elaborate coat of arms in the corner. The emblem looked familiar, but I could not place it, or the name written on the back: Sir Edward Cooper. *A haw-haw toff, I ventured.*

To pass the time, I surveyed the hundreds of books lining the walls. I could understand why Mr. Button was so keen on the sisters' library. I devoted little time to reading due to the sparseness of choices — that's what I told myself. Clearly that reason would no longer suffice. I owned two beloved books: Ruth Pitter's *First Poems*, and a collection of Yeats's poetry.

As I circumnavigated the library, an unassuming brown volume on a side table caught my eye: _Howards End_. I recall hearing Dr. Watson speaking about this novel. I picked it up and thumbed through it. Nearly every sentence was flawless and poignant, but one in particular jabbed at my heart: _She felt that those who prepare for all the emergencies of life beforehand may equip themselves at the expense of joy._

That described me—doing everything to survive . . . to be safe. I was driven by an underlying anxiety that shaped most of my choices. I feared that Rory and I could not care for my baby sister after our mother died. Later, as a teenager, afraid that I would be swept away in the gutters of Spitalfields, I made certain I had the arm of a man — Benjie. Most recently, I took refuge in the black dress and bonnet of a Salvation Army slum sister. My recent drug-induced dream told me that those abiding fears waited just below the surface of my day-to-day awareness. And, there was the big one: death. Not mine. The Grim Reaper had taken too many of the people I loved.

My musings ended when I saw Jeddie, Molly, and Mrs. Moss scurrying past the library door toward the front entrance. The sisters were arriving.

Emma and Jeddie waited under the portico as Mr. Button opened the limousine door. I wedged myself behind Mrs. Moss and a pillar as the sisters stepped from the auto. As the two august ladies emerged, I hoped my face did not betray my curiosity.

As Mr. Button had said, Gwendoline was purely and completely in her class — impeccably dressed and bejeweled. With queenly movements, she climbed the stairs — her silver-capped cane tapping each step as she ascended.

Margaret was another creature altogether. Her plentiful grey hair splayed down her back and swept over one shoulder. Her well-cut features were tanned and melded with her unadorned brown dress. She remained on the sidewalk for some time, chatting with Mr. Button.

I nudged my way forward, standing behind Jeddie and Emma as they offered a polite welcome. I added mine with a tentative smile and nod, but I did not go unnoticed.

"Ah! You are here, my dear," Gwendoline said, as she offered her hand. Jeddie stepped aside. Miss Gwendoline wore little makeup, but her eyebrows were perfectly penciled. The lady's eyes dilated with what seemed like genuine interest. She smiled and nodded as she took hold of my hand. She turned to her sister. "Margaret, Miss Wiggins has arrived."

Margaret was taking the last step as she caught my eye. She was a protean creation, having the look of some primeval dowager queen. Her hazel eyes were wide and alert. As she studied me, her mouth narrowed. A half-smile revealed a scar on her cheek that drew to the corner of her mouth.

"Miss Tessa Wiggins," she said, in a husky voice. "My sister tells me that you have given your life to helping the poor women and girls in the city. Pray, what attraction can two rich old ladies have for you?"

So much for small talk, I thought. "I believe that there are many ways to serve others," I replied.

"I am surprised that Major Dugmore let you go," Gwendoline chimed.

The shock of hearing the name of my former employer certainly registered in my face, for Margaret quickly changed the subject and mood.

"Gwendoline and I feel most fortunate to have you under our roof." She took my hand briefly before passing into the house and, looking over her shoulder added: "I look forward to a long chat."

Emma Moss took note of my unease, and the peculiar exchange between Margaret and myself. Mr. Button attempted to stifle an impish grin as he passed through with the luggage.

My curiosity about how and why the Davis sisters employed me was blossoming into discomfort. I assumed that their interest stemmed from my work at The Nest, but it was clear that something else was at work here. I too looked forward to chatting with Margaret Davis.

As the sisters retreated to their upstairs rooms, I busied myself by preparing their mail. I slit the envelopes and laid them in a row according to postmark, then readied a pad of paper and pencil. I sat to one side of the desk and waited.

A short time later the doorbell rang, and Jeddie bustled down the stairs to answer it. Returning from the door, she poked her head into the library. "Miss Wiggins?"

I waved her in. She proffered an envelope that bore my name in the unmistakable hand of Dr. Watson. The young woman smiled: "The sisters are settled into their rooms and wondered if you were free to join them. The sitting area is between their bedrooms on the second level. It's the one with the double doors in the middle of the hallway."

I thanked Jeddie and waited for her to leave before I opened the message. It read:

Tessa,

Holmes asked me to write to you to say that he is anxious to discuss plans for finding your girls. You are to come at your earliest convenience.

JHW

Drugs. I crumpled the note. A dreadful shame roiled in me. My sole experience with the needle had me regret procuring drugs for Mr. Holmes.

I took paper and pencil in hand and went upstairs. The doors to the sitting room were open — Gwendoline and Margaret were waiting. A teapot and three cups sat on a table before them.

I put on a cheerful expression and stepped in. "The mail is downstairs," I began. "I can retrieve —"

Gwendoline brought one hand up. "It can wait. Sit down, please Miss Wiggins."

As I found my seat, Margaret poured for me. She set the pot down and handed the cup to me. "You wonder why we offered you a position, do you not?" she asked.

I nodded affirmatively.

"You have done a marvelous job at The Nest," Gwendoline began, "there is no doubt of that. In particular, my sister and I marveled at how you employed the healing power of the earth — the gardens and vegetables to succor the girls."

"And the greenhouse," Margaret added.

"A gift . . . from my brother."

"Yes, a gift, from Rory."

Rory! I shot to my feet. "What is going on here? You seem to know a lot about me."

Gwendoline motioned for me to sit. Margaret rose and closed the doors.

I sat with my arms folded, unable to look at them.

Margaret returned and put her hand on her sister's shoulder. "We have handled this poorly, sister." She sat down and turned toward me in a contrite manner. "We have come to see you as an extraordinary woman."

"I'm far from that," I retorted.

"You come well recommended," Gwendoline added.

"Not by Major Dugmore, surely."

"No, not the Major."

My bewilderment boiled over into anger: "Who, then? Why am I here?"

Margaret glanced at her sister, and then to me, "Ganna."

235

CHAPTER 36

I FELT LIKE A TRAPPED ANIMAL, and no doubt looked it. The sisters seemed content to let me have my feelings and a long silence ensued. They waited for me to speak.

"Did Ganna tell you *everything* — how she and Maeve lured young women into a murderess sect?"

Margaret held up a forefinger. "We know of Maeve Murtagh. She shares blood with Ganna, but they do not share the same nature."

I bolted from my chair. "Really! Then, why doesn't Ganna bring my girls home?"

"You must ask her," Gwendoline replied.

"She's here?"

"No, but she will come soon."

I sat down and leaned back into my chair. *It is a blessing*, I reminded myself. "So then . . . about my position . . ."

Margaret smiled. "The position is real."

Gwendoline continued her sister's thought: "The job is yours, if you wish it, for as long as you require it."

With as much earnestness as I could muster, I said: "Thank you. That is extremely generous of you." My attempt at sincerity failed, for the two sisters could not stifle their grins.

"I am sorry," Gwendoline explained. "Naturally, you are wary. But you need to understand that all of us here in this room are part of a community."

"The Sisters of Scáthach?"

"No. Our tribe," Margaret said.

"The Iceni," I mumbled.

They nodded.

The threads dangling from this mysterious tapestry were beginning to be woven into a curious tableau. "When will I see Ganna?"

"Soon," Margaret noted. "Until then, I suggest you busy yourself with your new duties. Now, would you mind retrieving the mail from the library?"

I spent most of the day writing replies to correspondence. The uncommon red envelope was a letter from the Lord Mayor of London, Sir Edward Cooper. He was acting on the sister's suggestion to convene a group of influential people to discuss ways to bolster the declining Welsh economy. I learned that the largest slate quarries in Wales, and one of the largest coalfields, rest on lands the sisters own. As a result, they had the influence and power that comes with providing jobs, income and tax revenue.

I helped to craft an invitation for the Lord Mayor's reception, and listened as the sisters discussed the pros and cons of inviting various dignitaries, including the Prime Minister David Lloyd George. Of course, after the guests were identified, it was left to me to send the invitations that would number nearly thirty. Needless to say, I ended my first day at Grey House impressed with the breadth and depth of these ladies' influence in Britain.

I was drafting invitations when Jeddie appeared. "Apparently, no one has told you, but dinner is at seven downstairs, and we are asked to dine together."

Her announcement made me aware that I hadn't eaten since I had arrived that morning. As I came into the servant's hall, I found everyone gathered around the table — all except Mrs. Bell who was placing the sister's meals on two trays. I was told the ladies often take their meals in their sitting room on the second floor.

As I took my seat, Hedy balanced a large silver tray on one arm, picked up a pitcher of water, and headed upstairs. Jeddie followed with another tray. A whimsical thought had me placing the straw cross on that tray as a way to tell them that I was anxious to meet Ganna. That sublime thought surfaced my true angst — Eva. *I pray she's well.*

After dinner I returned to the library to finish my correspondence, hoping that one or both of the sisters might bring more news about Ganna. Mrs. Moss began her evening rounds about ten, ensuring that the windows and doors were latched. Jeddie trailed behind, turning off the electric lights. As the parlor maid passed the library, she waited in the doorway for my attention. When I looked up, she smiled. "I will leave the hall light on for you. And, one in the back stairway as well."

"Thank you, Jeddie," I said. "You are very kind."

She nodded, made a diminutive curtsy, and scampered off.

My hand was cramped from writing, and my back was stiff. I have never spent much time sitting. My duties at the Army and The Nest continually had me on my feet. Regular meals and sedentary duties would make me prone to fatten if I were not careful.

I turned off the lamp on the desk, closed the library doors, and walked toward the kitchen stairs. I paused at a tall mirror in the hallway. Peering at myself, I poked at my waistline. As I turned away, I caught myself looking back — a strange sight, as I only possess a small hand mirror for daily use. *Where was that cocky young girl that swaggered down Switon Street on Benjie's arm?* I continued to gaze into the looking glass. Like Dorian Grey it seemed my iniquities were showing on my face — not in wrinkles as much as a certain sadness that formed my features. My mouth tightened, and my eyes glared back. "Where did you go, Tessa Wiggins?"

My sleep was fitful. My new surroundings, and recent surprises, had my mind in a jumble. I must have drifted off, because I awoke with a start—my heart racing from a dream where I was wandering, lost in a strange dark cave.

I sat up in bed. Moonlight filtered through the curtains. My eyes were slow to adjust to the light as I studied the shadows in the room. A familiar one materialized at the foot of my bed. *Ganna!*

The old woman was sitting in a chair smiling at me.

Propping myself up in bed, I let my shock ease away. "I am pleased to see you."

"I could not come sooner," she replied. "We were forced to flee the city. Finding a safe haven was difficult. We traveled far," the old druidess said, in an even voice. She rose and went to the window.

"Spare me the details of your journey. What of Eva and the others?"

"They are well."

"When will they be allowed to come home?"

"The authorities make their return difficult."

"For you, or Maeve possibly. The girls are innocent."

Ganna did not answer. She placed her hand on the windowpane as if she were caressing the moon. The azure moonlight highlighted her face. "And, what of you? Your life is caught up in all of this. Are you well?"

"I will be when Eva and the others are safe."

Ganna turned. "Please believe me, they are safe."

"Among the Sisters of Scáthach?"

"No, within the folds of our tribe. Someday you may join with me and the others."

"With Maeve? Never."

"Not Maeve."

"The Davis sisters? Who?"

"There are many, but not nearly enough. The mother needs us all."

"You mean Nature . . . the Earth. Is that what you're talking about?" I asked.

"The Earth and its dwellers."

"So, you are going to save us, are you? From what?"

"Death by ignorance. The people have lost their connection with the Earth. They must be reminded and reunited."

"My first responsibilities are to Eva, Abigail and the others . . . and Mr. Holmes. He's crippled because of you and your crusade!"

"I will accept my role in Mr. Holmes's accident if you will concede yours."

Ganna turned from the window and stood as a dark specter, the moonlight tracing the edges of her body. "Stop giving into regret, Tessa. I will help you meet your responsibilities if you help me to meet mine."

Another devil's bargain, I thought. "So, you will bring Eva back?"

"If she wishes to return."

"And, what of Mr. Holmes, will you make him walk again?"

"If he chooses to walk, we may be able to help him."

"How?"

"I will teach you," Ganna replied as she moved to my bedside. "Let me teach you the ways of the druids. My spirit lives forever, but my body is tired. I need someone to carry the wisdom and keep up the olde ways."

"That's not me," I said.

"It is in your blood, and I believe it is your destiny."

I pushed my blankets away, rose from my bed, and looked down at Ganna. "So, you want to make a bargain, do you? I will accept your teaching. If you return Eva and heal Mr. Holmes, I will do whatever else you ask of me."

Ganna's eyes widened. "Very well. We have made a covenant: I will teach you, and you will learn. I will bring Eva to you and endeavor to heal Holmes, and you will study the olde ways. I have left some herbs for Mr. Holmes in a tin in the pantry. They will ease his pain until we can craft a healing linctus. The herbs will be ready in the morning. Mind you, they should be burned slowly."

As she turned to leave, I asked: "When will I see you again?"

"I have a matter to attend to before I can come back, but I will be close."

I was up early the next morning. Only Jeddie was about, making Grey House ready for a new day. I found a tin in the pantry with my name on it and took it to the library. A familiar scent arose as I opened the container to examine the herbs. I wrapped the tin in brown paper and addressed the package — tucking a note within:

Mr. Holmes,

Ganna has reappeared. I am hopeful she will lead me to Eva and the others. She mentioned that they have traveled far from the city.

The old woman gave me something that she says may help you to escape your wood and wicker prison. I believe it is similar to the potion Ganna used on All-Hallows-Eve. Burn it slowly. I can offer nothing more to ease your pain.

I will come on my next day off. Please be cautious. I do not know if Ganna can be trusted.

Tessa

CHAPTER 37

THE MOST AMAZING SIGHT greeted me as Sheen Lane came into view. A long line of women snaked down the street to Dr. Watson's flat. As I approached, a boisterous woman in a purple sports suit, with fox-fur hanging from her shoulders, waylaid me. "Here now! Back you go. The queue forms back 'ere." She pointed toward the corner.

I was incredulous. Two more women closed in with wary looks.

"Ladies," I began, "I am uncertain as to what is happening here, but I assure you —"

"Look 'ere, the livid lady continued, flashing a newspaper.

I read the boxed advertisement that was circled:

An Easy Shilling

Women of all ages sought. One shilling for three-minute interview and an impression of rouged lips on paper for research project.

Apply in person:
24 Sheen Lane, SW14 8AB.

I pushed, prodded and cajoled my way to the front door and up the stairs — passing a dozen women, and a number of girls, along the way. Pressing into the parlor, I saw Dr. Watson crumpled on the windowsill, as there seemed to be no place else to recline. The poor man held his ears to lessen the din from the chattering women waiting their turn.

Holmes was at the desk, scribbling in a notebook as he conversed with a young lady sitting beside him. When his interview ended, he handed her a piece of white blotting paper to which she promptly pressed her red lips. Holmes took the lip-print, wrote a number on it, placed it in a box, and handed the woman a coin. She held the shilling up for all to see. Ooh's and ah's echoed as the young lady pranced out of the parlor.

Holmes caught sight of me, but went on with his research — if I may call it such. I went to the window to comfort the Doctor. His desperation was apparent in his bloodshot eyes and anxious manner.

"What's all this?"

He shrugged. "I can't explain it. He called the *Daily Mail*, or sent a messenger to place an ad."

"I saw it."

His eyes swept the room. "His malady has affected his mind. He claims to be cataloguing women's lip-prints for use in criminal cases — where a print is left on a collar, cigarette butt, or the like."

"How long has this been going on?"

"Since yesterday evening. He hasn't eaten. He smokes all day — some new tobacco."

I grimaced.

"Better than his shag," Watson noted. "I don't know what to do. This simply cannot go on."

"Where's Nora?" I asked.

"She did not come this morning. I fear I may lose her. We could barely manage him before . . . now this."

"There are other maids," I said.

"Not like Nora," he answered.

She was a fetching lass, but he may have been referring to her skills, which I have yet to appreciate. And, to be fair, she is on the dainty side, and not equipped to deal with a grown man bound to a chair.

I walked to the table where Holmes sat. I did not see any evidence of the tin I had sent two days ago. Then, beside his smoldering pipe, I spotted a teacup filled with the herbs. When he was preoccupied, I snatched the cup, went to the kitchen, and emptied the contents into the drain. I fetched a glass of water for Dr. Watson and, with the teacup in hand, went back to the parlor.

I stealthily put the empty cup back on the desk and brought the water to the Doctor. "I suspect he will come to his senses soon."

"Not soon enough," Watson mumbled. "Look at this room!"

The furniture was scattered about to make way for the queue, the carpets were grimy, and the bouquet of colognes and toilet water made a full-out assault on my olfactory sense.

I helped the Doctor to the kitchen and hastily prepared a plate of cheese and fruit for him. I then put coffee on the stove.

It took longer for the parlor circus to end than I had hoped; but as the last of Ganna's herbs went up in smoke, the din in the parlor subsided. When it was quiet, I poked my head in and found Holmes with his head propped up on both arms — eyes closed. The marauding woman in purple was shaking him: "Look 'ere, now. I come a long ways. I wants me shilling!"

I found the stash of coins in Mr. Holmes's pocket and doled them out to the last three ladies in the parlor, ushered them down the stairs and out the door, and promptly locked it. Later others came by and shouted their displeasure, but within an hour the street returned to normal.

Watson and I helped Holmes to his bed. I suggested the Doctor do likewise. He eagerly acted upon my recommendation.

Returning to the parlor, I surveyed the wreckage, took a deep breath, and began cleaning. This was not the way I imagined spending my day off.

Around mid-day I heard steps treading softly on the stairs. I opened the door to find a dainty redhead — a fetching girl, maybe nineteen. Her jolly scarlet hair fell in ringlets about her head, and her pale blue eyes twinkled. Under an open coat, the young lady wore a dainty grey housedress trimmed with a white collar and lace cuffs. Nora had returned.

"Nora, thank you for coming. Dr. Watson will be so pleased."

She glanced about furtively. "They're gone, are they?"

"Yes. The Doctor and Mr. Holmes are resting. Let's us girls have a spot of tea."

We had a good chat, and I learned just how much things had changed since Mr. Holmes had moved back in. It was clear that, even with Nora's help, Dr. Watson was not able to care for him. "Something needs to be done," Nora summarized. I agreed, and made a call to an old friend at St. Bart's.

* * * * *

The moment I laid eyes on Sister Hilda MacAskill, I knew she was the woman for the job. She towered a good six inches above me, and was on the verge of bursting from her blue uniform, which she undoubtedly crafted herself. A cap was pinned to a mound of brunette hair with no less than a dozen pins. She wore thick black glasses that nearly hid her blissful brown eyes.

Nurse MacAskill had worked in the Billingsgate Fish Market as a girl, and so was accustomed to hard work. How she came to nursing would be a story for another time. She asked three guineas a week, which was reasonable. There was one problem. She also required room and board.

As my day off was almost at an end, I hurried back to Sheen Lane to bring Nurse MacAskill's work history, references and demands to Watson and Holmes. The comforting hum of daily life had once again settled on the street. Nora received me at the door with a smile. I found the Doctor stirring a cup of tea in the kitchen and humming.

"I have some news to share. Where is Mr. Holmes?" I asked.

"In his room." Watson lowered his head and his voice. "I believe he was embarrassed by recent events," he said, pushing the evening edition of the *Daily Mail* toward me.

A photograph of the women queued along Sheen Lane was accompanied by the headline: "*Ladies Line Up Lips for Sherlock Holmes.*"

"I imagine that got his goat," I said.

"He said he's moving out," Watson muttered. "I've failed him. I didn't provide proper care."

I wanted to blame Ganna for what happened, but it was my fault for trusting her. I should have told Dr. Watson about Ganna's herbal gift, but this was not the moment. Instead, I turned to the good news. "This may work out to the best," I said, going on to tell him about Hilda MacAskill.

"I won't have a nurse!" Holmes exclaimed, wheeling into the kitchen. "I hear you two scheming. I'm a cripple, not a child!"

Something inside me snapped. I turned and shouted: "Indeed, you are not a child. That's the point. You are a man — a brilliant one who has all his faculties, but one. You have a sound mind, good name, friends and colleagues, and — if you will stop feeling sorry for yourself, you may also consider that you have everything necessary to carry on the great work that you have been doing for four decades."

Holmes starred at me. Watson sat motionless and Nora poked her head into the kitchen.

Holmes's brow tightened and his eyes bore down on me. "Miss Tessa . . . after all these years, you still surprise me. I'm certain Watson agrees with you, as does little Nora. I might even agree with you myself . . . if I were not the one sentenced to spend the rest of my life in this bloody chair."

CHAPTER 38

WHEN I RETURNED TO GREY HOUSE, Mr. Button was polishing the Daimler limousine in the driveway. He smiled and waved as I made my way to the back door. "Have a good day?" he asked, wondering about my day off.

"Not the best," I replied.

He frowned and started toward me. I waved him off. "Sorry, I have things to attend to." *That was a mistake*, I immediately realized. A servant's society is a peculiar tribe that works well when burdens are shared. He looked as though he truly cared about my day. *Why did I do that . . . push him away?*

Jeddie was alone in the servant's hall, mending bed linens. She too looked genuinely pleased to see me. "Tell me all about it," she said, the moment I entered.

"Not much to tell. I visited a friend who's not doing well."

"Is he ill?"

"Crippled."

"Oh, I'm sorry. Would you like a cup of tea?"

"Maybe later. I'm tired. Anything I should know?"

She glanced around and beckoned with her finger. I came closer.

"Well . . . after the sisters left this morning, a strange old woman came . . . and to the back door. The lady bore a note from Margaret saying that she was to be given lodging in the . . ." she lowered her voice to a whisper . . . "the cottage at the back of the property. Do you know the place?"

"Mr. Button mentioned something about it."

"Mrs. Moss was baffled. She didn't know what to do. The old woman was potty. Scruffy dress, grey hair sprouting in all directions . . ."

I nodded. "So, is she there now?"

"I think so. The strange thing was, no one had a key to the place. When we told her that, she said that she did not need one. If she is there, I don't know how she got in or what she is eating."

"Nuts and berries," I said.

Jeddie laughed.

I wished it were a joke. "So the sisters are not here?"

Jeddie shook her head. "They are off to some event. Not in residence at the moment."

"I'll be in my room if anyone needs me."

I opened the door to my room and stood for a moment, still basking in the sheer wonder of it. Determined to enjoy the last part of my free day, I shed my city clothes, donned a shift, and curled up in bed. I would wait until dark to find Ganna.

Grey House has many strange noises at night: a downstairs shutter that rattles in the breeze, creaking pipes in the walls, and above it all, Mrs. Moss's nightly adenoidal symphony. *No sense trying to sleep.*

I picked up the book on my nightstand: *Ten Days that Shook the World.* It's not my kind of reading, but Clark's review prompted my curiosity — my interest being more in the man than the book.

I must have nodded off because I awoke to a voice . . . someone was calling my name. The book tumbled from the bed onto the floor as I came to attention.

"Tessa, I have returned," Ganna's voice said.

I scanned the shadows looking for her vague outline. There was nothing. No sound. No movement.

"Where are you?"

"I'm here," the voice said, echoing in my head. "With you."

The sound was inside me. My heart was pounding and I became light-headed.

I must be dreaming, I thought.

"You're not dreaming. I'm here in your presence."

"No! NO!" I rasped. "What are you doing?"

"Don't let the olde ways frighten you."

"How can this be?"

"It is possible for one person's presence to come into another's body."

"Or into another's dream?"

"That too."

"I should have known. You are a demon, or some kind of —"

"Yes. Demons and similar beings are of the olde way as well; but you will learn that even you can let your soul wander. It's called a *taistealach.*"

"Stop doing this!"

"There is no need to shout. I can hear your thoughts."

I'm going mad.

"I will go now, but if you wish to speak with me, come to the stone cottage."

"No wait!"

But, she was gone. Her presence within me was no more.

I went to the window and flung back the curtains. It was dark, but I could see the vague outline of the cottage in the ashen landscape. Maeve told me that Ganna possessed prodigious powers. Tonight I received proof of this. I sought to trap *her*, but instead she ensnared me.

I found my coat and slippers and tiptoed down the stairs. No one was about. I cautiously moved to the back door, unlocked it, and stepped outside. A small lamp burned in the window of the carriage house quarters. Clark was up late — *reading most likely.* Keeping to the shadows, I tiptoed past the carriage house along the stone path that led through the garden to the cottage. As my eyes adjusted to the moonlight, I saw the old stone building perched at the lane's end like a miniature blue-white castle. I searched for some speck of light between the shutters or under the door, but the dwelling was dark. When I got closer, the path split: One small trail led to the cottage entrance on the right, the other into a stand of trees. I recalled that Mr. Holmes taught me to choose the path on the left, as most people inevitably take the right one. Like the others, I usually took the right path — but no longer. I turned left and walked into the stand of trees.

The grove became thicker as I walked, until I was barely able to move between the trunks. They formed an almost impenetrable wall. I was about to turn back when I caught a light flickering through the leaves. I moved toward it, squeezing into a small clearing no more than four yards in diameter. There, at the center, stood Ganna holding a candle. The amber light played on her face revealing a sweet smile. She wore the same coarsely woven dress, but had a green hooded cloak about her shoulders. As I approached, I saw that she was standing over a well.

"So, you have come," she said.

"I have come for Eva and the others."

"And to satisfy your curiosity," she added. "You chose correctly. I knew you would."

"So, this was test?" I asked, moving closer.

"No. I already know you. Now, it only remains for *you* to learn who you are," Ganna said.

I stepped closer and looked into her eyes. "People who speak in riddles seldom speak the truth."

"That may be so. So, let me speak plainly. Your destiny is to wear the druid's mantle. My time is nearly gone, but I cannot leave until someone can stand in my place."

"What of Maeve?"

"She does not have the heart . . . nor your balanced mind and compassion. You and I share those gifts. I have waited for *you*, and now you have come."

"We . . . you and I . . . are not the same. I cannot see how this can happen. Are you planning to cast a spell on me?"

Ganna stepped back. "I understood that we had a bargain. I will heal Mr. Holmes, and bring Eva to you. In return, you will study with me." She raised her brows in a question. "That is all I ask."

My head was telling me to flee, but I knew I could not escape her.

She waited—arms folded—expectation playing in her eyes.

"I have responsibilities here," I finally countered.

"The sisters will understand. They are of our tribe."

"Our tribe, our tribe! The days of tribes are past. We no longer live in trees and dance in the moonlight. This is a new age!"

Ganna confronted me: "One thing has not changed. The Earth is our home. The druids serve the Earth and everything that dwells upon it and within it. We must find a way to bring my knowledge to this age. I do not understand the new ways. You do. You can bring together the new and the olde ways." She paused.

She seemed desperate. I could see it in her eyes, and I felt sorry for her.

So, this is where the left path brought me, I thought.

"So be it".

Ganna released a long breath, smiled, and held up a key. "For the cottage."

CHAPTER 39

GANNA AND I AGREED to meet every day: When the sisters were in residence, I would come in the evening, after they retired. When Gwendoline and Margaret were away, we would meet in the early morning before my duties commenced. I kept my days off.

As the evening of my first session approached, I girded myself for a strange experience, but I could never have guessed what I found when I entered the cottage.

In the center of the shuttered dwelling stood a dome woven from willows. Candlelight inside the dome filtered through the willow branches, wavering on the ceiling like a thousand dancing fairies. It sat upon a circle of stones that rose about two feet off of the dirt floor. Ganna was standing next to a small entry covered with a blanket. Without a word, she swept the cover back and, bowing low, ducked into the lodge.

I pushed the blanket aside and entered. When I straightened, the priestess was sitting cross-legged on a small rug behind a large flat stone that served as a low table. Three candles were on the stone alongside a large leather-bound book. Ganna pointed to a rug opposite her, and I took my place on it.

Despite the strangeness of it all, I was relaxed, maybe because as I grew up with candlelight. I missed the purity it brought to small spaces.

"Ask me a question, and then I will ask one of you," Ganna began.

I didn't know where to begin. "Trees — I know trees have a special significance to you. Why is that?"

255

Her beaming face told me that Ganna was delighted with my question. "Nothing is holier than a tree. If you learn to listen to them you can learn the truth. They do not preach ideas or beliefs, but rather the ancient laws of life. They say 'Listen: Observe that in me is revealed the way of Nature. My powerful trunk is rooted in infinity that branches out through all the tiny veins in my leaves. Listen: You are anxious because you are far from home, but I will lead you back to the Mother. Be like me. I want nothing, except to be who I am. In this thought you will find that you *are* at home with the Mother.'"

I was touched by Ganna's eloquence, even as I struggled to understand her words. Her answer was unfathomable, yet it rang as genuine and true. "Thank you. Now you may ask me a question."

Her first question surprised me: "Tell me about your older brother."

"I don't see what —"

Ganna held up her hand and repeated the question.

"Very well. Rory was seven years older than I. And, almost from the first day I could walk, I became his shadow. Even now, I can picture him in his black galero and dusty coat." The image brought a smile to my face. "His cuffs were bell-shaped and covered his hands, which were usually filled with another's belongings," I added, with a chuckle. "His 'run,' as he called it, was in and about Exmouth Market on London's east side." A wave of sorrow rippled through me, and what felt like a fist tightened in my chest.

Ganna's eyes remained riveted upon me. "Go on. And your brother brought Mr. Holmes into your life."

"Yes. Mr. Holmes was searching for a stolen pearl necklace. The thief's wife had the loot and, unfortunately for her, she walked through Exmouth Market. Rory pinched them. Mr. Holmes, who was on the trail of the thieves, nabbed my brother. The crooks thought Rory had given the necklace to Holmes, so they held him for ransom. I was there when they whisked Rory off in a growler."

Ganna's eyes widened. "You must have been frightened!"

"I was seven at the time. The thieves tucked a note into my pocket and told me to deliver it to Mr. Holmes."

"And he has remained in your life, Ganna said softly."

"Yes. Our father left us after Evangeline was born. Our mother struggled to eke out a living as a rag picker, and by selling flowers. She died of pneumonia when I was twelve. Rory was nineteen then, and my baby sister three.

"I'm sorry your life was so difficult," Ganna offered. "How did you get on after your mother died?"

I closed my eyes. "How did we get on? We didn't. We stole food from carts on the street and slept in doorways and abandoned buildings. Evangeline fell ill in the winter because there was no warm place to stay — no medicine." Tears gathered in my eyes. "I was afraid my sister would die. Something had to be done. Rory was against it, but one night, while he was asleep, I took Evangeline to an orphanage, left her on the step . . . rang the bell . . . and ran." I was crying. "She was so very sick."

"Go on," Ganna urged.

"The next morning, Rory learned what I had done. He was angry. A few days later, he packed his things, pushed a one-pound note in my hand, and told me to go to a friend of our mother's who would give me a place to sleep. He kissed my forehead and left."

"But, he came home again," Ganna predicted.

"Never for long. So, when he joined the Irish patriots during the Easter Rising, I went with him."

Tears began flowing in earnest now, and my body was shaking.

"What happened?"

"Rory begged me to stay home, but I followed. Our cause was doomed from the start. Commander Ashe ordered him to take me, and another woman, to safety. When Rory returned, the battle at

Swords was over. Rory was the lone survivor of the Fingal Battalion."

I began to sob—speaking in gasps. "Because of my pigheadedness Rory lived the life of a fugitive . . . until the day he died."

"A great loss," Ganna said. "You have had many losses."

A bitter bile rose in my throat. My tears dried up. I glared at Ganna: "I don't know why you must know these things, old woman, but I did not come here to have you gawk at my sins."

I rose to leave.

"Stop!" Ganna said. "Be with your feelings."

I sat.

"It is painful — I know," she said. "But it is not me causing your pain. You carry it inside you. Stop waiting for your memories to fade. They won't. Ask your heart to accept what happened."

"No more tonight . . . please."

Ganna took a long breath. "Very well. Ask me another question."

I composed myself. "When first we met in the boathouse, you said: *I know you.* What did you mean?"

She paused and pursed her lips. "I understand that you have a religious practice."

"I am a Catholic — though not a good one."

"Do Catholics believe that a spirit inhabits our bodies?"

I nodded.

"And, what happens when the body dies?"

"Their soul goes back to God."

"Does their soul remain with God?"

"Yes, in heaven."

Ganna leaned closer. "Would it be so strange if a soul chose to come back into another body?"

"That's what you believe?"

"Yes, Tessa. That day in the boathouse, when I said: 'I know you,' I recognized your soul."

"So, you claim to see a person's soul?"

"Not in most people, but your soul is one I've known before. I knew you as Isolda."

I stifled my laugh.

She continued: "Have you heard of Queen Boudicca?"

"Professor Stone said she defeated the Romans a long time ago."

Ganna nodded. "Isolda was Queen Boudicca's daughter."

I could no longer keep a straight face. "So, I am the latest incarnation of Isolda, am I? How can you know this?"

"The same way I know that you have a birthmark on you right hip that you keep hidden."

"Not a birthmark — it's a burn scar from my mother's stove when I was young."

"It appears like three letters."

How could she know this! I thought.

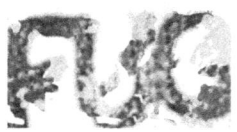

Ganna continued: "It is the letters F - U - G. Isolda and her sister Siora were taken as slaves and branded with those letters — Latin for *fugitivus* — runaway. With every incarnation, Isolda has chosen to keep that mark as a reminder of who she is."

I was trembling. "No . . ."

"Yes, and Maeve carries the soul of your sister, Siora."

259

CHAPTER 40

GANNA'S WORDS SHOOK MY SANITY: *You carry Isolda's soul. Maeve has the soul of your sister Siora.*

The existence of a soul is an article of faith. However, the whole notion may be a trick of a mind that cannot imagine not existing . . . or a childlike answer to the greatest question of all: who we are?

The entry in my diary summed up my feelings:

> *Tomorrow it is heaped at my feet*
> *I'm remade in another's memory,*
> *another's time, place and people.*
> *I walk in a druid's dream.*

My beliefs were irrelevant, I finally told myself. Ganna believes it, and it explains much about what has happened and why. More importantly, it will help me to predict what may happen. I needed Mr. Holmes's advice before my next meeting with Ganna. But, I wondered if the sisters would give me the time off to pay him a visit.

Any trepidation I had about requesting an extra half-day was allayed the moment I approached Gwendoline at breakfast.

"My dear, your wan face tells me you spent a dreadful night," the younger sister remarked as I took my place at the dining room table with my pad and pencil.

Margret chimed in: "Yes, there is no pressing business at the moment, take some time to restore yourself."

I was certain that this was *not* the result of my wanly appearance. It was Ganna's work. "Thank you," I replied. I appreciate your generosity. Of course, I do not expect to be paid for —"

"Nonsense," Gwendoline chided.

"Thank you." As I turned to leave, I noticed Emma Moss glowering from the doorway, holding a pot of coffee in her hand. I beat a hasty retreat.

It had been only two days since I visited Mr. Holmes at the Doctor's abode, so I was surprised to learn that my friend had found new lodgings at a mews house on nearby Shrewsbury Avenue. Dr. Watson walked me to Holmes's new domicile pointing out the amenities — never mentioning the chief convenience being that he, and little Nora, no longer needed to look after Holmes on a daily basis.

"Quite spacious, as you will see," Watson pointed out. "Makes me rather envious — all necessary though, as a second bedroom is required for Mrs. MacAskill. She should be quite pleased to have an entire floor to herself."

"So, Mr. Holmes is getting on with the new nurse?"

Watson chuckled. "It would appear so, but . . ." he continued in a droll manner: "I do not believe Holmes's eccentricities are yet in full blossom."

Upon arrival, I was pleased to see Mr. Holmes busy at his desk. The parlor had already been transformed into a workshop and laboratory.

"You have more holidays than a Whitehall bureaucrat," the Detective exclaimed, as I entered. He swung his chair around to greet me.

"You seem to be well entrenched in your new residence," Watson noted.

I seconded that assessment. "Indeed, how are you spending your time, Mr. Holmes?"

Spreading his arms wide to emphasize his restricted condition, he answered: "As you can imagine, clients are not flocking to engage me, but I am putting my unsolicited talents to work, nonetheless." He placed his hand on a stack of newspapers. "The press offers some small mysteries that I like to work out."

Watson shook his head. "Well Holmes, you've solved many a mystery from your armchair."

"Only after evidence had been meticulously gathered," he snapped. "The clues . . . the miniscule traces . . . must be gathered and presented to me."

Watson shrugged. "You could hire people to gather the pieces . . . as the Irregulars once did."

"Yes, the Irregulars were my eyes, ears and —"

"And feet," I added. A smile found my face as I recalled the sheer joy that I, and the other Irregulars, felt as we scoured the city on a mission for Sherlock Holmes. He gave us the gift of adventure, and a few sorely needed coins as well.

Holmes grimaced. "People can barely see what is there . . . for example . . ." He jerked his chair about and thumbed through today's edition of the *Daily Mail*.

A clattering on the stairway above signaled that Hilda MacAskill's arrival was imminent. Dr. Watson and I turned to see the hefty woman posed in the doorway with her hands on her hips.

"Hello, sister," I said. "You and Mr. Holmes are managing admirably."

The nurse cackled. "A man of action, this one," she said. "I heard his lordship's bellowin' and thought I'd better come to see that he doesn't bite yer 'ead off."

"No one here needs your tender ministrations, Mrs. MacAskill," Holmes barked. "Although, 'tender' is not a word I should use to describe your manner."

Hilda roared with laughter. "If nasty words were bullets, I'd have been dead long ago," she said. Then turning to us: "I hope you will stay. Some company will do him good. I was just preparing lunch."

"No thank you," Watson began. "Just a wee visit for me."

"Are ya sure now, Doctor? I'm making bubble and squeak, and I still have some fine pork pies left over. Simple fare, but mighty good, if I do say so meself."

"That will invigorate his blood," I said. "I for one would love to stay for lunch."

"Yes," Watson added, "I suppose I can find the time as well."

Watson, an epicure of British fare, hunched over his plate in earnest, while Holmes picked at his food. I waited to bring up my conundrum about Ganna. As the clatter of knife and fork dissipated Watson bowed out: "Lovely lunch, but I'm afraid I must be off," the Doctor said, placing his napkin on the table. "I need to waylay Nora before she begins preparing my evening repast." He patted his belly. "I fear there is room for little more than fruit and cheese." He held up a hand in goodbye. "I'll see myself off. Good to see you my dear—and you as always Holmes."

Holmes looked up whimsically. "Thank you, my friend."

For a moment the two men looked upon each other, their eyes unable to hold back their sadness.

When Watson departed, Mrs. MacAskill carried off the dishes on a large tray she balanced in the crook of one arm.

"You have something playing on your mind, Tessa," Holmes remarked. He turned his chair around and rolled into the parlor. "Is it Ganna?"

He patted the arm of his old Morris chair. When I was seated, he continued: "Of course, I too am pleased she has reemerged. Have you lain eyes on her again?"

I suddenly became hesitant to share my problem with him. When I did not answer, he went on: "You've seen her, haven't you?"

"I was with her last night."

"Out with it," he said.

"She believes I am a Celtic princess . . . rather, that I possess the soul of the princess."

He laughed. "My, my . . . tell me what occurred."

I laid the events down, beginning with the straw insigne in my room and ending with the proceedings behind the cottage last evening. I omitted the bargain Ganna and I made as it related to him.

"You doubt your own rational mind only because she knew of your birthmark," he said. "Where might she have seen it?"

"I've been thinking about that," I mumbled. "Maybe . . . at *Samhain*. She took my coat and loosened my blouse."

"Very good, where else?"

"Having the blessing of the Davis sisters, she has access to Grey House. She may have seen it when I was sleeping."

"Now tell me, are those possibilities more likely than the tale she tells?"

"You're saying Ganna is a charlatan?"

"Yes, a skillful one. She knows that she can ensnare you, because she promises access to Eva. She also knows you and I are friends, and wishes to diminish my influence." He lowered his head and looked up mischievously. "She had you send herbs to me that made me act the fool, did she not?"

I grimaced. "I'm sorry about that."

"We must be cruel, only to be kind," he quoted.

"Nonetheless, do not rebuke Ganna," Holmes instructed. "You are correct in thinking that she may lead us to Eva and the others — if we keep our wits about us. This is all working to our advantage, for she will also lead us to Maeve. But, mind you, move with caution. Maeve may be closer than we think. I believe that she still walks in her murderous ways. In the last two months, there have been two men slashed to death in a manner similar to Goodnow. Walls has been investigating these murders, and I expect a report soon."

"Where did these occur?"

"One in Birmingham and the other in Manchester."

"West of the city, then? That seems to verify Ganna's claim that Maeve and the others had traveled away from the city."

"Indeed. If it is Maeve, the Sisters of Scáthach are moving ever westward."

"And Eva with them."

"In that regard, I am curious about Eva Allsop. Your single-mindedness regarding the young woman is admirable, but it borders on the obsessive." He paused and raised a brow. "Am I missing something?"

"Nothing gets by you, Mr. Holmes. Eva is special to me . . . someday I may tell you why."

"Ah, a mystery is it?"

CHAPTER 41

I WAS NOT ABLE TO SLEEP, so I went to the Davis library. I was surprised to find Margaret at the desk. Before I could apologize, the older sister rose and took me in hand. "I hope you are not doing any work at this hour, my dear."

"I came to find a book."

"Possibly I can help. What are you seeking?"

"The Celts. I want to know more about Celtic women."

Margaret smiled and guided me to a shelf behind the desk and pointed to, what I later learned, was a sixteenth century translation of Diodorus Siculus's *Bibliotheke Historike*. She pulled two volumes from the collection, cautioning me to be gentle with the bindings. I knew little of such things, but I judged that these were rare and valuable folios. She put the books in my hands and said goodnight.

Ensconced in a comfortable Chesterfield, I read snippets of Siculus's accounts, which were numerous and detailed. I was struck by the attention he gave to the Celtic women — for who is more unsung than the women of history? My limited schooling had taught me that primeval women were no better than broodmares, often left to die in infancy for the effrontery of arriving in this world without a penis. To the contrary, Diodorus did not hide his admiration for Celtic women — comparing them to their Roman counterparts:

> *"A Celtic woman is the equal of any Roman man in hand-to-hand combat. She is as beautiful as she is strong. Her body is comely but fierce. The physiques of our Roman women pale in comparison."*

My mind turned to Maeve as I read how Celtic women choose to be trained as warriors:

> *"The women of the Celtic tribes are bigger and stronger than our Roman women. This is most likely due to their natures, as well as their peculiar fondness for all things martial and robust. The flaxen-haired maidens of the north are trained in sports and war while our gentle ladies are content to do their womanly duties and thus are less powerful than most young girls from Gaul and the hinterlands."*

And so, I began to understand why Ganna recognized, honored, and supported Maeve's choice. Accounts of these women in battle, rekindled my memory of Maeve fighting off the witch-hunter and his hound:

> *"Here the women met our soldiers holding swords and axes in their hands. With hideous shrieks of rage they tried to drive back the hunted and the hunters. If a Celt calls in his wife, she comes with flashing eyes; and poising her huge white arms, begins to rain blows mingled with kicks, like shots discharged by the twisted cords of a catapult. And, with bare hands, such women tore away the shields of our warriors and grasped their swords, enduring mutilating wounds."*

Celtic women were allowed and encouraged to express their true nature. Far from primitive, they were educated in religion, herbalism, bard-craft and weaponry. They inherited and kept their wealth separate from their husband's.

As I set down the book, I was aware of an enigmatic mingling of pride and wonder at the thought that I share the blood of these ancient Celtic women. Contrary to what I've been told all my life, I would be wise to embrace my boldness (some call pig-headedness). Instead of hesitant and doubtful, I felt a growing pride, and the possibility that I might rise from the ashes of my past life to walk in the Celtic ways. No doubt, similar thoughts were what attracted young women to the Sisters of Scáthach. In her own perverse way, Maeve was endeavoring to protect and honor the feminine aspect in Nature.

"Knock, knock."

I turned.

"Mr. Button, what brings you here?"

He pointed to the bookshelves. "Lovely library, is it not?" He ambled up to my chair. "A small thing, but you asked that we call you by your first name, yet you feel compelled to use my proper one."

"We're above stairs . . . but, I will risk Mrs. Moss's ire, Clark."

"Thank you." He pointed to the large book in my lap. "Looks like serious reading."

"It's about the Celts . . . Celtic women."

"Of which you are one."

"I am, and proud of it. Oh, by the way, I picked up John Reed's book, *Ten Days that Shook the World*."

"Did you read it, or just pick it up?"

"Hm-m-m. I know you are attempting to be clever, but the truth is, I couldn't get through it.

"Yes, knowing the ending rather spoils it."

I laughed. "Are you looking for a particular book?"

"Our last conversation about Conan Doyle has me desirous of delving into some of his works. One in particular, *The Mystery of Cloomber* — one of his early works."

"I hope you find it. If you do, please don't spoil the ending for me."

"Hardly, I understand it's all about strange priests from another world come to seek revenge," he said, mimicking a frightened face. Then he paused, looking sideways at me.

"Well . . . what is it Mister . . . Clark?"

"Please excuse me, if I am being bold or presumptuous . . ."

"Yes?"

"The other night . . . I was restless and went outside for a smoke. When I returned, I saw you behind the cottage."

I did my best to keep a straight face.

"It was rather late," he said, hesitantly.

"And?"

"I'm trying not to be impolite . . ."

"Then how do you characterize this conversation?"

"*Concerned*, is the word I would use."

"Have you mentioned this to anyone else?" I asked.

"No. I reckon it's your business . . ." His voice trailed off, and he looked at me expectantly.

I appreciated his caring, but I let him dig his "grave" a little deeper with a long silence.

"With the goings on at the cottage . . . you remember . . . I told you about that . . . I just . . ."

"You are concerned for my safety, is that it?"

"You strike me as a woman who can take care of herself, and . . . I suppose . . . you might have been meeting someone."

I stifled a smile. "So, you think I was keeping a rendezvous?"

His feet shuffled and he fidgeted with his hands. "No, Miss Wiggins, I wouldn't presume anything of the sort."

"Good. Because, I was not meeting anyone, and I wouldn't want something like that to get around," I chided. "And, it's Tessa, remember."

He beamed. "As I say, not to worry."

"Thank you, Clark, I will leave you to the books. I believe I will retire. Good night."

With the curious chauffeur in the library, I deemed it was safe to slip out to the cottage.

Ganna received me in silence. We sat quietly in the willow dome for some time before she spoke: "I apologize for frightening you last evening. I was probing a chink in your well-armored mind. You must understand that you have an essential destiny. You need not be certain of what I said about you — but you must come to understand how important it is that my knowledge finds its way into the world."

"You expect me to be a druidess? Such things are not possible nowadays."

"Some would say that there is no place in the world for a woman warrior, yet one exists. Maeve was born a warrior — although there is a bit of warrior in every woman, if she will honor it. I was born with the spirit of a priestess, and you a bàrd."

I winched. "A story-teller?"

"Yes, a teller of tales and a poet. You already know this."

"I enjoy playing with words and rhymes, but that is all."

"We will see," Ganna said. "Are you ready to begin?"

I nodded.

"We are in a sacred place. The grove of trees behind this cottage, and the spring that flows below us, has been untouched for hundreds of years."

"Professor Stone said the *bandrui* hold rivers, and all flowing water, in high regard."

"We hold reverence for everything in Nature, but trees, rivers and springs are distinctive because they span several realms: water flows beneath the earth, on the earth, and in the sky. Because our bodies carry mostly water, they connect *us* to these realms."

I took my journal and a pencil from my pocket, but Ganna stayed my hand. "You must learn these things, but do not write them down."

"It will help me study."

"When you write, you are recording, not learning. Sacred knowledge must pass from one being to another. This is the way true knowledge moves."

I put away the diary. "I fear I may not remember all you tell me."

Ganna smiled. "I expect to tell you these things a hundred times. That is my task. Yours is to listen."

"There is so much to learn. Maybe we need to lengthen our meeting time?"

"It is important that you have your sleep. It is the time when your soul connects with time-spirits from other realms."

I undoubtedly looked perplexed, for Ganna held up both hands in acquiescence. "Too much, too soon. I have been waiting so long for you, I have difficulty controlling my eagerness."

"I am keen to learn — especially how to heal Mr. Holmes."

"Ah, yes . . . our bargain. I have not forgotten. There is not enough time to teach you the herb-craft required. For now, you must trust me. I will give you what is needed. The understanding will come later."

"But, the last herbs . . ."

"The cojóbana seeds? You said that he took the herb directly into his lungs. It was meant to burn slowly and be breathed in over a long time. It will not happen again."

"I know him. He will not take herbs."

"Mr. Holmes has cultivated his mind as a wheat farmer does his field," Ganna explained. "The wheat farmer does not plant other crops. In the same way, Holmes does not entertain possibilities that lay beyond his senses. So, we will plant new seeds. We will begin with his body — the herbs . . . then his mind, and finally his spirit — each in turn. You must help him believe that healing is possible; for the body always seeks to be in harmony with the mind."

"You expect much from me."

"Just a little more than you expect from yourself."

With that, our lessons began.

Ganna laid the foundation for my new knowledge — appreciation and respect for the inspirited Natural world.

"Your awful factories and mines with their machines are diminishing the human creature," Ganna explained. "Human beings are among the most inventive, adaptable, and intelligent animals on earth. For thousands of years there was no separation between work and living. It was one and the same because we lived within the natural world — hunting, cultivating, building shelters, and making clothing needed to survive. Now, work is detached from making a living, and consequently, from Nature."

"But, we cannot live that way today," I argued.

"I hope that is not true, because, if we cannot work as part of Nature, we will destroy our own Nature—our essence as human animals."

"You want to change the world!" I exclaimed.

Ganna grinned. "Presently, I only wish to change your mind."

It was all very strange, and yet it made sense to me. Ganna's teachings flew in the face of everything I had been taught. Father O'Malley would be turning in his grave.

As our time together came to an end, Ganna looked at me. A beatific smile appeared, and tears streamed down her cheeks. She cried silently for a minute before she spoke: "These are tears of gratitude. They have welled up in me for centuries. I must let them flow. We will continue tomorrow."

As I rose to go, she added: "When next you visit Mr. Holmes, you will have what he needs to begin healing his body."

CHAPTER 42

MRS. MACASKILL'S BROW WRINKLED when I showed her the powdered grey granules in the canning jar. "It's intended to treat many injuries, from burns to broken bones. I've seen it work wonders, and thought it couldn't hurt," I said.

"And, what is your medical background, Miss Wiggins?"

"More than a decade in Spitalfields and the East End. Assisting midwives, and treating the poor, gave me insights to homespun medicine. The poor cannot afford doctors or drugs, so they rely upon simple treatments and herbal remedies. I made note of those preparations that have a good effect."

The nurse opened the jar and sniffed. "I recognize the turmeric, what else is in this?"

"All natural herbs," I lied.

Ganna had hesitated when I asked the same question of her. "We call it *cascabel*," the priestess said.

"Which is . . .?"

"The baked and finely ground bones of a snake," the druidess answered.

"A poisonous snake?"

She nodded. "A viper, but there is nothing of the poison in this. It is a regenerative linctus used for hundreds of years. If it will ease your mind, you can make a tea, and I will drink it."

This offer from Ganna had me accept the concoction without proof, but Hilde MacAskill was a Doubting Thomas.

"Very well, let us make a tea," the nurse said. "It may do my arthritis some good."

It was a gritty bitter tea that tasted like spicy dirt.

"It tastes so bad, it must be good medicine," Hilde said, as the tea went down. "Though how you expect to get Mr. Holmes to take it is another matter."

"You might sprinkle it in his food."

She agreed. "Mind you, if I notice any adverse effects . . ."

"Of course, you must do what is best for Mr. Holmes . . . always."

And with that, Holmes's herbal regimen began. *Improving his mindset would be more challenging,* I told myself, as I found my way to his parlor office.

Holmes had a newspaper in his lap and a pipe stuffed halfway in his lips. Wafts of smoke obscured his face, so his mood was not immediately apparent.

"Something in the newspaper has your interest?" I asked.

"Yes, a diamond robbery." A whimsical look flashed across his face as he turned to me. "I am anxious to hear your report on Ganna."

"Don't change the subject. What makes this theft so interesting?"

Holmes rolled his chair toward me. "It is one of the largest jewel thefts ever in London, and the circumstances are said to be inexplicable."

"A real mystery."

"Yes. In the past, I would have expected a knock on the door of 221 Baker Street."

"What was stolen?"

"A rare red diamond. The theft occurred at a private showing above Hemming's. Details are unknown—including the owner of the gem."

"Insured?"

"Doesn't say. The stone is a great loss, but the reputation of Hemming Jewelers is as valuable." He folded the paper and set it back on his desk."

"Why not call Scotland Yard?" I inquired.

His silence suggested he was considering my suggestion, until he remarked: "Do you think they might take pity on a crippled old detective?" he asked.

"Self-pity is not your way, Mr. Holmes."

He glared at me. "You are taking advantage of our friendship. Sit here for a couple months and tell me how you feel."

"I don't presume to know how you feel, but unlike you, I can see beyond this room. Call Inspector Walls."

He eyed me. "Tessa, I've lost the use of my legs, not my pride. I will find my way. Let MacAskill do the nursing."

It was clear that when his mind engaged a crime, his mood and demeanor improved; so my highest hopes were realized when, after our luncheon, a knock came to the door.

Watson's vociferous voice burst into the room. "Short notice . . . sorry . . . sorry, but I needed to show the Inspector the way here."

I ushered the two men inside and showed them to a *settee* facing Holmes's desk.

"I have more information on those grizzly murders," Walls began. "Beyond the style of the attacks, they may be in keeping with Maeve Murtagh's targets: one of the men had a reputation as a womanizer, and the other was the managing director of a girl's home — a rather poor one we were led to believe. So, there you are."

"So, what is your opinion?" Holmes asked.

"I think it is she, and I've put two of my best men on it. If Maeve Murtagh is about, the locals will notice her. We're making inquiries thereabouts." Walls suddenly became more animated. "Oh, and I have news about Basil Zaharoff." Expectant looks turned his way. "Evidently, he continued to pursue that actress . . ."

"Edna Avery," Holmes prompted.

"Yes. Well . . . he sailed his floating palace to Vigo, Spain, to see the lovely Miss Avery in a strange little play about a love affair between a butterfly and a cockroach."

"Let me guess," I exclaimed, "Miss Avery plays the butterfly."

"And Zaharoff the cockroach," Watson chortled.

Walls held up his hands. "The play aside, Zaharoff nearly met his death at an opening night dinner party — poison."

"Attempted murder?" Watson asked.

Walls grinned. "Yes, by a bird."

We stood dumfounded as the Inspector explained: "Quail was served at the dinner party, and Zaharoff's quail —"

"Had eaten hemlock," Holmes exclaimed. "There are a number of poisonings by coturnism every year. The quail eats the hemlock and the diner eats the quail."

"How unfortunate for the Greek," Walls exclaimed.

"Not bad luck, but bad company, I would venture," Holmes surmised.

"Not Maeve, certainly" Watson declared. "Not sufficiently gruesome."

"Gruesome enough," Holmes countered. "Coturnism is an agonizing way to go — rapid heartbeat, seizures, and finally, respiratory paralysis."

Watson grinned. "So Holmes, you believe it was . . . *foul play* after all."

Walls grimaced and then continued: "Difficult to prove," Walls said. "But, I've come on another matter, Mr. Holmes, Something more in your bailiwick. I was hoping that you might put your mind to —"

"Before you tell me *what* Inspector, I am curious as to why you believe I can help," he said, widening his arms to bring attention to his fixed state.

"Unless your injury has affected your brain, you are still the best detective in Britain. And, if I can presume to know your ways, I would guess that you know why I am here."

"A diamond," Holmes answered.

"Not just a diamond," Walls said, "but a nine carat stone with an estimated worth of more than a quarter million pounds."

The collective mouths of Watson and I gaped.

Watson reminisced: "You recall the blue carbuncle, do you Holmes? Found it in the crop of a goose. Hah!"

"You might call this the *red* carbuncle," Walls said. "And, it wasn't insured."

Watson pulled a notebook from his pocket. "So, there goes one possibility."

"Yes. We do not know the owner, but they must have some acquaintance with Hemming's — or someone with ties to the royal family."

"Rather hush-hush," I noted.

The Scotland Yard detective grimaced. "Yes, royal eyes have been set upon The Yard with the caveat that we make a special effort to abate any embarrassment to Sir Wallace Hemming and his family."

"Holmes is just the man!" Watson exclaimed.

We all turned to the eminent detective who had refilled his pipe, and was tamping the tobacco with a finger. "I suppose the entire police force has tramped through the crime scene."

"On the contrary, the entire area has been secluded pending your arrival," Walls said. "Transportation awaits."

There was a tug on my heart as I watched Mr. Holmes helped into the car by Watson and Walls. This would mark the first time he had ventured into the larger world since the accident. *A turning point.*

Not wishing to impose unnecessarily on the generosity of the Davis sisters, I immediately returned to Grey House. As I made my way inside, I caught site of the stone cottage and wondered if Ganna were in residence. In my visits, I did not see any signs that Ganna actually abided in the cottage. So, when I was sure that no one was lurking about, I went to the rear door of the cottage. Before I could knock, a faint moaning caught my ear — it came from the grove of trees behind the cottage.

I followed the sounds that resolved into a rhythmic lament. *Ganna.*

I made my way through the underbrush and found the druidess on her knees, eyes closed, slowly rocking and quietly chanting:

> *"Mother enfold me,*
> *Mother surround me,*
> *Mother show the way."*

Then — she stopped — aware of my presence. Her eyes opened.

"I'm sorry for interrupting your . . . ."

"Entreaty. I suppose you might say prayer." She came to her feet. "Curiosity is a good thing in a student. So, what have you learned?"

"That you believe in prayer."

"To whom was I praying?"

"You used the word 'mother' — a feminine deity."

Ganna put her arm about me and guided me toward the cottage. "No. I was not praying to a deity." The druidess' eyes rolled upward in thought. "Let me simply say that the collective essences of the Natural world form a web, much like a spider's web. When we connect with that web, we are not only aware of events or disturbances when our part of the web quivers, but like the spider, we can know of occurrences that may impact us anywhere across the web."

"Anywhere in the world?"

"Yes, we can hone our awareness to that level. But understand, that even if you are not in communion with the web, it still touches you, because every creature on earth comprises one of its threads."

"I must be back to my duties now, but I am curious about how you put yourself at the center of that web. I will come this evening at the usual time."

"Very well, I am eager to learn how you spent your time with Mr. Holmes."

I had become accustomed to Ganna knowing my every step, so I did not offer a rejoinder.

Returning to Grey House, I gathered the mail, grabbed pad and pen, and went to the dayroom. After I delivered their mail, the sisters had me go to a bookstore to retrieve a package and post letters *en route*. My workday ended with my taking instructions for a charitable event in support of the National Kitchen, a canteen created to serve struggling families during and after the war.

My meeting with Ganna in the offing, I once again decided it was best not to sleep beforehand — not that I could have. My mind was whirling. Something within me was moving. As I awaited the meeting, I took pen to hand:

> *Arrogant certitude*
> *Borrowed convictions*
> *Undeserved confidence —*
> *the consequences of conceit.*
> *Within my poor choices,*
> *perhaps I've paid the price*
> *to know what's real and true.*

I found Ganna waiting when I entered my nighttime classroom — as usual, her eyes were closed — her breaths shallow and slow.

I thought she might be asleep. Then, her eyelids rose and her dark pupils adjusted to the candlelight.

"What happened today?"

I told her about enlisting Nurse MacAskill in delivering the medicine to Holmes, and the surprising turn of events that had prodded Mr. Holmes from his flat.

"Then Mr. Holmes's spirits improved when he engaged the theft?"

"Indeed."

Ganna's vague smugness had me ask: "Did you have anything to do with the Scotland Yarder's appearance?"

"How would I do that?"

"You did not answer my question."

"Does it matter? Reengaging the world is part of Mr. Holmes's healing regimen."

CHAPTER 43

MR. HOLMES GREW STRONGER each day. Ganna's linctuses, and the application of his mind and talents, were working just as she had predicted.

I visited his flat regularly now, bringing the latest elixir and leaving with the latest news about the diamond robbery. The crime proved to be a true mystery befitting Holmes's talents.

Inspector Walls felt the kind of pressure that only the royal family can apply. He pressed Holmes for his insights and ideas almost daily. As the two put their minds to the theft, I sipped tea and listened in.

"Trupp is our man," Walls declared. "The windowless gallery where the theft occurred suggests an inside job, and Trupp is a diamond cutter. He can split the stone making it easier to fence."

"I believe him innocent for those very reasons," Holmes countered. "He would know that he is the primary suspect. My inquiries within the criminal underworld tell me that no red diamonds have come on the market."

Holmes swung his chair back to his desk and retrieved an envelope. He took a six-inch black feather from it.

"This again," Walls grumbled.

"This was on the floor of the gallery," Holmes said to me. "What do you make of it, Tessa?"

I leaned closer. "A bird feather. Rather strange."

"Exactly!" Holmes agreed.

Walls was unimpressed. "It may have come in on someone's clothing, or wafted through an open window."

Holmes pointed a finger at Walls. "You said yourself the windows were sealed. Now . . . there are vents to the roof."

"Well, there you have it," Walls replied, "pigeons on the roof . . . a feather flutters through the venting . . ."

I took the quill in hand. "But, this is not a pigeon feather. The rooftop at the Salvation Army is paved in pigeon feathers, and I can tell you it belongs to another bird altogether."

"I agree, Tessa," Holmes said. "I have not had the time or opportunity to look into it — but it appears to be a species of black bird."

"Maybe I can help. The Davis library is very complete."

"Excellent!" he said, handing the envelope to me.

Walls threw up his hands. "I must be off. I'm going to question Trupp again. I need to find some solid evidence . . . something more than an errant bird feather."

"I'll continue to make inquiries," Holmes promised. "Thank you for coming, Inspector."

Walls gone, I turned to Holmes. "Mrs. MacAskill tells me that your health is improving."

"I do feel better."

"The human body is a wonder, don't give up hope," I said.

"Don't make too much of MacAskill's reports, Tessa. I prefer harsh reality over false hope."

"But she tells me the blood circulation in your legs has improved."

"Legs are one thing. Broken backs do not mend." He was anxious to change the subject: "More encounters with Ganna?"

I nodded and gave an abbreviated report, essentially telling him that she had taken on a role of tutor — schooling me about the Natural world. As I took my leave, he once again, cautioned me: "She may lead you to Eva, but she can also bring you face to face with Maeve."

"I understand. I'll say my goodbyes to Mrs. MacAskill and be on my way."

I found the nurse tidying up in the parlor. "I have the newest linctus," I told her, taking it from my purse.

She put a finger to her lips and waved me toward the kitchen. "I fear he suspects something. I found him snooping about in my kitchen yesterday. He may have seen me sprinkling it in the cooking."

"Could he have tasted it?"

"No. I only use it in strong or spicy sauces and the like. I'll be more discrete."

"But you believe it is healing him?"

"I can see that muscle-tone in his legs has returned. And, just the other day, I caught him shifting his feet in the chair stirrups without the use of his hands."

"But, he claims little improvement there."

"Miss Tessa, I think he's afraid to believe."

*****

Ganna was pleased with my report: "Our cure is working then."

"Will he walk again?"

"When his mind lets him, or requires him to." Ganna stated. "He's not a man to accept failure. He will walk when he knows he will succeed. But, it's clear he is ready for the final linctus."

"What is that?"

"A tincture made from mistletoe, mugwort, and hemlock. Very powerful and it requires a ritual be performed.

"Hemlock? That's poison."

"Mistletoe also, but in small amounts they are medicinal."

Tessa's eyes narrowed.

"What I say is true," Ganna told me.

"Then there must be another way. For one thing, I know that Mr. Holmes will not participate in a ritual."

"He need not. If you can obtain a personal object of his, you can make the petition on his behalf."

I offered a hesitant nod.

"Shall we begin?" she asked.

"Yes, but before we do, I need your opinion." I pulled the black feather from the envelope and handed it to her.

Ganna ran her finger over the feather's edge. "Morrighan," she mumbled. Then turning to me added: "It is a feather from a crow."

"And, Morrighan is . . .?"

"An illustrious Celtic warrior that legend elevated to a godlike level. Someday you may write a poem about her."

"A woman then?"

"Yes — the crow is her talisman. You know," she said coyly, "crows are more intelligent than most people."

Seeing the glint in her eyes, I asked: "Could a crow be trained to steal a gem?"

A cackle escaped Ganna. When her eyes caught mine, she laughed and stomped her feet. "Ha! You have caught me," she exclaimed, holding her arms up to mimic surrender.

"You stole the gem?"

"My crow Morrighan did."

I was flummoxed. And, seeing the bewildered expression on my face, she flung into uncontrollable laughter.

When she was again composed, she said: "I told you the cure for Holmes requires healing his mind as well as his body and spirit. It must be done in that order, for while the soul is the great healer, the body and mind will not let the soul do its work unless we honor them first.

"You faked a theft in order to —"

"Faked! I assure you, it was a real theft." She reached into her satchel and drew out a crimson gem the size of a large hazelnut and held it up to the candlelight. "It may be time to return this bauble."

*****

"*Corvus corone*," Holmes remarked when I returned the feather the next day. "You are an excellent detective, Tessa. The crow is a clever and bold fowl, to be sure, and your news presents a rather novel possibility."

The confirmation that the feather was that of a crow was all that was required for Holmes to bring the "thief" to justice. He sent Watson to set a trap atop the roof of Hemming Jewelers, baiting it with a hunk of rose quartz. They trapped the creature that afternoon, and after Holmes posted a small army of street urchins around Hemming's, Watson released the bird. Within an hour, a young runner reported they had found the nest in Green Park. Watson and Holmes hurried to the location, and nestled among twigs, shiny objects, and bits of fabric in Morrighan's nest, lay the red diamond.

They returned to Holmes's flat where I anxiously awaited news. Holmes was beaming.

Walls arrived soon after, and though happy with the outcome, wanted to have the creature destroyed. This went against Holmes's iconoclastic nature. "You know, Inspector, the animal presents no real danger. This bird was crafty, fearless, and possessed nearly enough intelligence to deceive us both. I feel the fellow has earned his freedom."

Walls laughed. "Birds of a feather, is it? Very well, you may let him go."

"Him?" Watson exclaimed, "It was, after all, attracted to pretty jewels. I rather think this fowl is a female."

"So, Doctor," I remarked, "what will you title this adventure: The case of the conniving crow?"

Holmes shook a finger. "I would not write this one up, Watson. But, if you should, give the credit to Tessa." Then, he turned to me: "How did you learn the feather was that of a crow?"

"I consulted an expert."

"Let me guess: Ganna."

"She was simply trying to help."

"Help me, or you?

"Why are you so skeptical?" I asked.

"Of Ganna, I am . . . and you should be also."

"I believe you have a deep-seated mistrust of women," I said.

"You sound like Watson."

"Thank you for the compliment. And, I can tell you that Ganna is not evil."

"She may not be evil, but she could be dangerously deluded. She has baited her trap with Eva, and you are falling into it. Have you ever asked yourself why she has engages you?"

"She hopes that I will follow in her footsteps."

"To be a druid priestess!" He raised his brows. "Mark my words young lady, you are heading into danger."

CHAPTER 44

I MADE MY WAY back to Grey House, well behind my time, but I was not concerned. The Davises were generous with regard to my schedule. However, a battle was raging within me.

Mr. Holmes's warning weighed heavily on me. I'd known him all my life; and, if he is one thing, he is right most of the time.

And, there is Ganna who speaks of spirits and souls . . . sleeps in trees, and prays to life forces no one can see. She seems wise and sincere but, as Holmes suggests, she may be demented.

Yet . . . something in me comes alive when I am with her. When she shares her teachings, a little voice within says: *of course*.

Absorbed in my inner debate, I did not see Mr. Button leaning against the carriage house having a smoke.

"Oye, Miss Wiggins . . . Tessa."

I indicated that I needed to keep moving. But, he waved frantically, urging me to come. He flicked his cigarette aside and walked toward me. His characteristic grin was absent.

"What is it?" I said.

"Are you okay?"

A sweet man, I thought. "Not really. Just a situation—you know, where your heart says one thing, and your head something else."

"Ah-h-h, I know it well," he replied, with the silliest grin.

"What?"

"Do you really want to know?"

I nodded.

"Right now, my heart wants me to take your hand and have you in my arms, but my head says that would not go well for me."

"Mr. Button!"

"Clark."

"Mr. Button, I'm . . . you are a foolhardy man if you believe that . . . well, I advise you to listen to your head. Good afternoon, Mr. Button," I replied, turning to leave.

"Wait, stop. That's not why I called you over. It's Mrs. Moss — she's beside herself with jealousy, and I fear she will take it out on you."

"Envy? But why?"

"She believes you are taking advantage of the Davis sisters — or so she claims. I am certain she is envious because you receive special treatment from them."

"Special treatment?"

He smirked. "Tessa, everyone can see it."

"Oh. I thought . . ."

"Yes, well . . . be careful," Button said, awkwardly reaching out, then pulling his hand back. "Moss has a nasty side."

"Thank you . . . Clark."

A Cheshire Cat *smile blossomed on his face.*

When I entered the servant's hall, Hedy Bell was at her stove and Moss had her faced buried in a note she was scribbling. The cook turned: "Good afternoon, Tessa," she said, motioning with her eyes toward the housekeeper and grimacing.

"Good afternoon, Hedy — and to you, Mrs. Moss."

Still writing, she replied: "Ah, so pleased you could make time for us. The sisters are waiting to chat with you."

"Anything special?" I asked.

"You seem to know their ways better than I," she replied. "They are in the dayroom." Then, she deigned to address me face-to-face: "Would you bring their tea up when you go?"

Hedy filled the pot on the tray that held two cups. As I reached for the tray, the cook winked and placed a third cup and saucer on it.

Here I go again, I thought, mounting the stairs — *in a jam with the governor.*

I could hear Gwendoline and Margaret chatting as I approached their sitting area. Balancing the tray in my arms, I made a feeble knock.

"Ah, Tessa . . . and with our tea," Gwendoline said. "Come in my dear. Please set the tray down and close the door."

Margaret turned and settled in her chair. I closed the door and returned to take the pot in hand.

"Please, let me serve," Margaret said. "Sit down, we'd like a word with you." She began filling the cups. "As you know, our family home is in Wales, between Blaenau Ffestiniog and the Irish Sea. We will be leaving, two days hence, to celebrate *imbolc*."

"*Imbolc* is a special time for Margaret and me," the younger sister continued. "And, we would like you to accompany us."

My shoulders lowered, and a sigh of relief escaped my lips. "I thought . . ."

"Yes, yes," Gwendoline said, "Mrs. Moss shared her concerns. Margaret and I did not fully appreciate how our household might see your . . . shall we say . . . varied duties."

Margaret chimed in: "We will do our best to manage Mrs. Moss's expectations, and those of the others." Seriousness came over her as she went on: "Your time with Ganna is paramount. Your secretarial responsibilities are needed and appreciated, to be sure, but they are ancillary."

"Ganna tells us," Gwendoline said, "that she believes you are ready to take the next step. We trust her judgment, and wish to take you into our confidence. In so doing, my sister and I beg your discretion." She paused, and looked deeply into my eyes. "Tessa, Ganna, Margaret and . . . and many others have been waiting for you our entire lives — Ganna so much longer. Your coming to us is a blessing. And, as imbolc is a time of new beginnings, it is appropriate that we celebrate your advent in Wales three days hence. Ganna will tell you more when you meet with her this evening."

As I departed, Gwendoline asked me to have Mr. Button bring their trunks to their rooms.

Evidently, tongues had been wagging while I was upstairs because I returned to the kitchen to find the whole crew assembled: Hedy, Jeddie, Clark and, of course, Mrs. Moss. Eyes bounced between Moss and me.

"Did things go well with the sisters?" the housekeeper asked.

"Yes," I replied, with the biggest smile I could muster. "It appears they are returning to Wales tomorrow and I am to accompany them."

Mrs. Moss's head snapped around toward me. "Really? Was that all?"

I put on a thoughtful expression. "Oh, no." I turned to Clark. "The sisters asked if I would see to it that their trunks were brought to their rooms. Can you help me with that, Clark?"

For a frozen moment, everyone — but Mrs. Moss—shared a look of surprise and satisfaction.

I marched out of the kitchen to the carriage house. Clark followed.

"Where are the trunks?" I asked, upon entering the garage.

"Upstairs," he said, pointing with his finger. "The storeroom is next to my quarters."

Not wishing him to think I was uncomfortable, I quipped: "What are you waiting for? Show the way."

Any uneasiness I felt climbing the stairs to his quarters was due to his brazenness — his sad attempt to woo me earlier — and, to be fair, my own disquieting reflections. I've not considered a relationship with a man for a long while.

He opened the door at the top and stepped aside. As I passed him, I could smell the tobacco on his breath and clothing. He pointed down the hall toward two doors.

"The one on the left is the storeroom."

I went to the door and tried the knob. Locked.

"The key is above the door, on the molding."

I reached up — my fingers just short of the top.

"I'm sorry," he said. "I should get that. It's that you come on like a woman who must do everything herself."

"Do I?"

"Yes," he replied. Reaching over my head. His body pressed against my back. He came down with the key and held it up. "Shall I, or do you wish to unlock the door?"

I gestured with my hand toward the lock.

He put the key in and twisted it. I jumped a little when it clicked open.

"Excuse me," he said, brushing me aside as he opened the door. He went inside and retrieved a lantern. Holding it up he patted his pockets. "Here, hold this," he said, jiggling the dusty lantern. It smelled of kerosene, and was laden with grime. I suppose that is why I hesitated to take it.

"Well," he said, "it's either that or get the matches from my pocket."

I snatched the lantern from his hand. I needed to stop these puerile games. "Clark, your behavior earlier today prompts me to suggest that you get any unwarranted notions out of your head."

"Unwarranted notions?"

"You know to what I am referring."

"Oh, that. I don't know what I was thinking. You were a Salvationist, after all, and me . . . well, I was a bit of a rake in my younger days."

"Really? What was it? Wine? Women? Gambling?"

He shook his head. "Stop it, Tessa," he said. "I don't want to play games either. It's true I have a past that I'm not proud of, but I'm not the same person. I've learned my lesson."

There was sadness in his voice — remorse in his eyes. "I'm sorry, Clark. What lesson did you learn?"

His face reddened. "You'll think me foolish."

"I won't. What did you learn?"

He glanced down for a moment before he brought his eyes to mine. "You have the prettiest green eyes."

"Clark! Is it that you cannot put the lesson into words?"

"No, it's simple really. I learned that the only way to be a happy person is to embrace the broken parts of ourselves."

His eyes were soft, and his words tugged at my heart. *Does he see the broken parts of me . . . is that what attracts him?* "That's a good lesson," I said, reaching up to touch his cheek.

I felt Clark's hand come around my waist. He pulled me toward him. His fingers were warm against by back, and his hips pressed against mine. His scent filled my lungs. He waited — for just a moment — then he kissed me with an urgency that echoed within me.

CHAPTER 45

I ASKED JEDDIE to dust the trunks that Clark set by the back door. "They need to be cleaned up before Mr. Button takes them upstairs," I told her.

"So, I can see," Jeddie said. "You have some dust on the back of your dress. Do you wish me to brush it off?"

"No. I'll see to it in my room. You might hurry as Clark is waiting to take them up."

I hurried through the kitchen and raced up the back stairway because I had the ridiculous notion that my encounter with Clark would show on my face. When I got to my room I snatched my mirror and stared at the image. I did look different . . . wide-eyed . . . dazed. My heart was still beating fast. Clark's kiss had stirred long dormant desires. I touched my lips. The taste of him was still there.

I slapped the mirror down. *Silly woman. My life is chaotic enough*, I thought. *The last thing I need is a man.* But the truth was: I was afraid of what I really wanted.

A knock on the door startled me. *Clark?*

Another knock. "Tessa?"

It was Jeddie.

"Just a moment." I cracked the door.

"May I have a word with you?"

"Certainly, Jeddie. Come in."

I showed her to the chair and sat down on the edge of my bed. "What is it? You look as if something is worrying you."

"Well, I thought we should have a talk . . . woman to woman."

"About?"

"Clark, Mr. Button."

"Go on."

"I don't believe it's common knowledge, but I am rather fond of Clark."

"And, how does that concern me?"

"I see . . . we all see, how he looks at you."

"You're imagining things, Jeddie."

"I wish I were." Her shoulders shook and tears began to flow. "I wished he looked at me the way he does you." She covered her face with her hands. "I love him, Tessa."

"Have you told him?"

"Not in those words, but I think he knows."

"He may, I don't know. But even if he feels something for you, he may see the age difference as a difficulty."

"What's a few years?"

"I would say near twenty years."

"So, you think he prefers someone your age."

"Jeddie, I have no designs on Mr. Button."

"Why not, he's handsome, worldly, and I know he has a good heart."

Her tears stopped. A clear-cut resolve appeared. She stiffened. "I just came by to say that I'm going to tell him how I feel . . . in no uncertain terms. He will have to choose."

"He may have to choose, but the choice is not between you and me."

"You are deceiving me . . . or yourself. I just wished to give you fair warning."

"Thank you. I am warned."

She turned to leave.

"Jeddie, your heart is precious, and a young heart is tender. I can tell you that, the only thing worse than unrequited love is rejection. Guard your heart well."

When Jeddie was gone, I held the mirror up again, pointing at my image: "What is it with you? A few kisses and things are already cocked up. Lord help you if you fall in love."

Thankfully, the rest of my day was uneventful, and at the dinner table, Clark and I successfully managed to hide what we were feeling. Later, as my meeting with Ganna approached, I was aware that I needed to be especially discreet going to the cottage. Jeddie would be looking for any suggestion of a tryst between Clark and me — and I did not wish to run into him again. Sitting atop this jumble of concerns was Holmes's warning.

Nonetheless, when the appointed time arrived, I made my way to the cottage, keeping well in the shadows.

The druidess was waiting — eyes closed as usual. She spoke, even as her eyes remained shut: "The question we will explore tonight is: do we trust our heads or our hearts?"

I chuckled. "That *is* the question."

Ganna's eyes opened in mild alarm — disturbed by my laughter.

"The sisters told me you would explain this trip to Wales, so I assume you are going as well," I said.

"Yes. We will celebrate *imbolc*. Just before this festivity you will perform the ritual that complements the powerful remedy we will craft for Mr. Holmes. It is important that it be dispensed on the same evening we perform the ritual — three nights from now. As I told you, for the ritual, you must have an object that belongs exclusively to Mr. Holmes — an item he uses nearly every day. Mind you, he must not know you have taken it." She paused and cocked her head in thought.

"There is more?"

"Yes, there is. I am aware that our time together may be limited — Maeve continues her bloody campaign. There are forces moving against her and the others — closing in every day."

"What does that have to do with you and I?"

"As you said once yourself, this world has no place for the likes of me. When the day of reckoning arrives for the Sisters of Scáthach, they will come for me as well."

"I won't let that happen."

"You will not be able to prevent it. And, any judgment against me may be justified. I should have done more for Maeve. I can see that now."

"Mr. Holmes will —"

"Help me?" Ganna smiled. "You know better. What is important here is that *you* must believe, beyond any shadow of a doubt, that the knowledge I offer is needed here on earth." She waited.

"I believe it is, but the world is a big place and you and I are but two people."

"I believe we can do it. Your words, like seeds, will be scattered over the earth and take root in the minds and hearts of the people."

"My words?"

"Your words and my knowledge — a potent combination. You are a bàrd. That is your gift. I am a druidess — that is mine."

"But, if time is short, as you say, how can I learn all you have to teach?"

"I will answer that question later. For now, I would simply ask if you are willing to walk in my place?"

"I do not think I can answer your question."

"That is your head speaking. What does your heart say?" The priestess smiled. "My child. Living is a string of choices. For some choices, you need facts and information, for others intuition.

The choice I am asking you to make can only be made with intuition."

"Mine has been proven wrong many times."

"I wonder. Maybe it wasn't intuition at work in those choices. Maybe it was fear, or wishful thinking, or guilt. The word intuition comes from the Latin: *inturei* — immediate spiritual communication."

"How do I know when it is intuition speaking to me?"

"I cannot answer for you, but I will tell you my experience," the druidess continued. "Intuition comes *into* me. It is not a thought. I feel it in my body. Wishful thinking is in my head — there is no visceral sensation. Intuition urges immediate action — it prompts me to do this, or go there. Wishful thinking emphasizes outcomes: I want this or need that. Now . . . close your eyes and quiet yourself . . . be aware."

I did as the priestess instructed.

After several minutes, Ganna asked: What did you see . . . and how did you feel when you saw it?"

"I saw you smiling and I was excited. But, it was strange?"

"In what way?"

"There was no urgent voice that told me to follow you. It was as if . . . whatever it was . . . did not care one way or the other about what I did."

Ganna nodded. "Intuition does work by force or fear. It stands, a little ahead of us on the side of the road, and points. It doesn't reveal, or sometimes even know, our final destination."

"This is good, Ganna. I realize that many of my poor choices came from fear, anger or selfishness, and not from intuition."

"You're not alone in that, my dear. You are human." She chuckled. "Let's make the most of our time, shall we? And, there is one thing that *must* be accomplished tonight. Sherlock Holmes's body is healing rapidly and we must prepare the final linctus. Tomorrow, you will bring the potion with the instructions that it is to be given to Mr. Holmes on the first of February — in the evening."

* * * * *

The next morning, I paid a visit to Mr. Holmes and was pleased to find Doctor Watson there as well. It was a simple matter to deliver the new herbal remedy to the nurse, but more difficult to explain why she had to wait to dispense it. I told her that the ingredients needed time to blend properly. Mrs. MacAskill believed me.

Later, as I was visiting with Mr. Holmes and Dr. Watson, my eyes tactfully searched the room for the object I would need for the ritual. The task proved more difficult than I imagined. He would miss his pipe or hand-glass. Other objects he used only infrequently. Then, I saw it — his leatherback knife. He used it in many ways — in lieu of a paperweight, he would stab it into a stack of papers. He sometimes used it to scrape the bowls of his pipe. But, it was most often employed as a letter opener. As far as I knew, he was the only one to use it, as others were continually admonished to never move his personal items. *Yes, the leatherback knife.*

Near the end of our visit, we went to the kitchen for a cup of coffee and some fresh-baked shortbread. I made an excuse that I had mislaid my purse and returned to the parlor. It took but a few seconds to secret the knife away in my handbag.

As I left for Grey House, I asked both the nurse and Dr. Watson to send word to me if there were any change in Mr. Holmes's condition, explaining that I was leaving early tomorrow and would be gone several days. I wrote down the address of Grey House.

As I took my leave, Mr. Holmes, once again, cautioned me: "Be careful, my dear. I believe Ganna is baiting you for her own purposes."

A week ago, his words might have caused me to abandon my trip to Wales, but now . . . I trusted my intuition and heart.

CHAPTER 46

CLARK BUTTON'S EYES continually shifted between the road and the rearview mirror during the long drive to Ceridwen Manor — the estate of the Davis sisters in north Wales. The object of his curiosity was a long-limbed woman wearing a rough woven pea green cloak. Ganna pulled the cowl up around her neck, and the hood over her eyes. It had taken some convincing to get her to ride in the limousine. Logic won out as there were only two days until *imbolc*, and it was not possible for her to travel by foot, or on the back of a beast — as was her custom.

Gwendoline and Margaret, like laconic bookends, wedged themselves into the back seat on either side of the old druidess. I braved the elements, sitting in front with Clark. When we stopped for refreshments at an old Cotswold inn near Carterton, Clark nudged me and, with a tilt of his head, beckoned for a word. When we were beyond earshot, he asked: "Who is the mystery lady?"

"An old friend of the sisters."

"Why the cover-up?"

I grinned. "She is nervous. She does not trust machinery and the like."

"That would make life challenging," he remarked. "You would have to live in the woods to avoid machines."

"Exactly," I agreed. "Come, I'm a bit peckish and could use a strong cup of tea."

As I turned back toward the inn, he tugged at my sleeve. "I am getting an uncomfortable feeling about all of this . . . silent sisters . . . mystery woman and all. Are you going to be . . . ." He gave me a worried look. "Are you fine with all this?"

"You worry too much."

"He surprised me by putting his hand on my waist and leaning in for a kiss. Just as quickly, I brushed his hand away put my finger on his lips. He kissed my fingertip and grinned.

As the sun was moving toward the horizon, we came upon a sprawling slate quarry. A row of empty wagons lined the road to the pit. "Our lands begin here and continue to the cliffs over the Irish Sea," Gwendoline remarked. "As you can see, this quarry, like another nearby, is mostly idle these days."

An inclement wind blew, whirling the dust into dervishes and veiling the landscape. Rough russet crags rose up like fortress walls against the stormy sky. However, the blustery weather quickly retreated just as we dipped into a wild flower meadow dotted with sheep. The sparse and ethereal terrain possessed a transcendent beauty that suited me. *I could fall in love with this place.* Ganna seemed to share my sentiments, for I saw her peeking out from the edges of her hood and smiling. The silence in the auto and the rolling landscape cast a hypnotic spell over us until Clark pointed to a cathedral of trees in the distance. "I didn't think trees like those still existed," he remarked.

"We call it our deer park," Margaret said. "Gwen and I are blessed to have this patch of native forest for which to care." Her words trailed off as the auto passed into a dark green tunnel that pierced the woodland. Slowly, my eyes adjusted to the iridescent light filtering through the leaves. Ten minutes later, as if someone had drawn aside a curtain, we entered another lush meadow. Ahead lay a massive wall and gateway like none I've ever seen. The portal, made of stone, was circular, only flattening at the bottom where the road passed through it. The rough-wrought iron bars of the gate were devoid of décor except for two ornaments on the gateposts that looked like the horns of some great beast.

Button brought the vehicle to a stop before the gate. "I'll pop out and . . ." But, before the driver could finish his sentence, a large man appeared inside the gate and waved through the bars.

"Oghma will get the gates," Gwendoline said.

As the portal opened, and the auto slowly crawled forward, Oghma stood at attention smiling. His shoulders and chest were massive and tugged at the buttons on his jacket. *He likely worked in the quarry,* I told myself.

It was another mile or more before we came upon Ceridwen Manor itself, spanning the horizon ahead. An amalgamation of Jacobean and Victorian styles, the façade had an openwork parapet running across the length of the sprawling two-story building. Jutting from the angular slate roofs were many chimneys, the hallmark of a wealthy home.

As Clark pulled to the entrance, outsized hobnailed doors parted. Two elderly women in neat grey dresses trimmed in white stepped out. They waited for the chauffeur to come around, eagerly greeting the sisters as they exited the car: "Welcome home," the shorter one said. "Your rooms are ready," the other reported.

The sisters and Ganna scurried up the stairs as the wind tried to snatch their hats and hood. I hurried around to the back of the limousine to get my portmanteau. Clark followed. "I'll get that." Then, glancing about to ensure that we were alone: "A bit of all right." he remarked, loosening the belts on the luggage.

"Then, you've not been here before?" I asked.

"No. The sisters usually travel by train." He studied the building, which loomed above us. "Do you feel it? This place has a mysterious quality."

"You've been reading too many penny dreadfuls," I said.

"I suppose, but I'd keep my eyes open, if I were you." He lifted my bag from the rack: "Wouldn't want anything to happen to ya."

His sweet comment prompted a request: "I'll be fine, Clark. But, there is something you can do for me, if you will."

"Say the word, lass."

"If any messages should come to Grey House for me — from a Dr. John Watson or Sherlock Holmes, immediately send word to me?"

"You know Sherlock Holmes?"

"That's a story for another time."

"Was he the bloke we visited when first I picked you up at the Sally Army?"

"That's the Doctor's flat on Sheen Lane. Mr. Holmes lives nearby, and is recovering from serious injuries. Please keep an eye out for any messages. It's important."

"Certainly — don't worry, I'll send word if anything comes to Grey House."

His hand came down over mine as I reached for my bag. He grinned. "You go on in and get warm. I'll get your bag."

I followed voices to the parlor where I found the sisters enjoying a hot cup. A short time later, Clark warmed himself in the kitchen before heading back to London. As he left, he glanced over his shoulder with a concerned look.

The room grew quiet after the chauffeur departed — the sisters seemed contented to sip their tea in silence. I risked intruding on their contemplative mood: "Where is Ganna?" I asked.

"She's in the garden," Margaret explained. "I'm sorry. Would you like a small tour, or do you wish to rest in your room, my dear?"

"There's much to see," I noted. "But, I would appreciate a brief look while there is still light, would be nice."

I followed the older sister into an enormous medieval hall that was crowned with massive wood trusses. "My sister and I have not been able to place this part of the house in time, however we are told it dates back sometime before 1470."

The stone floors were worn and stained. Our footsteps echoed as we strolled. A circular open hearth stood in the center of the hall — a spit was set on one side. The wind blew through a copula high above the fire pit and chased dry leaves across the floor.

"You will have time to see more of the manor and grounds tomorrow, but you must see this," the Margaret said, hurrying toward a passageway at the far end of the hall. She disappeared into the gloom beyond the entrance. I hastened to keep up.

We entered a chamber not more than eight yards square. The only light came through a single tall window opening high on the wall opposite the doorway. Margaret stood next to a waist-high stone ring in the center. "This is what Gwen and I call our boundless well. It is fed by a spring below. It has provided water for this manor house for centuries, and undoubtedly for others long before the building was here."

I walked to the well and looked down. My distorted twin was reflected in the water below. A small current undulated on the surface, putting tiny wrinkles in my reflection. *I look like Ganna.*

"We hold rituals and ceremonies here, Tessa."

"We?" I asked.

"You will meet the others on *imbolc*. Come now, why don't you rest before dinner. There is much to see and discuss, but it can wait."

As we made our way from the hall, we passed through a windowed gallery that looked out into a woodland garden behind the manor house. There, at the far end of the garden, was Ganna — her back to us. She stood at the head of a long avenue made from crushed rock and lime mortar. She clutched at the neck of her cloak and pulled the hood over her face.

"What is she doing out there?" I asked. "Is she waiting for someone?"

"I might say so," Margaret answered. "She has waited a long while for someone to take her mantle."

Neither of us took our eyes from Ganna. "She believes I'm the person she has waited for. I fear I am deceiving her."

Margaret chuckled. "If you are deceiving Ganna, you would be the first. But, you are correct. Ganna has chosen you. That is why we invited you to *imbolc*. It marks the season of new beginnings. There are many others in our tribe, but a special and distinctive vessel is required to carry Ganna's knowledge." She turned and put a hand on my shoulder. "Gwen and I believe you are that vessel, Tessa."

CHAPTER 47

A GALE WIND BLEW ALL THROUGH THE NIGHT, scaling the seaside cliffs and beating on the windows of my room. I was surprised to awake to sunlit skies. I promptly dressed and, retrieving my pad and pencil, followed the smell of coffee to the dining room. I was amazed to see Ganna sitting at the table like a proper lady. Her camaraderie with the Davis sisters was that of old friends.

"Good morning. Apologies for my tardiness," I said.

A maid pulled a chair back for me.

"Did you sleep well?" Gwendoline inquired.

"Well enough," I lied.

As I took my place, a plate loaded with bacon, pork patties, eggs, blood sausage and mushrooms was set before me. I must have gawked at the feast for Margaret remarked: "Will this suffice, Tessa?"

Still gawped by the plentiful platter, I answered: "It would be if I were splitting slate."

My remark proved amusing. Ganna's laughter was the hardiest.

"We seldom ask our guests to quarry, so if you wish a lighter fare, that can be arranged," Gwendoline offered.

"No, this will be fine. What does the day hold?" I asked.

"There is much to do before *imbolc*," Margaret said. So, I think your time is best spent with Ganna."

The druidess took her napkin from her lap. "Tessa, I must attend to a matter before we can meet." She looked at my plate and chuckled. "Enjoy your breakfast, then you might let the bàrd out to play in the garden. I will look for you there."

When everyone departed, I pushed my plate aside, finished my coffee and, wrapping myself in a warm sweater, went into the garden. I was aware that there were secrets lurking behind the polite breakfast conversation; and I was growing uneasy. I harkened to Clark's advice: *I would keep my eyes open, if I were you.*

I twisted the pencil in my fingers as I strolled, jotting down phrases and thoughts. Then, looking up from my musings, I spied someone at the far edge of the garden. A green hooded cloak told me who it was. It appeared that the old druidess was again waiting on the limed pathway that led to the cliffs. As I returned to the manor, I was surprised to come upon Ganna, who wore a long sweater. "I will join you shortly," she said, as she passed."

Staying well behind, I followed her. As I suspected, Ganna was on her way to meet the mystery person. As she approached, the green-cloaked creature pulled its hood back.

Maeve!

The plan had worked: Ganna led me to Maeve, and maybe to Eva. They chatted for some time. Though I could not hear their words, their movements suggested an amiable interaction. When their conversation ended, Ganna turned back toward the manor. I scurried ahead and found a chair on the terrace. I was scribbling on my pad when the druidess approached. "You saw Maeve?"

I struggled to control my voice: "Why didn't you tell me she was here?"

"Because you're not ready to confront her. There are things you do not know."

"What — that she's my two thousand year old sister!"

"You are mocking me," Ganna said, lowering her head.

"You're keeping secrets from me."

"I am giving you what you want: Heal Mr. Holmes . . . find Eva. I bowed to your wishes because you have respected mine. I am honoring our agreement. Will you?"

"I intend to, but Maeve will not permit it. She will not let Eva —"

"If you take my mantle, Maeve will submit. You must trust me."

"Trust me, trust me. I have trusted you but . . ."

"But now you do not," the priestess said, completing my thought.

I needed time to think, but there was no time. "You have only made promises. Will you bring me to Eva? Can you really heal Mr. Holmes?"

"Yes. The moon is waxing and the time approaches to mend Mr. Holmes. Come to the boundless well tonight when the moon rises in the east. Bring the knife and your petition. I will fashion an altar from which you can make your entreaty. When the time comes, speak plainly and from the heart."

As the sun slipped away, I lit a candle and made my way to the small chamber adjoining the great hall. A familiar aroma greeted me — cojóbana. Ganna and the Davises were waiting — all three wore green hooded cloaks. The only light came from four candles arranged on the ledge of the well. I stopped at the doorway.

Ganna looked at me. "What do you fear?"

"This . . . all of this. I don't trust that drug you burn."

"The cojóbana? We do not need it, I burn it to relax you, but I see it is doing the opposite. We will not use the cojóbana. Come."

The priestess directed me to the well, and took up a position opposite me. The sisters stood silently behind Ganna.

As the ritual began, I realized that I was witnessing a rite that was thousands of years old — maybe even from a time before there was language. The druidess took a scrap of wood and held it over a candle. As it smoldered, the scent from the cedar kindling filled the room. Ganna gave it to Margaret who walked around the well twice, encircling us in a ring of smoke. She returned it to the priestess who laid it aside and began an invocation in Gaelic. I would later learn that, having cleansed the area, the priestess was calling on everyone to be present and attentive.

Step by step the old druidess moved through the ritual: sanctifying the space, and calling on the elemental forces of Nature to be present. Then came my part — the invocation.

"Give me the knife," Ganna said, "and offer your petition."

I handed over the leatherback knife. The priestess snuffed three of the candles and nodded to me.

I began:

> *I call upon you — Mother:*
> *Go to him,*
> *Surround him.*
> *Revitalize Sherlock Holmes.*

Ganna did not react to my reading, but went on with the working: She rubbed the knife handle briskly in the palms of her hands as if she were polishing it. Then, with both hands, held it above her head and closed her eyes.

> *Blow your breath o'r him.*
> *Mend his body,*
> *his heart,*
> *and his spirit.*

The wind whistled through the window flagging the flame of the one remaining candle. From where I stood, I could see the moon framed in the narrow window high on the wall — its azure light filtered through the opening — falling on the silver blade.

Present him with miracles.
Strengthen his back
Restore his legs.
And render Sherlock Holmes whole again.

As I watched the illuminated knife above Ganna's head, I realized I was holding my breath. I felt dizzy. I gasped, and reached for the edge of the well. As I did so, I saw the radiant reflection of the blade on the surface of the water below. I felt Ganna's power, and the power of the olde way. It was as if, at this moment, Sherlock Holmes was being healed.

The druidess brought the knife down, but its reflection seemed to linger on the surface of the water for a moment before it faded away.

The ritual was nearly complete. Ganna chanted again. I did not understand the words, but I knew it was a prayer of thanksgiving. Then, she threw her arms wide as if she were releasing the spirits that had gathered.

The sisters silently left the chamber, leaving only Ganna and me. Her eyes were glassy, and I could see tear-tracks on her cheeks. A look of deep peace and gladness was on her face — and, I am certain, on mine as well. In that moment my desire to walk in the druidess' footsteps took hold of my heart.

CHAPTER 48

WHEN I AWOKE, my first thoughts were of Mr. Holmes. The certainty I felt last evening, that Holmes had been healed, faded in the morning light. There were no telephones at the manor, so if word came, it would be by telegraph or messenger.

It was *imbolc*, and Ceridwen Manor was abuzz. As if summoned by magic, a small army of maids, gardeners and cooks appeared and were busily cleaning rooms, tidying the gardens, and preparing meals. I made my way to the dining room and found the sisters hunched over their plates. Ganna was absent. I waved off the full-fry breakfast, requesting only a cup of coffee.

"You don't enjoy our Welsh breakfasts, then," Gwendoline remarked.

"It's the same fare in London," I answered. "What makes it Welsh?"

A look of surprise upon her face, Gwendoline explained: "All the ingredients are Welsh — and the cook as well."

"Thank you, all the same. I am content to enjoy my Welsh coffee."

My feeble witticism went unnoticed. The sister's had hardy appetites and knew how to work a plate. They were not predisposed to let frivolous conversation disturb their mealtime. I risked interrupting: "This is a busy day. I wish to be of help."

Margaret waved her hand as she finished chewing a morsel, "We've all the help required. Seek Ganna."

"Where is she?"

"She went out, but will return soon," Gwendoline noted. "You might wait for her on the terrace."

Seeing no sign of the druidess on the terrace, or amongst the gardens, I walked to the trail beyond. It was an antiquated avenue made of crushed stone overlaid with lime mortar. The mortar hardened the lane to prevent it from being washed away or overgrown.

I was told the pathway went to the cliffs, but what I wasn't told was that it went *over* the cliffs and snaked downward toward the choppy waters below.

I buttoned my sweater, pulled up my collar, and headed down. The rocky face of the cliffs undulated along the shoreline, so I could not see where the pathway ultimately led until I turned the last corner and saw the pallid path disappear into the granite cliff itself. When I reached the termination of the footpath, I could see that the lane narrowed into a crevice four feet across. I went no more than five feet into the crevice before it widened again to reveal a towering stone wall. The fortification stretched to either side of the now twenty-foot wide crevice, and soared to the top of the cliff. There was one entry point, and above it a single window. A door, of wood and metal straps, had no handles or locks — only a rusty iron knocker. I tugged on the knocker, but the door did not budge. I was only thinking of Eva when I impulsively knocked, for I suspected Maeve was within. I heard hushed voices and feet scrambling behind the door, but no reply. I knocked again.

"Tessa, you should not be here," a voice shouted from above. I looked up to see Ganna in the window.

"Eva. I want to see Eva!" I shouted.

"You will see her tonight. She will —"

"Now! I will not leave until I see her."

My certainty must have been carried in my words, for I only waited a minute before Eva appeared in the window. She was pale, thin and frightened.

"Eva, I've come to take you home. Come with me now."

"I can't," she said. "I can never go home. My place is here with my sisters. But, you're in danger. You must go!"

"Just a word," I begged. "Come down and talk with me."

Eva vanished from the window.

Minutes later I heard the clatter of a bolt behind the door. It opened — but only a little. Ganna slipped out and the door slammed closed again.

"Tonight," the druidess promised. "You will see Eva tonight. Maeve is here. It may be hard for you to believe, but Maeve loves Eva, and is trying to protect her."

"Protect her? Imprison her, you mean."

Ganna took my hand. "Listen to me. Eva has blood on her hands."

"What are you saying?"

"Eva killed Goodnow."

"I don't believe it. Maeve did it. She admitted it."

"Maeve was there, but Eva wielded the fatal blow."

I was stunned. "But, Maeve . . ."

"Maeve confessed to the crime to protect Eva. There have been other killings since Goodnow. I do not know if Eva or the others took part in those. It is only a matter of time before the authorities track them here. They plan to escape to the Isle of Man. The Davis sisters offered temporary shelter, but they must leave after *imbolc*. As I told you, because of my association with Maeve, I may be caught in the net as well. Now, come away and help me prepare for *imbolc*."

Ganna tugged on my arm. Grudgingly I put one foot before the other. In a daze of disbelief I walked back up toward the summit of the cliff.

Upon reaching the top, I turned to Ganna. "Eva is so very dear to me." I could not look Ganna in the eye. "Eva came from the London Orphan Asylum — the same orphanage where I left my sister Evangeline."

Shame now had me fully in its maw. No longer content to devour my heart, hope and self-respect, it held me up — sins and all — before the world. I was weeping. My words spit from my lips half formed. "When Dr. Watson told me Eva was fostered at the London Orphan Asylum, it all came back to me. I went there saying I was looking for a child of a friend. I couldn't even claim her as my own sister."

Ganna's head tilted and her eyes narrowed: "What did you learn there?"

"Evangeline died." My body trembled. Sobbing, I fell to my knees. "My sister . . . died . . . alone."

Ganna struggled to lift me, and wrapped her arms around me: "My poor child."

The druidess got me to my room and helped me into bed. The tempest of feelings and shame swirling within me seemingly pushed Ganna away as she went to the far corner of the bedroom, where she sat in the shadows.

I propped myself up on my pillow. "I . . . have a question," I said in a whisper.

"You hesitate. Why?"

"I fear the answer will cause you pain."

She smiled. "Ask it."

"How did you come to be here . . . in these circumstances."

Ganna eyes widened and her breaths came more rapidly. "Shame sticks in my throat even now. I violated a sacred *geasa*: respect for the cycles of life. I should be long dead." She straightened in the chair. "You say you know about Queen Boudicca's struggle against the black clad, but you do not know what caused her and her daughters to take to the battlefield."

"She was pushing back the Roman invaders."

"Indeed, and as we would say, Boudicca rode in the chariot of Andraste."

"Andraste?"

"The goddess of revenge. She sought retribution for the slaughter of the druids on Ynys Môn — Anglesey today. Those who taught and studied the olde way lived on that island, which is not far from here. And later, when the Romans came, fugitives sought refuge on our isle as well."

Ganna's face became a ghastly mask. "Suetonius Paulinus . . . that was his name. He wanted to eradicate the druids and break the spirit of our people. In the end, he did."

"And you were on the island when he attacked?"

"I can recall seeing him on his white stallion, staring in wonder across the shallow strait that protected our isle. Our warriors had lined the shore hurling taunts at the Romans, and trumpeting their carnyx. My fellow druids and I formed a circle around a huge fire to gather our power in support of our fighters."

Ganna's eyes grew dim. "We were overwhelmed. In one horrible day, Suetonius's garrison slaughtered everyone on the island — men, women and children. They heaped the bodies into our own bonfire, and burned everything on the island to the ground — including the great oaks."

"How did you escape?"

"I was the youngest of the druid initiates. So, when it was clear that our cause was lost, my brothers and sisters hid me in a bread oven, and then they took poison to free their spirits.

"Years later, I awoke to find that I was the last druid of the Iceni. I retreated to a cave near Gilmerton and communed with the spirits of my druid brothers and sisters. They gave me the secret of prolonging my life. From that time on, I have wandered this island nation seeking one of my tribe who had the healing spirit. I hoped it was Maeve, but . . ." Her eyes closed.

I was engulfed in Ganna's sadness and could not speak.

"You have that spirit, Tessa."

I felt a tightness in my chest and belly.

"I know, it is a heavy burden that I lay at your feet," she said. "But, you must banish any pity for me from your mind. Rest now and take the counsel of your heart."

I must have drifted off, because I awoke to the sound of carriages and automobiles outside, and voices downstairs.

Ganna was still with me. "They are arriving for the celebration," she explained.

"Members of the tribe?"

"Our tribe? Not all of them. Kindred spirits. They are anxious to meet you because they hope you will take my mantle and walk in my footsteps." She paused, leaving space for a reply, then she continued: "I had intended this as a naming ceremony — you as my successor. But now, you must be ready to truly walk in my path. Our inspirited world needs a voice, and mine is fading." Her eyes were heavy with sorrow. "I am out of my time, Tessa. My body is weary, and the authorities are closing in." The priestess clutched at my hand. "Will you do this?"

"I have just begun to plumb the depths of your knowledge. It will take years . . . decades, before I can walk in your ways."

"I know. But there is a way." She straightened in her chair. "Do you recall when I came to you in your dream?"

I nodded. "I will never forget that dream."

"I have learned to let my spirit travel — a skill one must use carefully and thoughtfully, for our souls are keen to travel. But, they always . . . eventually return to our body because they require a home."

Caught in the wonder of Ganna's words, I was struck dumb.

"I know, my child, such a thing seems impossible because you do not know the true way of things — the olde way. But trust me, what I say is possible." Her head lowered and her eyes narrowed. "There is a way for you to possess all my knowledge and wisdom . . . if you will allow my soul to reside in your body."

CHAPTER 49

I FROZE as Ganna's proposal took hold in my mind.

"But, what of you?" I asked. "What happens to you?"

"My body will pass away . . . as do all things . . . as should have happened long ago."

A whirlpool of fear and awe churned inside me. Ganna sensed this. "You must take some time to consider this," she said.

"I have many questions. What of *my* soul?"

"Of course — your soul is just that, your soul. It will remain with you. My spirit would be a guest. It will only venture forth when summoned or when sorely needed."

I got up from my bed and walked to the window. Pulling back the curtain, I watched a carriage pull up to the entrance. Margaret was greeting two older women and a man on the steps below.

"As you say, I need time to consider these things. I am not certain I can give you an answer tonight."

"I understand," Ganna said. "If you cannot decide, or if you decline to assume my mantle, stay in your room tonight. No one will disturb you. If you decide to accept my invitation, come down and celebrate with us. *Imbolc* is a wonderful time. '*I mblog*' means 'in the belly.' It is a celebration of new life yet to come."

"And Eva will be there . . . and Maeve?"

"Yes. Maeve will not blemish *imbolc* with violence. And, if you decide to give shelter to my soul, she will honor you as she does me."

I looked into the pleading eyes of the old druidess. "I am not certain I have the courage to do this thing."

"I believe your spirit is that of Isolda, daughter of Queen Boudicca. Together with your mother, and sister, Siora, you faced the mighty Roman legions and defeated them. Think on that . . . and know, that whatever you decide, I love you. There is nothing you can do that will disappoint me or diminish my love for you."

She turned from the door, as she departed: "One more thing, Tessa: you do not need to do this to redeem yourself . . . there was never anything to be redeemed. You may have been afraid, but your past choices were inspired by the love of others. Tonight offers a new way to love, and a new vision for your life. Think on these things." Ganna said, as she closed the door.

A new vision for my life. That's what I've been seeking. But, maybe it was too late. Where was that vision when I was eighteen? I had dreams, but I let shame shape my destiny. I devoted my life to good works to compensate for the death of my sister and brother. I strived to be, and be seen as, a good person. I was. I did good things, but maybe for the wrong reason . . . I left dreams behind. I left myself behind.

As the western sky turned a dusky red, I descended the stairs. The eyes of the strangers in the hallway turned upward in expectation. I did not see it then, but sitting on a silver tray near the front door, was a telegram for me.

I followed the music and singing into the great hall, searching all the while for Eva's face. The crowd parted as Gwendoline swooped through the crowd to greet me. "Hurry Tessa, we're welcoming Brigid."

A procession of forty or more persons gamboled in a circle chanting: *A Bhirid, a Bhirid, thighas as gabh do leabaidh*, to invite the goddess of fertility, healing and poetry into the room. A large candle burned next to a pile of rushes at the center of the floor — a bed for Brigid in the hope that she would stay the night.

The innocent gaiety of the group lifted my heart. While most of the revelers were long in the tooth, they sang, pranced and played like children. Some of them reached out to me as they paraded by. I turned to see Ganna walking toward me holding her insigne — Brigid's cross.

I took the symbol woven of rushes from her hand: *I have come full circle*. This cross was how Ganna came into my life, and now our lives were going to unite in a miraculous new way.

The celebrating continued and moved to a great banquet table set with dozens of candles to fend off the darkness. There was an empty chair placed at the head of the table for Brigid.

Bowls, plates and platters of unfamiliar and wonderful foods were passed around: colcannon — mashed potatoes and cabbage; sowans — a kind of porridge; dumplings, and, of course, still warm bannock, a delicious quick bread. Korma, a barley-based beer, flowed freely. And after a time, o-o-ohs and ah-h-h's abounded as the kouign was carried into the hall, still steaming from the ovens. I could smell the sweet butter and tantalizing burnt sugar as guests sliced into it.

The din diminished as the revelers' appetites were slaked. A fiddler rose and took a place near the head of the table, behind Brigid's chair. As he played, two young women joined him and sang: '*A ghaoil, leig dhachaigh gum mhàthair mi . . .*'

I leaned toward Ganna. What are they singing?

The old druidess turned to me, tears rolling down her cheeks. "A song for me." She bit her lip, wiped her tears, and smiled. They are saying: 'Let me go home to my mother.' It's an ancient song . . . an endless one."

Conversations ceased as the plaintive song released an avalanche of longings in our hearts. Then, while the melody was still echoing, Ganna rose and took a candle from the table. Others followed suit, removing a taper and standing in place. She nodded to the fiddler who began playing again. The priestess, with me behind her, led a procession into the adjoining room and around the sacred well before we went out toward the cliffs. The lime path ahead was lined with torches. Ganna took my hand as we walked toward the cliffs — the fiddler's mournful music rising from the rear of the procession.

"Eva's waiting for you," Ganna told me.

When the pathway rounded and we approached the door to the cliffside fortress, I hesitated.

"Don't be afraid," the priestess told me.

"I am afraid, but not for myself. You are going to —"

"Do you see the moon there," Ganna said. "When it dips below the horizon you will say, 'It is gone.' Gone where? Just gone from sight. It still moves on . . . as I will."

The door to the fortress was open as we drew near. Maeve was standing on the threshold in full warrior dress, her beloved *gae bolga* at her side and the *naofa* stone pendant gleaming on her breast. She did not give me notice, but took up a place on Ganna's other side. The three of us moved on into a large chamber, a granite hall alive with burning torches.

There! It was Eva and the Sisters of Scáthach lined along the wall holding candles before them. Ganna squeezed my hand to say: *As I promised.* It took all my strength to keep from running to her.

In the center of the hall stood a large wooden altar with a bed of rushes upon it. Maeve guided us there, and we turned to face the celebrants as they encircled us. The fiddler's music stopped when all were assembled.

Ganna surveyed the gathering and spread her arms. "Words fall short of expressing what I feel in this moment with my two daughters at my side." She smiled. "I say words fail me, but I will keep chattering on."

People laughed.

"I have walked this world a long time. I have known great joy and countless sorrows, and within them all I hold an indescribable gratitude for every human soul that cast a shadow on my life. But, my body is weary. Now, Tessa will lead us, and Maeve will protect us." She glanced about the room, taking in all the faces and feelings. "Let my last words be from a poem I wrote a long time ago. Only tonight did I come to understand its true meaning:

> *"I will find the green woods*
> *at the edge of the wasteland;*
> *and walk amid the tall grass and wild thyme*
> *kissing the earth of that kind field,*
> *pitching a tent by a quicken tree,*
> *and lying the night,*
> *all resting in love and contentment,*
> *leaving ancient grief behind."*

Ganna turned to Maeve: "Help me, please."

Maeve took the druidess by the waist and helped her onto the altar. Again, Ganna's eyes swept the room. People smiled, nodded, or raised a hand in farewell. Then Eva appeared. She walked toward us with a wooden bowl. Her attention was on the bowl, careful not to spill a drop. I beckoned to her with my eyes, but she did not see me.

When Eva was at the altar, she looked at Maeve, who nodded. Eva approached Ganna. The old druidess put her hand on Eva's cheek and smiled. "Thank you, Eva."

Ganna took the bowl in both hands and Eva retreated back to the edge of the chamber with nary a glance at me.

The priestess brought the bowl to her lips and, in one long draft, drank it down. The old druidess pulled her feet up and lay down. Maeve took up a place at the foot of the altar.

The priestess reached for my hand. When I took it, she pulled me close. There was a musty smell on her breath. She whispered: "*Coinín . . . coinín.*" Her eyes fluttered and closed.

I held her hand in both of mine and watched her chest slowly rise and fall. Silence enveloped the gathering. The only sound was the fluttering of torch flames.

Then — a shout from the back of the hall: "Stop. Stop. Step aside!"

A frightened uproar arose from the guests — shouts and threats. A melee broke out at the entrance to the chamber — people pushing and yelling. Maeve leaped in front of the altar, swinging her blade overhead and cocking it over her right shoulder.

Ganna's hand clutched mine tighter.

Maeve stepped out as the invaders pushed their way past the guests who were unable to fend them off. One of the intruders broke through.

"Clark . . . NO!"

CHAPTER 50

MAEVE SWUNG THE BELLY-RIPPER. Clark twisted away and ducked, but the razor-edged saber sliced into his shoulder, sending him to the ground.

Maeve turned to me: "Ganna?"

Her hand still had life in it. "Still here."

Policemen were successfully pushing back the throng of guests. A huge bear of a man, Oghma, was trying to rip a pistol from Holmes's hand.

"Stay here with her. I'll draw them away." Maeve ordered. She called out to her sisters and dashed toward the back of the chamber. Candles in hand, Eva and the others followed Maeve deeper into the cavern.

It was all a horrible dream: Clark rolling on the floor clutching his bloody shoulder, Holmes reigning blows on Oghma, and a dozen policemen swinging truncheons and shoving guests aside. Maeve's command rang in my head: *Stay with her!*

Then . . . Ganna's arm fell slack . . . and she was gone.

I gripped her hand more tightly now, waiting for some feeling . . . a sensation, awareness . . . a sign.

Nothing. Her hand grew cool. I sensed nothing within me. "She died for nothing!"

"Tessa, are you well?" Holmes shouted, coming to my side.

"I'm . . ."

He looked at Ganna.

"She's gone," I told him, releasing her hand.

He nodded. "Where did Maeve go?"

327

I pointed toward the back of the hall. "Eva and others are with her, be careful."

Holmes signaled one of the approaching policemen. "Look after this man," he said, pointing to Clark Button. And, turning to me: "Stay with him, Tessa." He took a small pistol from his pocket and offered it to me.

"Put that gun away! I'm going with you."

"Very well, stay behind me."

He paused to catch his breath. "I have my legs, but they are weak. Bear with me. Clark sent word but . . . never mind. Let's go!"

We each grabbed a candle and dashed to the rear tunnel that extended into the heart of the stone cliff. We could see no more than ten feet before us. The going was slow as we protected our candles from drafts in the tunnel. The uproar in the chamber tapered off as we moved deeper into the chasm.

We both drew a calming breath as the narrow tunnel emptied into a small chamber that formed an intersection with two more passages. Holmes held his finger to his lips and crept toward the first opening—bending an ear. Then he moved to the second. There were no sounds. He pointed to the left tunnel, which is his custom. I pointed to the right. He agreed with a nod, and took a revolver from his pocket and handed it to me. "Keep the pistol up in front of you."

I watched him disappear into the left passage in slow, deliberate strides. I followed into the right one, advancing slowly — stopping often to listen. Then, I saw light coming into the passage from beyond. I doused my candle and, holding my pistol before me, slid along the wall toward the opening.

It was a grotto lit with a single candle on the floor near the edge of a pool. The water scattered the candlelight and speckled the damp cave walls, making it difficult to see.

I called out: "Maeve! Maeve, are you here?"

"Are you alone?" a voice echoed back.

"For now."

Maeve's indigo and blue face emerged from the shadows beyond the pool. Her *gae bolga* rested on her shoulder. She was calm and steady. "Ganna had a good death?"

"Yes . . . I believe so, but . . ."

My hand was shaking and tightened around the revolver still pointed at her.

My body shuddered as if buffeted by a cold draft. *Don't* a voice said.

I startled and looked about. "Who . . . who is it?"

It is I. I am with you . . . very strange.

"Ganna?"

Yes

"My god, it happened."

Maeve nodded. "So, it has come to pass. The old one is with you. It is good that you are here, Ganna."

Holmes is coming, tell her.

"Holmes is coming. You must hide."

Maeve shook her head. "Why? Are you going to shoot me?"

I dropped the revolver to the floor.

"Very well then, hear me Tessa: Eva and the others are innocent. Do you understand? I did all the killing."

"Ganna told me . . ."

"Alone — I did all the killing myself. I confess."

"They may not believe me."

"Holmes will believe you. You will make him believe — for Eva's sake. I love her also, and gladly give my life for her and the others with but one request: I claim a warrior's death," she said, extending the *gae bolga* toward me, grip first.

"I cannot do that!"

She shook her head. "You and Ganna are so alike — afraid to shed blood. Very well." She took the blade in hand. Her eyes became fixed and vacant. Standing still and silent for a moment, she shifted her feet to balance her stance and brought her saber up before her eyes. It glistened — fracturing the darkness.

She brought the cold blade tenderly to her cheek: The lover, and her beloved *gae bolga*. Lowering it reverently, she placed the pommel on the ground between her feet. She bent over until the jagged point of the saber bit into her bare belly. Then, gripping the tip with one hand to steady it, she held the other out to the side— her body stretching low, like an august lady before a monarch.

The moment slowed and became heavy . . . . .

Her eyes beg me to look.

I do.

Her face takes on a set look of hardness. Her back stiffens. She looks at me — tears of farewell pooling in her eyes.

Help her, Ganna tells me.

"Wait!"

Maeve pauses and straightens. I hold out my hand. "Tell me what to do."

Taking the grip of the *gae bolga* in both of my hands, I hold it before me — the tip pointing toward Maeve.

"Keep your elbows at your sides and your feet spread wide. Lean forward as I come at you."

She smiles. "Thank you Ganna . . . and you also sister. This is for Rory too, and all deprived of an honorable death," the warrior declares.

Her arms spread wide. Her eyes close. Then . . . in a flash, she charges me screaming: *"Faugh a Ballagh!"*

Oh! She hits the blade. My grip tenses as the metal slices into her breast, splitting her ribs and twisting her body. Eyes open, her lips tremble in a whisper of concentrated agony. I clutch the sword tighter. Her eyes rivet on mine. "I can't hold you," I say — my arms shaking.

I let go. She falls, clutching the blade that was her salvation.

Maeve! Ganna screams.

I look at her, resting at my feet, still, devoid of all traces of grievous hurt, safe from the hole and corner evils that afflicted her.

"For Rory and the warrior Maeve," I say.

Hearing footsteps behind me, I turn as Holmes rushes into the grotto. "Tessa!" He slows when he sees Maeve's body, and walks quietly toward me. His questioning look is not rendered into words. His fierce expression softens when he sees my face. Taking his fingertip, he wipes a single small tear from my cheek.

"Eva?" I ask.

"Safe. All safe. They are malnourished, but Eva, and the others are ready to go home. How did this happen?"

"I couldn't let her die on the gallows."

"You pitied her?"

"I do . . . did."

"Maybe this is just as well," Holmes said. "It will spare Eva and the others the ordeal of a trial. When Walls comes, let me do the talking."

"And the walking. Who believes in miracles now, Mr. Holmes?"

* * * * *

I never told him the entire story, but offered a poem instead. For reasoning alone cannot mount what happened in that ancient grotto. Sherlock Holmes is the master of mysteries, but even he cannot fathom the mystery of the intrepid human heart.

EPILOGUE

JULY 7, 1939

"HERE YOU ARE MOTHER," Eva said, when she found me behind his desk. "Is it hard for you to be in his office . . . with all his things around you?"

"It's comforting. You know . . . memories tend to magnify the good, and diminish the bad. It is a little trick our hearts play to make the loss of a loved one bearable."

"I hope so, because, judging from the crates father is putting in the boot, we're taking a lot of memories home."

"It's people, not things that make memories, Eva. And, I already carry a heart full of wonderful ones thanks to Mr. Holmes."

Eva walked behind me and wrapped her arms around my shoulders. "What's that in your hand?"

"A poem I wrote long ago. I gave it to Mr. Holmes. He kept it all these years."

She took the torn page from my fingers and started reading. "The Tear . . . I don't know this one. It's beautiful."

"I could never bring myself to publish it."

"You must tell me the story behind it," Eva said.

"Maybe some day. They say tears are just salty water, but there is a good amount of joy, pain, and wonder in each one of them."

I patted Eva's hand and got up from the desk. "Come along, get that crate over there. We have packing to do."

"Where's father when you need him," Eva grumbled.

A head with shaggy auburn hair poked into the room. "Hey, you two, we'll never get out of here if you . . ." His jaw dropped as he saw the hundreds of books lining the shelves. "So, these books are ours too?"

"Yes, Clark, he gave me his books and his bees. I think you now have all the books you will ever read in a lifetime."

I started to cry.

Clark and Eva wrapped me in their arms, not understanding that these were not tears of sorrow. I was simply surprised to find myself so happy.

Clark kissed my forehead. "Endings are not a bad thing, Tess. It just means something new is about to begin."

And then, there are those things that never end, Ganna said.

THE TEAR

Wet from the womb
a baby knows
the quintessence
of the human animal.

And it cries.
And we cry.
Only we cry.

History has taught
that a tear
can launch an army
and bring peace.

We use this native tool
as it uses us.
Tears are the blood of love
coursing through, into and long after.

Tears are the telltale sign
of what lies betwixt and between.
Our salty bond.

So, let us dip deeply from our hearts
and dredge up our tears.

Let them burst forth in an embrace.
Let them signal defeat,
catapault a laugh,
drown a desolation,
announce guilt
and bless forgiveness.

And above all,

hale reunion
and warm relationship,
wherein our tears await.

The mighty tear is
just for you.
It does not exist afar,
nor in a separate room.

It is just
for you
and
for me.

The tear is my religion.

ACKNOWLEDGEMENTS

When good things happen in my life, I have but to look to my side to find Sara Rose. This is not a coincidence. Sara has walked with me as I wrote this book, offering continual encouragement, providing ideas and criticism, and keeping my prose flowing. Any insights into the psyche of women characters in this novel have their genesis in Sara Rose — my warrior, lover and spiritual guide.

Working more than a year on this novel, it's easy to lose perspective. But, with the help of two "reviewer-critics" in my local community, I was able to steer the plot and maintain consistent and credible characters. My heartfelt thanks goes out to Cathy Moser and Tom Potter — both masters of the written word. Cathy is the feature editor at *The Chronicle News*, and Tom is the Teen/Adult Services Specialist at the Trinidad Carnegie Public Library.

Finally, my heartfelt thanks goes to you — my readers, who are always top of mind. Your kind words in reviews, blog postings, and in personal contacts are "coin of the realm."

ABOUT THE AUTHOR

KIM KRISCO is the author of two previous Sherlock Holmes novels: *Sherlock Holmes — The Golden Years* and *Irregular Lives: The Untold Story of Sherlock Holmes and the Baker Street Irregulars*. He continues in the footsteps of the master storyteller, Sir Arthur Conan Doyle, by adding yet another, tale to the popular canon — *The Celtic Phoenix*.

Meticulously researched, Krisco's stories read as mini historical novels. His attention to detail, which includes on-location research, adds a welcome richness to his exciting stories.

Prior to writing full-time, Kim served as a consultant, trainer, and coach for business and non-profit organizations, and their leaders. You can find out more about Kim and his current activities at: www. kimkrisco.com.

He and his partner, Sara Rose Ferguson, live in south-central Colorado (USA) in tiny homes that they built themselves on the North Fork of the Purgatory River—"a writer's paradise."

www.ingramcontent.com/pod-product-compliance
Lightning Source LLC
Chambersburg PA
CBHW051230260626
47162CB00002B/365